GOLF WIDOWS

GOLF
WIDOWS

Samantha Marcham

Fernando

Words and Music by Benny Andersson, Bjorn Ulvaeus and Stig Anderson
Copyright © 1975 UNIVERSAL/UNION SONGS MUSIKFORLAG AB
All Rights Reserved Used by Permission
Reprinted by Permission of Hal Leonard Europe Ltd.

Matador
Unit E2 Airfield Business Park,
Harrison Road, Market Harborough,
Leicestershire. LE16 7UL
Tel: 0116 2792299
Email: books@troubador.co.uk
Web: www.troubador.co.uk/matador
Twitter: @matadorbooks

ISBN 978 1803131 443

British Library Cataloguing in Publication Data.
A catalogue record for this book is available from the British Library.

Printed and bound in the UK by TJ Books Limited, Padstow, Cornwall
Typeset in 11pt Minion Pro by Troubador Publishing Ltd, Leicester, UK

Matador is an imprint of Troubador Publishing Ltd

An elderly lady once said to me, upon hearing that I was getting divorced:

"You are so lucky. I wasn't brave enough. It wasn't the done-thing in my day. I have wasted my life"

"I have wasted my life"... That sentence has stayed with me.

I dedicate this book to all the women out there who are struggling, either with lack of confidence, with fear, or with guilt. You might have others to look after, but don't forget self-care. You owe it to yourself to live your best and true life. Be brave.

You are only here once!

I also dedicate this book to my darling twins Max and Olivia. You made my life complete.

I continue to be blown away and so proud of you both every single day.

Be brave and follow your dreams. Know your self-worth and have faith in yourself.

I love you so much x

ONE

BELINDA

It was a Saturday afternoon at the West Seale Golf Club in Hampshire, where a group of self-confessed golf widows greeted each other with familiarity as they arrived for their usual weekly get-together.

The circular table, around which they were now seated, was situated in a large bay window, overlooking the course. With ample light flooding in from the open green, it was the best spot in the restaurant and was already laid out in preparation for their 2pm lunch reservation. They hadn't needed to call ahead to make their booking. The same table and the same time were set in stone, week in, week out.

Their husbands, having earlier shared a large platter of various sandwiches and sausage rolls, were already out on the green, so their wives prepared to do what they did every single week, which was to eat and share polite chat whilst they dutifully waited for their husbands to finish at 4pm.

Post-golf, the men would have a drink, or few, after which the obedient wives all drove them home around 7pm. This was what happened every Saturday, come rain or shine, but there was something different this time. Something was missing, or rather someone was missing. Belinda.

To their dismay, the golf widows genuinely felt her absence, made even more glaringly obvious by the now empty seat where she normally sat. The restaurant staff had laid five covers on this table for years. They probably didn't even realise yet that their group was now down to four.

Janet was the first to speak. "It just doesn't seem right. I will miss her dreadfully."

"I don't see why she can't still come," Tracey said.

Amanda replied, "She could do, but she said she'd find it too upsetting. Seeing him. The Pig."

Louise added, "She must be so embarrassed, bless her. How could he? Belinda is the nicest person I've ever met."

"She certainly didn't deserve this," Janet concluded.

The women solemnly devoured the poached salmon, asparagus tips and Jersey new potatoes. The food was delicious, greatly improved recently, courtesy of a new chef, which was a welcome relief to them all, but their mood was still low.

Earlier that day
Plop. A solitary tear landed in the white mountain of self-raising flour that was piled up high in an old-fashioned traditional mixing bowl. Belinda used the cuff of her plain navy Marks & Spencer jumper to wipe her eyes, keen that he didn't catch her crying again. Not that she was ashamed.

Her self-respect went AWOL the week before, when she had asked, pleaded even, that he stay. But no, the heartless bastard thought it was for the best.

"Best for who?" she had screamed. "Best for you? Best for your fancy bit?"

Belinda cried now because she was angry. Furious even. The estate agent, that her so-called husband had organised, without even having the decency to pre-warn her, had turned up that morning, and after just a few minutes of bashing, a shiny new 'For Sale' sign now stood proudly at the front of their garden, as though it were a good thing.

The young man who had erected it disappeared just moments after he had arrived, whistling to himself, totally oblivious of the devastation that his one minute and thirty seconds of swinging his chunky mallet had caused.

She was distraught, livid, that the home she loved, still loved, would soon be snatched, so swiftly, so unfairly, from right under her chubby nose. She seethed inwardly at the thought that some other family would now get to have the happy ever after that she had worked thirty-two years to achieve in her home, absolutely gutted that some other lucky cow would soon get to stand at the island of her beloved, perfect English country kitchen.

This wasn't just a kitchen to Belinda; it was her favourite place in the whole wide world. Her sanctuary. Where she baked, making cakes, her true passion in life, apart from her son Max of course, but he flew the nest straight after university. It transpired that none of the men in her life needed her anymore now. She was superfluous to requirements. Redundant. Useless. Unwanted.

She had partly realised this a few years ago when Max left home to travel the world with his Rock Band 'King'. They had hoped to become the next 'Queen' but he is soon to turn thirty. Surely, they should have given up by now; the big time is clearly not going to happen for them. He might have managed to earn himself a few bob, but Belinda wished he would just come home, get a steady job, meet a local girl and give her a few grandchildren in as quick succession as possible. She would never tell him this of course because she wanted him to be happy, so she had done the decent thing, had wished him well, along with a huge chunk of her savings, and she'd waited until after he'd left until she sobbed for her loss. Her loss of her role as a mother.

If she had been honest with herself, and not stuck her head in the sand, like the pathetic, weak woman that she was, she should have seen this day coming. Roger had always been a selfish sod, but since Max had left, she had hardly seen him. He was always out; if not working, he was on his beloved golf course.

She had consoled herself with her baking, consuming almost as much as she gave away to friends. She looked down at herself, ashamed of her bulging, sticky-out tummy and the handles of fat surrounding her wide hips and spilling over the top of her size sixteen jeans. *No wonder he is leaving me*, she thought. *I only have myself to blame. What man would want a whale of a wife when he could have a minx of a mistress?* Even more sickening was that the minx was only thirty-flippin'-one, only a year older than their own son. How on earth could she compete with that? Belinda was fifty-five, and she looked it.

Who was she fooling? There was no competition. It was game over, and she was the loser.

At least the skinny bitch wouldn't be getting her kitchen though, thank God. Neither of them could afford to buy the other out, so Roger was insisting that they sell up. It was alright for him – he didn't give a toss about their beautiful home. He wanted to buy a swanky, modern apartment in the town centre with his half of the sale proceeds. Apparently, he and the minx wanted to be able to stroll out to trendy bars and restaurants without having to drive home to the boring old sticks.

Poor Belinda loved where she lived, in the leafy Hampshire village of Seale. It would kill her to leave, but it would have certainly finished her off if the minx was going to get her home as well as her husband. She looked down at the cream marble Venetian worktop that matched her cream trusty old Aga. She stroked it lovingly, thinking of the years that she had spent in that kitchen. She'd baked a cake at this island for every single birthday that Max has ever had, as well as for the many special occasions of her friends too.

"Belinda, would you mind baking a cake for so-and-so?" they would request, and she was always only too happy to oblige. She was genuinely proud of her creations. It was the only thing she excelled at, and the only thing that made her happy these days.

Oh, she wished she could turn the clock back. She should have put her foot down with Roger, kept him on a shorter leash like the other women did to their husbands. But no, easy-going, boring old Belinda didn't want to upset anyone. She berated herself for being such a doormat. "And now I'm going to pay for it," she told herself out loud. "Silly old fool."

Belinda knew that Carrie wasn't the first. Roger by name and Roger by nature. He had clearly been at it for the whole of their marriage. She first suspected an affair when she was pregnant with their only child Max. She was a new wife then and hadn't been ground down so much, so she still had a small amount of feistiness left in her. She was brave enough to confront him in the early years, and she did so furiously but also hysterically and tearfully, due to her raging hormones. Roger had sworn on the life of their unborn child that he 'was a hundred per cent not shagging anybody else whatsoever'. So, she took him at his word, thinking that even Roger wouldn't stoop so low to swear on their unborn baby's life. Then her Max was born.

Dear little Maximillian, with a spout of golden thick hair from day one. The most beautiful baby that she had ever seen in her life and to whom she has devoted her life to ever since.

There were many occasions after that when her gut told her that Roger was up to no good. The tell-tale signs were obvious: more working away from home, suddenly making more of an effort with his appearance, buying new aftershave and clothes and the out-of-character gifts for her. He would bring her bunches of garage-bought flowers, snatched as a guilty afterthought whilst refuelling his car on the way home from his adulterous trysts.

Belinda never questioned him again though. This house, her baby boy, their family, it was all she had ever wanted. There was no way she would let anything take that away from Max.

Her son was going to grow up in a family home, with both parents present, no matter what. From then onwards, she always turned a blind eye to Roger's activities, knowing that it would soon blow over, until the next time of course, but that was until Carrie Carpenter came along. Owner of exotic, curly, long, dark hair, athletic long legs that went on forever, neat, Pilates-honed, perky bottom and sun-kissed caramel skin from being mixed-race. She was like a flippin' supermodel, the bitch. If Belinda were attracted to women, she would have fancied her too.

Roger hadn't wanted Belinda to work. He wanted her at home, to do the school run and have a proper home-cooked dinner waiting on the table for him when he arrived home from work each evening.

It was 'tradition', he had insisted. "Men should go out to work, and women should stay home and look after the family," he had told her. "You're my wife, and I want to look after you."

So, Belinda had obeyed his wishes, feeling all warm inside that he must really love her and that she was being taken care of.

The reality was that he had wanted his wife where no one else could touch her. He knew what other men were like because he was one of the very worst. He particularly loved shagging other men's wives behind their backs. Colleagues' wives, friends' wives, any wives would do, but Roger had an enormous ego, and there was no way anyone was going to be shagging his.

Another thing about Roger: he did love his food, so he could not have married a more perfect woman in that department. His favourite day of the week was Sunday when he liked to come home from playing golf to a traditional roast dinner with all the trimmings, followed by one of Belinda's legendary apple and blackberry pies with vanilla custard.

Belinda would have liked to have had the occasional family day out on a Sunday, but Roger said that he couldn't let the team down. They needed him, apparently. He boasted that it was mainly due to his efforts that they won so many competitions. Anyway, he claimed that he needed to play golf at weekends to reduce the stress of work, and he reminded her that it was his job that paid for their house, so she kept quiet, like the good little wife she was.

She was brought back to earth from her thoughts by a snuffling noise. She looked down at the Italian rustic stone floor that she had spent years scrubbing and making smell fresh with extra generous dilutions of Country Garden Zoflora. A chunky golden Labrador lay in his favourite bed, dozing due to the comforting warmth of the underfloor heating. At least she still had him, although he was almost twelve now. *Oh God, please don't let anything happen to the dog*, she suddenly thought in her anxious, panicky state. She gazed adoringly at Hugo. Fat, easy-going and never any trouble. *If I were a dog then I would probably be a Labrador too*, thought Belinda, thinking negatively of herself as usual. Beside Hugo, she spotted Roger's green Hunter wellies. As she went to call out, he suddenly appeared. He had stopped by to collect the last of his belongings from their home, and he stood there now, brazenly, in the doorway, holding an expensive Mulberry tanned-leather holdall in one hand, leaning against the door frame with his other. Belinda was annoyed at herself that she still found him attractive. His dark hair had silver streaks now, but they only served to enhance his golfer's tan. Annoyingly, it hadn't all fallen out, or rapidly receded, which was what seemed to have happened to most of the men his age. She never had found baldies attractive, but, *maybe if he had gone bald, he wouldn't have pulled a young bird*, she thought. Angry at herself for even thinking he looked good, she snapped at him, "Taking the best luggage I see?" and then, "And don't forget your bloody wellies."

"Well, you won't need it, will you? It's not as though you ever go anywhere," he responded causally, without thinking how callous he sounded. "And I won't need wellies in the town, will I? Just chuck 'em in the bin."

"What, like you have to me?" Belinda replied sadly. She couldn't help herself.

Roger was not going to hang about. He didn't want her trying to make him feel guilty again because he didn't. In his eyes, he had worked hard for years, had supported her and his son and now it was *his* time. To do what *he* wanted to do. Ironically, he always had, but it was how he justified himself to anyone who dared to comment on their break-up.

The boys at the golf club had been great, jealous even. They had all admitted that they wished they could trade in their wives for someone like Carrie, and although said in jest, he knew that deep down, they all meant it. The wives though, it was all that they could do to even glance in his direction now. They already generally disliked him, and had done for years, but this had now been upgraded to being furious with him. Despising him.

Roger remained calm. He was not going to waste any more time arguing over the same old stuff. As far as he was concerned, they covered everything, and said what needed to be said, the week before when he had moved out. Besides, he needed to be at the golf club for 12pm, and he was late enough as it was.

"If we get any offers for the house, let me know, will you?"

Hugo plodded up to him, thinking a nice walk might be on the cards, but Roger pushed him coldly away with the holdall. "Anyway, I let you keep the dog, didn't I?" he said, as though he had done her a huge favour.

Then, Roger briskly turned away and left, their front door slamming loudly behind him. He couldn't get away quick enough.

"Arrrghh," screamed Belinda, throwing her tea towel across the room as she watched him saunter off down the winding stone path as though he didn't have a care in the world.

It's so unfair, she thought. *Why now?* This was meant to be their time. They had only just finished paying off the mortgage. Finally, they were going to have extra money to do things that she wanted to do, such as a nice holiday, maybe visit Max to see him play in whichever country he would be in.

Belinda returned to the cake that she had begun to create. She cracked, then dropped in, two large organic eggs and began to mix furiously, incandescent with rage and frustration at her situation. Her bingo wings slapped unattractively from side to side as she stirred like a mad woman, imagining that the mixture was Roger's fat, arrogant head.

With the concoction more than prepared, she turned to her ingredient cupboard to reach for a tub of baking powder.

She eyed the rows of neatly organised glass bottles, full of every spice known to man. She would have to pack this all up into cardboard boxes soon. She started to cry again. She didn't want to leave. This was her home. Where would she go?

She walked away from the cupboard and over to her enormous, double-fronted American fridge, where she poured herself a large glass of white wine. This wasn't like Belinda, but she didn't know what else to do. She wanted to call Max, but why ruin his day? And she didn't want him worrying. He was still young, and she wanted him to have fun. They hadn't even told him yet and had both agreed that they would wait until he next came home, whenever that would be.

She didn't really have any close friends. Roger made her up sticks from where she grew up in Derbyshire, so she lost touch with all her old school and college friends. She had never been one to go and visit them, to keep up the friendships, because Roger had preferred that she stay at home to look after him.

The only women she socialised with now were the other ladies at the golf club. The wives of Roger's golf pals. She couldn't call them. They might feel awkward. *Maybe Carrie is already sat in my seat at the wives' table right now*, she thought. *Maybe they really like her? Maybe they like her more than me?*

Belinda had never been sure of herself. A chubby, plain child, she lacked in confidence. Her mother had always cut her thick, wiry hair into a short bob which did nothing for her strong jawline. Roger had been her first-ever boyfriend. She had been working as a receptionist for her father's building company. The job had given her a little more confidence, and as a consequence, she had started to grow her hair longer and lose some weight due to religiously attending Weight Watchers every Monday and Friday evening. She could have gone once a week and maybe used the extra night to do an aerobics class or go for a swim, but Belinda was never a sporty type of girl.

By the time that Roger Morris walked into their office and introduced himself as the new trainee quantity surveyor, she looked the best that she was ever going to look, and she was utterly smitten from day one.

Roger had already won over her father, and he was clearly very ambitious. Looking back now, Belinda realised that it was she who was actually 'the catch' in the beginning, with her being the privately educated convent girl and virgin daughter of his boss.

Him, he was a chancer, a council house boy at the very start of his career but with not a penny to his name to set up on his own. Roger had been super keen and had impressed her father, but he had especially flattered and charmed her, which was a first for Belinda. He was tanned, cheeky and cocksure of himself. She was a sitting duck. She never stood a chance. So, they married within the year, and his success was sealed. He always bragged that it was his hard work that had supported the family, but it was her inheritance that had set him up in his company, and it was her father's money which enabled them to buy their home, with him generously stumping up a hefty fifty per cent deposit for this house as his wedding gift to them.

Now look how Roger was going to repay her daddy's trust in him. By spending his share on floozies whilst she was losing the roof over her head. Her parents would both turn in their graves if they could witness how he was treating her now.

She gazed out of the window and looked up and down the road. She thought she would remain in this house until the day she was carried out in a wooden box or an ethical wicker casket or whatever the most current sarcophagus was these days. Her days of tree-lined avenues and electric gates were clearly soon to be over. She surveyed the lounge in a daze. She stroked the heavy curtains, reminiscing how she'd handmade every pair in the house herself, along with the co-ordinating cushions. She had devoted so many hours to her home, sat at her trusty old Singer sewing machine that was a wedding gift from her mother. The amount of money she'd spent in Laura Ashley, she should have bought shares in the company. She wondered if the new owners of the house would just pull them down and bung them in the bin. Maybe they were too old-fashioned now. Like her.

She supposed she could take them with her.

She knew that she needed to sit down and work out how much she would receive from the proceeds of the sale and, more to the point, what she could afford to buy with her share. She clearly wouldn't be able to afford to stay in Seale. It was far too expensive. But where would she go? Where did rejected wives go?

She wondered if she was old enough to get a retirement apartment at the new McCarthy & Stone complex down the road. It was literally the only place in the area that she might be able to afford, but most probably only a one-bedroomed apartment. She thought of her future, abandoned with all the other old, lonely women. The thought of it filled her with despair.

Belinda had always wished she'd had a daughter, but now more than ever. Right now, she needed one. Roger hadn't allowed her to have any more children after Max. He had insisted that one was enough. How come he had got his own way? Why hadn't she put her foot down? She might not be so lonely now if she had another kid or two. Especially if she had been lucky enough to have a girl.

Years ago, she had yearned for a daughter, to make clothes for, to organise pretty, girly birthday parties for, to bake pink cupcakes with icing ballet shoes on top. As much as she loved her Max, boys just didn't appreciate the finer details. As long as their mates could come over, and there was football and food, then they were happy. Simple creatures really.

She desperately wished that she had a daughter, one to go shopping with and one who would have popped out a few babies by now, making her a grandma, her greatest desire in the world.

She wasn't holding out much hope of Max producing any grandchildren. Maybe she deserved to lose the big house if it was only going to be her in it, all by herself. What a waste.

Belinda walked upstairs, continuing to wander aimlessly around her house. She sat on the end of their, sorry, *her* bed, and stared at her sad reflection in the mirror. *Will I ever meet anyone again?* she wondered. *Who would even fancy me?*

Belinda didn't think she would particularly want sex even if George Clooney knocked on her door holding a magnum of chilled Dom Perignon and with a red rose clenched between his luminous white teeth. Suffering through her menopause without succumbing to HRT had been brutal, and quite frankly, she never had any sexual thoughts or desires these days, and she hadn't done so for years.

Before he had left, her and Roger had still had sex, albeit infrequently. She never enjoyed it, though, because it wasn't making love. That hadn't happened since Max was about three years old. Since then, it had been just sex. Unsatisfactory sex. He hadn't wanted to make love to her; he'd just wanted to empty his bollocks, and it was only ever on the odd Sunday morning, just before he went to play golf, and always a quickie, because he didn't want to be late to his beloved golf club.

Belinda wondered what would happen to her. Would she ever date again? She very much doubted it. What would a new man think of her? She didn't think she would ever be brave enough to even strip off in front of another man, and who the hell would want to look at her body?

She hadn't invested in herself like the other women at the golf club had. She had never joined the running clubs or gone off to the gym at weekends because Max needed driving around to his various clubs. She hadn't gone in the week either because in between school runs, she would be busy with the shopping, cooking and cleaning.

Neither had she ever gone for facials, her nails done nor any other beauty treatments. She was far too busy running her home to neglect her family for all that nonsense. She'd spent her whole life looking after her husband and son, and she had taken immense pride in doing so. But had she made a mistake? Had she been stupid for not putting herself first?

Maybe she should warn the new buyer of the house, the wife that is, not to make the same mistakes as her. But no, better not, they might think she was crazy or bitter. Maybe she was.

She stood at her bedroom window now staring out, admiring the back garden, with its perfect lawn mown into straight stripes. Soon, the giant acer trees that stand tall in each corner would turn a shade of exotic deep red, and the rose bushes all around the borders would bloom in an array of pastel colours, in soft shades of cream, pale yellow and peach. The house always looked its best in the summer, but she doubted she would get to enjoy it this year, not if they got a quick sale. She prayed that they didn't.

Belinda flopped down onto the bed, picked her up iPad and started searching on Rightmove to see if any retirement apartments were up for sale. She couldn't bear to leave the area so she reasoned that it would be far better to be dumped in with the old ladies rather than the alternative of having to move away from her local village to somewhere she didn't know anybody at all. There were a few men in the complex too, but it was mainly women. For some reason, the men always tended to die first. Was that because the bastards deserved it? She thought of the widows who already resided there. They probably moved there because they were lonely after their husbands had died, or maybe they couldn't cope looking after a big house by themselves. For one second, Belinda wished that Roger had died instead of absconding. At least her heartbreak would be deserved. Surely it must be better to be a widow than to be abandoned. These old women were lucky. Their husbands love for them didn't die, they did.

Belinda wished she was a widow. She could forgive Roger for dying but not for deserting her for another woman.

Belinda secretly felt ashamed for being a divorcee, although she technically wasn't one yet.

She knew there was still a stigma surrounding women when their marriages ended. They were looked upon as failures or strumpets or desperate. Or all three. How come divorced men got away without being tainted with the same labels? They didn't get judged. They could slip back into being a bachelor and still be seen as a catch. They didn't stop getting invited to events and dinner parties. It was the opposite for them – they got all the sympathy and the respect. *Yes*, she thought, *it would be much better if I were a widow.*

She suddenly felt ashamed of herself for even contemplating it. She shook her head, disappointed in herself for thinking such a bad thing. Then she had a realisation. She had already been a widow. She'd been a long-suffering golf widow.

TWO

AMANDA

A stylish designer tap continued to dribble out a stream of piping hot water, topping up her luxuriant Jo-Malone-scented bath, increasing the volume of bubbles, not that more were required, but Amanda was always over the top. The more the merrier for her. Bath bubbles, champagne bubbles – she was a huge fan of both, often at the same time. But right now, it was 8am, so she clutched a warm china mug of Earl Grey tea whilst reading a copy of *The Times Travel Magazine*.

She gazed longingly at the images of pure, white sands and shallow, calm waters of the Andaman Sea. The perfect virgin beach, with not one footprint to ruin the creamy, pale sand that sat in perfect unison beside the most tranquil aqua-blue sea she had ever seen. She was desperate to be there. She needed a holiday, a proper one, somewhere exotic and decadent.

Amanda worked full-time, always had done, but she'd be fifty soon, and her husband Christopher had just received a very generous inheritance, meaning that she could afford to go part-time now or even retire altogether. *Part-time*, she thought, *for a while at least*. She was sick of working, and she had been getting more tired lately, but she feared being bored. It was bad enough being fed up at home in a failing marriage, but at least her job got her out of the house.

She didn't have any proper hobbies. There hadn't really been any time. In between ferrying Sophie to school, her pony clubs, swimming galas and then working full-time to pay for them all, there was never any time left for her. Regardless, there was only one thing that really ignited any passion in her, and that was to travel, and they could finally afford to now, seeing as her husband's mother Josie had recently passed away. Finally. Thank God. Wasn't she an evil old bat? Josie had never bothered with her, nor even Sophie, her only grandchild, but she had been totally obsessed with her darling Christopher. And didn't he just love it? Wasn't he such a typical mummy's boy?

Josie had always disapproved of Amanda. Many years before, when they had both gone to see her, all giddy and in love, to announce their celebratory news that they were engaged, she had pulled him to one side to warn him that he was marrying a girl from the 'wrong side of the tracks'.

"Jesus Christ, Mother, her family aren't a bunch of criminals," protested Christopher. He had stuck up for her in the early days, but the fact that Amanda had been born working class meant that she was lowest of the low in Josie's spiteful, stuck-up eyes. She was even overheard calling

Amanda's family 'ne'er-do-wells' at their wedding, which she had proclaimed to be the worst day of her life. Josie had wanted her only son to marry the only daughter of her best friend Valerie. Good job he didn't though; the perfect girl that Josie thought was better than Amanda turned out to be a work-shy, anorexic alcoholic. Not too dissimilar, in fact, to lots of the other posh girls who he could have married. They obviously didn't all have these conditions, but most of them tended to have at least one of them. They wouldn't have pulled their weight and worked full-time for thirty years like Amanda had. She had been a damn good wife to him, but in return, she didn't feel that she had got as much back as she put in, which only leads to one thing in a marriage. Resentment.

Amanda totally blamed her mother-in-law for the fact that she was married to an arrogant, entitled, selfish prick.

When they had first met, Amanda was an ambitious, hard-working career girl. Head of PR and fiercely independent. He was an architect, eight years her senior.

In Amanda, Christopher just saw a very pretty girl. A beautiful face and a slim body. That's basically all that was on his checklist. He liked to look flash, to show off. He already had the Porsche 911, so the only thing missing was a fit bird, arm candy, a trophy to sit in his passenger seat and ride around with him to make himself look good, and Amanda was the nearest he would ever get to a model. It wasn't that he was ugly, but with his red, ruddy, posh cheeks, blond, thinning hair and chubby physique, he was more chunk than hunk. He was well and truly batting above his weight with Amanda, and he knew it.

They had met at a trade show at the National Exhibition Centre in Birmingham. They were on rival stands, opposite one another. Christopher asked her out because all the other men on his stand fancied her. The one advantage of his arrogance was that he appeared super confident.

For all his bravado, though, he was inexperienced with women, especially sexually, but this time it worked, and he couldn't believe his luck.

She hadn't particularly fancied him at first, but it was a Tuesday night, so it was either accepting an invite for a meal at the trendy new Indian Fusion restaurant from a man who had been flattering her all week, or a room-service meal for one alone in her hotel room… and Amanda did love a curry!

To her surprise, they hit if off immediately. She loved his confidence and his public-school manners. He loved her feistiness and the fact that she didn't take any crap from anyone.

He was sick of the girls his mother kept introducing him to. The wet lettuces, desperate to get a husband to look after them. Amanda Adams did not need saving, and he found that very attractive indeed. She was a challenge.

In Christopher she saw a stable, solid, decent man, with whom she would have a comfortable, sensible, middle-class life. She thought he would be a potential perfect father for her future children. He never exactly turned out to be one, mind, leaving her to do everything, so she stuck at just the one child. She was more than content with her choice, though, because there was absolutely no way she was ever going through the pain of childbirth again, and more to the point, she couldn't imagine ever loving another child as much as she adored her beautiful, clever daughter Sophie.

Amanda had always known that she didn't want a working-class husband and most definitely not one like a builder. There was no way she would have ever married some slob who showed his arse crack by day and downed four cans of lager in front of the TV by night. So, when Christopher proposed after only two months, she gladly accepted, and they were married within the year. Thinking about it, hadn't she ended up with the same anyway? Christopher spent his days having to put his nose up his VIP clients' backsides by day, and he knocked back four large glasses of Sauvignon Blanc in front of the TV every night. Same shit really, or was that most marriages?

She had thought about leaving him so many times during their marriage, but a divorced friend had once warned her, "When you swap your man for a new one, you just swap one problem for another." This had stopped her in her tracks. Maybe her friend was right. Was there something wrong with all of them? The next one might be even worse. She thought about the grass rarely being greener on the other side. So, she'd stayed put.

Amanda's daydreams of blue skies and sunny days were brought to a sudden halt by the appearance of her husband who had entered the bathroom. Without acknowledging her, without speaking to her and without even making eye contact with his wife, he walked over to the loo to take his morning wee, clearly the first of the day due to its strong stench and dark yellow colour from drinking too much wine and not enough water. Mid-stream, and without any embarrassment whatsoever, he let out an enormous, blustery fart. *Romance is truly dead*, thought an unimpressed Amanda. "And a good morning to you too, my darling," she joked.

Christopher turned his head as though confused. "Huh?" he grunted back obliviously at her, before doing up his flies and leaving the room without bothering to flush. He left behind three splashes of urine on the toilet seat.

She looked at the back of him now as he slovenly sauntered off, his bald patch getting bigger by the day, his flat-as-a-pancake, unsexy bottom clad in unflattering chinos that he insisted on wearing even though she had told him so many times that they did absolutely nothing for his non-existent bum and even less for his bulging gut.

"Don't worry, I'll flush the loo and wipe the dribbles off the seat," she shouted sarcastically after him which landed on deaf ears. She received no reply. First thing in the morning, Christopher was like a Neanderthal until he'd had at least two cups of coffee.

She didn't even particularly mind the fart, but what really narked her was that if she had ever dared to do that to him, he would have been absolutely outraged. He had insisted very early on in their relationship that women should never ever trump nor burp, and he made it very clear that he never wanted to hear either from her; then, years later, he insisted on the same standards of conduct from their daughter.

Amanda smiled to herself, reminiscing of the days when a young Sophie would defiantly and purposefully let rip most mornings as soon as he walked out of the door. They would then both burst into girly giggles in their shared conspiracy of rebelling against Christopher's rules.

Gurrrrgle – a loud rumbling came from under the bath water as Amanda let out her own rebellion of flatulence. She giggled to herself and spoke out loud, "And a good morning to you too, my darling husband." Toilet humour had always appealed to Amanda or anything crude or non-PC. She hated rules. She pondered on the question she had thought about many times: why do farts smell worse when they come from underneath the bath water?

She smiled to herself, amused at her own filthy sense of humour. She bet the women at the golf club would never dare think such a thing. She could be closer to them if they would just loosen up a bit, but they were all so fucking polite. For all she knew, they could be getting a beating every night and they still would turn up for their Saturday afternoon lunches with a spring in their step and an affable 'good afternoon, ladies'. Why did they never come in and moan about what their fuckwits of husbands had done that week to really piss them off?

Sometimes, she daydreamed that they had secret lives, that Lady Janet and Major Charles were swingers, or sensible, adorable Belinda was a secret service agent. She knew that wasn't true though because Belinda hadn't even suspected that Roger was shagging around behind her back. Or had she? See, that was the problem with the ladies from the golf club, they never let on what happened behind closed doors. They never washed their dirty linen in public.

It was one of the things she missed about her friends from the olden days, the ones she left back in Wolverhampton. In the West Midlands, what you saw was what you got. People were open with their friends, warts and all. She much preferred that.

She would hate to go back, though. It was all too working class for her. Not the people, they were salt of the earth, but their lifestyle. She didn't want to have BBQs in ugly back gardens with blokes drinking from cans comparing their latest tattoos, their beer bellies covered by a football shirt. And that was just most of her relatives. Yet, was it any better here in the leafy suburbs of the affluent south? As her mother would say, 'they were all lace curtains and no knickers'.

She was lucky – she had escaped. She had left school and started work at sixteen and had worked her way up through sheer grit and hard graft. She might have been brought up in a council house, but her future would never be in one; of that she was certain. Her parents had purchased theirs from the council, thanks to good old Maggie Thatcher. It had been such a big deal to them at the time, you'd have thought they'd won the lottery, and although they eventually upgraded it for a normal house, it was still crappy in Amanda's eyes. She could not wait to get the hell out of there. She had always had extravagant taste and was never cut out for an average life.

Although Christopher's fat salary might have paid their mortgage, Amanda was proud of the fact that it was her wages that paid for Sophie. Everything that Sophie had needed, or wanted, she got. Pony club, ski holidays, foreign holidays. She wanted her child to live the best life possible, so it was her who'd paid for a private education, something that had never been an option for Amanda, but it had so been worth it. The confidence that it gave her, the friends that she made and the opportunities that she received were worth every single penny. That was why she was travelling around the world right now with Poppy, Arabella and Olivia.

Amanda's mother didn't understand her at all. She simply couldn't grasp why she always wanted better. You would have thought that after the hard, miserable, mundane life that she'd endured, that she would have encouraged her daughter to aim higher, but no, unfortunately she seemed to resent her for it. Amanda was glad she had never listened to her mother's advice, for if she had, and had stayed put and settled down in Wolverhampton, she might now be married to a plumber called Gary, and her daughter might now be knocking back shots in Benidorm with Chantelle, Chanel and Leanne. Amanda felt guilty when she had such condescending thoughts. She was not really a snob, far from it, and she was in fact a big softy, despite her feisty, outspoken ways.

Amanda was sure the other women at the golf club secretly judged her. She often said things to shock them, desperate to bring them out of their shells, but alas, she'd had no luck so far. They were all so bloody prim. They all probably needed a damn good seeing-to. Talking of shagging, who was she to talk? She could have done with one herself if she had the energy. That bastard menopause was knocking the shit out of her on a daily basis, so by the time she got home from work each evening, it took the last of her energy to dump down her bag, clip her hair up, whip her bra off and bung a Marks & Spencer meal for two in the oven.

After she'd eaten, she would watch the clock, waiting until it was acceptable before she could sneak upstairs to watch the TV in bed. 7.30pm was the point at which she usually allowed herself to slope off. She'd got into a habit of watching *Emmerdale* from 7–7.30pm first. She knew it was naff to watch soaps, but you can take the girl out of Wolverhampton…

She'd tell Christopher that she was just nipping up for a bath, but the reality was she'd dash up to her big, wooden sleigh bed, taking with her a cup of green tea and one chunk of Green and Black's organic chocolate. The higher the percentage of cocoa the better; it made her feel less guilty. If she'd had a bad day, she'd switch to a hot chocolate and a whole box of Jaffa cakes, the lowest fat biscuits apparently, so eating the entire box was only as bad as having a few Hobnobs, wasn't it?

Christopher never moaned, nor cared, because it suited him too. He got to watch golf all night, and this way he had the lounge, the sofa and, more importantly, the big telly all to himself. Just how he liked it.

So, where did Amanda fit in? She didn't know, but she just knew that she wanted something different. She was no longer satisfied with her life anymore now that her daughter was all grown up. She was envious of Sophie, running free without a care in the world. She had encouraged her daughter to go, and she'd had to fight vigorously with Christopher, who was insisting that she began her law career straight away. Amanda didn't want their feisty girl trapped on some corporate treadmill until she married some bore, who would take her for granted as soon as she'd popped out a couple of kids, so Sophie, having achieved a First in Law at Warwick University, was now thoroughly enjoying her well-deserved gap year with a group of her equally bright and exciting girlfriends.

Amanda wouldn't let Sophie make the same mistakes that she had, but she didn't need to worry because her daughter was far smarter, yet just as feisty. She was her mother's daughter alright. Amanda called her 'apple' because she never fell far from the tree. Her tree. She was relieved that Sophie neither looked, nor acted, anything like Christopher. Sophie was her girl, inside and out. She was so proud of her.

How Amanda envied her daughter and those girls right now. She hadn't had the chance to do a gap year when she was young. She wasn't sure she'd even heard of one back then. Amanda was an average working-class kid from the Midlands. Neither she nor her friends had the money to go on a gap year. In their day, they went straight out to work, unless of course they were already knocked up, and the poor cows that were, it was usually by some spotty git who would be long gone nine months later. Amanda saw Sophie off with one piece of advice: "Run free, my girl, while you still can."

It was also what Amanda wanted for herself. She was forty-nine now. She didn't want to be fifty and unfulfilled. Where had all the years gone to? She wanted to escape, to run away. To get as far away as possible from her bore of a husband and her nine-to-five regular life as she could. She needed a new purpose to fill her days, and she yearned to do the things that made her happy. She wanted to stop blow-drying her hair, and to leave it to its own curly devices, to wear flowing maxi dresses with flip-flops, travel the world and write a book. She wanted adventures. She wanted out. She didn't want to be a golf widow anymore.

THREE

TRACEY

Poor Andy.

That's what most people called him. It was never Andy the golfer, Andy the accountant; it was always poor Andy. He was the good guy of the group. The only one of the golfers who wasn't an absolute selfish tosser.

This didn't mean he loved his wife, though. He didn't anymore. She had killed that love years ago. There was only so much a man could take before he switched off. Thank God for golf. It was his saviour.

He'd never leave Tracey. He was far too decent, and he intended to keep the vows that he'd made in church all those years ago. Besides, he was too worried about how she would cope without him. Left on her own, the house would never get cleaned; the bills would never get paid. She'd probably invite a group of homeless people to move in if they happened to bump into her when she was inebriated.

Their home would have an open-door policy for any waifs and strays, because although she was a nightmare, she had a heart of gold underneath.

He was wasted on Tracey. She couldn't care less what he did, not realising how lucky she was. The other men reminded him regularly that he had the patience of a saint, and they all admitted they would have strangled Tracey by now, and with very good reason, but they only knew the half of it. Andy had never told anyone the full story. He was far too embarrassed. He was ashamed of her behaviour, but even more so, he was ashamed of himself for putting up with it.

He had really loved her once. She had bounced energetically into his office, auburn, curly hair, like a wild temptress. He had never met anyone like her. A free spirit, a wild child, an artist, but that was the thing with artists, they had a crazy side that made them creative.

For a steady, sensible accountant, she was a breath of fresh air, a girl who brought colour to his dull, grey life. She dragged him out of his shell until he loosened up, had a drink, went to parties. But all play and no work was alright, if you didn't have to go to work. Tracey was a trust fund babe. Her equally crazy grandma had left her in the fortunate position of not having to work for a living, which left her at liberty to do as she wished. Tracey didn't live in the real world; she lived in Tracey-Land. As a friend, she was good fun, in small doses, but as a partner, she was spoilt and selfish. Andy had started off their marriage by indulging her, so as far as she was concerned, he only had himself to blame. He knew what he was marrying, so why should she change?

The problem for poor Andy was that he did have to work. He couldn't, and didn't want to, drink until 3am on a Sunday night. He simply couldn't keep up with her. What was fun when they were young had now turned distinctly unattractive. She was a lush. A functioning alcoholic. Maybe if they had kids, that might have made her change, calmed her down, but no, she didn't want any attention to be given to some brat. Attention had to be on her, and her alone.

Andy had hoped that she might change her mind in the early days, but now he was relieved that no child had her as a mother or had to live in their house with her slovenly behaviour. Thank goodness they hadn't had kids. They would have ended up well and truly fucked-up.

Tracey described herself as an artist and a social butterfly. She often described Andy as a bore. If he had a pound for every time she screamed 'boring bastard' at him, he'd be a millionaire. In fact, they would almost be millionaires if she didn't spend so much money on Botox and fillers or in their local Waitrose where her trolley would be stacked high with ready meals and her beloved alcohol. Tracey would regularly accuse anyone who dared to stop drinking before the early hours as being boring. She would host extravagant dinner parties and fancy nights out, but her revolving door of friends was ever-changing. People would only be in favour for a while, until they refused to carry on drinking with her until the early hours. If you were a drinker, you were in, but if you dared to stop when you'd had enough, you would be replaced by someone more fun. None of the couples that they socialised with lasted for long.

She could be great company when she was the artist – the crazy, bubbly, chatty girl – and if you met her for lunch, you would thoroughly enjoy it, but if you met her for the evening, then God help you, because naughty, wild Tracey came out to play.

Andy thought she might be on the spectrum, but he would never dare to suggest it. He didn't want scratches and bruises on his face again, it didn't look good for work, so he put his head down, worked hard, paid the bills, and left her to fill her days with whatever she chose to do. She was a very gifted artist, with oil painting being her true passion, but unfortunately, she wasn't dedicated enough to knuckle down and make a proper living from it. She didn't want deadlines and managers. She just wanted to have fun.

Andy had tried many times to put his foot down. He attempted to restrict her drinking, begging her to keep it to weekends only, but that soon slipped to include Fridays, and then Thursdays. She said it was none of his business what she drank or when she drank, but poor Andy was the one who would end up on his knees, clearing up the vomit from their carpets, and it was he who had to scrub their mattress clean when she very often wet, or had occasionally shat, their super king bed.

He had spent one New Year's Eve silently crying, and hating his life, whilst he vigorously scrubbed orange hues of spaghetti bolognaise vomit from a new, cream stair carpet. Once, he found her passed out and fast asleep in their hot tub, but when he had gone to pull her out to safety, he had cut his feet open on the broken glass that she had left all around. His yelps awoke her, and the ensuing abuse that spewed out of her mouth at him caused him to wish that he had left her there to drown.

He didn't know what was worse, when she threw up and passed out at various places around the house or garden or when she wasn't too drunk but was in an amorous mood. He didn't fancy her anymore whatsoever. Not only was she overweight and bloated, but she had chopped off the long, wild, dark ginger hair he once loved and had cropped it into a short bob and dyed it a strange tint of burgundy. She persisted in going to a local salon every week, where some eighteen-year-old trainee dyed her eyebrows a tad too dark and painted her nails in too bright a colour. She was trying to look young, but she was starting to look cheap. He had tried to resist her drunken seduction once, but she hadn't given up and had more or less forced him. Was it possible for a woman to rape a man? All that he knew was that it was easier to oblige and get it over with than to face another fight. Most people never saw this side of her. Her guests had always long gone before she got into these states. She had a knack of being on her best behaviour when she needed to.

From Tracey's point of view, she was fine. She just wanted Andy to stop judging her. She wanted him to accept her as she was and to stop trying to ruin her fun. What she really yearned for was to go and live in Spain, but Andy wouldn't agree, dreading an expat lifestyle where she would easily be able to find an abundance of company and plenty of excuses to drink all day, every day. She denied this, claiming that she only drank to rebel against his restrictions. She maintained that all she desired in life was a terrace overlooking the sea, to spend her days painting and to eat every meal outside, with the sun on her face.

Tracey had been brought up by a constantly depressed mother, who never ventured from her bedroom, and an overbearing, controlling father. She had no siblings, so she'd spent most of her time in her bedroom with her own imagination for company. Now grown up, she wanted to play in the light, to be free, to spread her wings like the butterfly she used to imagine she was when she was the lonely, trapped child. Tracey said she would rather live to sixty and be liberated than to live to eighty but with no joy and no colour in her life.

She needed to be understood, to be accepted for her choices in life, and she wanted someone to love her just the way she was.

FOUR

LOUISE

'So quiet, I hardly notice she's there'. That's what Louise's teacher wrote about her in her school report when she was eight years old.

She was never any trouble for her parents, not even in the dreaded teenage years. The only bad thing she ever did in her life was to steal a chocolate bar when she failed to put some money into the honesty box at the Girl Guides tuck shop because she had forgotten her purse, but even then, she had felt so bad about it that it had given her sleepless nights for a week, sick with worry, so much so that she went back the very next week and she slipped a fifty pence piece into the box, which was more than she even owed.

Louise always achieved acceptable Bs, rather than dynamic As. She was ordinary. Her hair was shoulder length, neat and mousy, her body average. Her eyes blue but not a dazzling sky blue, instead a dull, greyish blue, like a cloudy day. She had never done one thing that you could describe as wild or rebellious in the forty years of her life. So far.

She was married to Chris. They called him Chris so as not to confuse him with Amanda's Christopher. He was the local estate agent, and she his dutiful wife, who sat beside him in their smart town office every day, Monday to Friday, nine to five. She was his secretary, his PA, and his office manager. She even worked extra hours on Saturday morning, doing house viewings whilst he went off to play his beloved golf.

Sunday was her only day off, but it was no day of rest for her because this was catch-up day when she did the cleaning, the washing and then cooked a full Sunday roast dinner for Chris's parents who insisted on coming round. Every. Single. Fucking. Week.

She didn't really like them coming, but she had never complained. It was just what happened. She accepted that was just the way it was. Chris liked to see them. He wanted them there. Clearly, her company was not enough for him. Her parents had died in a car accident years ago, so his parents were the only close family they had, so she couldn't deny him his folks just because she hadn't got hers anymore, could she?

To the dismay of his staid parents, they had no children. It was a conscious choice. Louise had never wanted them, and neither had Chris. She thought that it was this preference that had drawn them together. It was something they had in common. Maybe it was the only thing they had in common. They were the only ones in their peer group who were adamant that they didn't want any kids, ever. She knew what the others thought of them, 'the boring freaks'. Maybe that's why they stayed together. She would describe their relationship as companionship. It had never been a great, passionate affair.

Her confidence never did get the chance to blossom. She never found herself. Instead, she had found Chris, and he found her. They had married young, so she never knew anything else. Chris liked routine. Louise was pliable. He had moulded her into what he wanted from a wife. Supportive, reliable, subservient. Louise would have loved a dog, but they had no pets because he didn't like animals and he insisted on a clean and tidy house. She would have settled on a cat, but he was allergic, so he claimed.

Her life was safe. Predictable. Was she happy? Well, she wasn't unhappy, so why rock the boat? There wasn't anything better she had to do, or anywhere better to go, so that was that. It was what it was. Or was it?

Because Louise had a secret.

A little monster had been festering away inside her for a while now, one that had started on her fortieth birthday. She'd had her eyes well and truly opened, but she was keeping the monster contained, for now. She was fearful to let it out because she was too scared of the repercussions.

It happened when their salesgirl, Samantha, had asked what she was doing for her fortieth.

"Nothing special," replied Louise. Chris hadn't done anything special for her thirtieth, so she didn't expect that her fortieth would be any different. He didn't go in for romantic gestures or spontaneous surprises. Left to him, it would no doubt be the usual takeaway and a bottle of wine. Every birthday, he always ordered the same. Crispy duck and pancakes and a special chow mein from Mr Cheung's Diner in the high street, and it would all be washed down with a bottle of Prosecco, or maybe two seeing as it was a special occasion. That was as exciting as it got.

Samantha had put both Louise and Chris on the spot. She'd announced in the middle of their office that there was no way she was allowing Louise to let her fortieth birthday pass without a celebration. Chris went to take over the conversation, but Samantha had raised her hand to silence him. "Sorry, Chris, it's girls only," and before they knew it, she had told Louise what time she was picking her up on Friday night.

"Just a few drinks and nibbles with the girls," she ordered to a bewildered Louise and a miffed Chris. He didn't dare to object; Samantha was the best salesperson they'd ever had, and their business would be lost without her. His rival agents in their town were always trying to poach her, so she got away with anything she wanted. Louise was in awe of her, wishing she were that brave, that dynamic. When Louise was a little girl, she used to watch the popular girls at school and wish she had their outgoing natures and sexual confidence. She was an observer of life, not a participator.

Louise did love Chris. At least she thought she did, seeing as she had nothing else to compare it with. He once compared them to twins – "Two peas in a pod," he had proclaimed. She disagreed; it was more like bossy big brother and spineless, silly sister, but he was right about one thing – it was more of a sibling relationship. Companions. They shared a passion for board games and box sets, in that order. Their rigid routine consisted of a fish and chip supper every Friday night, followed by a game of Scrabble, then a box set at the weekends, not that he ever watched anything until the end. By the time whatever they were watching was fifteen minutes in, he would always fall asleep, worn out from the hours of walking and the fresh air from the local golf course.

Did he love her? She wasn't sure. He always told her so when he pecked her on the top of the head, but this only occurred when he went away for his regular golf trips. She wished she could go away with a group of girls, but she didn't know anyone that did that sort of thing, and if she did, they'd never invite her, she thought. Samantha from their office went all over the place, but her friends were younger than Louise, and far more glamorous, and anyway, she couldn't leave their office, especially if Samantha or Chris went away. She had to hold the fort. Chris needed her, she reminded herself. It was her duty to support him.

Anyway, back to the night where it all changed. Her fortieth birthday. Samantha must have pre-warned her friends that Louise was a nerd, a bore, too straight, because they clearly had an agenda for the evening, and that was to get her pissed and to make her loosen up and enjoy herself. After being plied with drink, Louise found that she was thoroughly enjoying the night out that she had genuinely been dreading all week. She had worn her second-favourite dress. Chris had complained about her first choice. He couldn't have 'the wife of the town's finest estate agency boozing in bars and looking like an old slapper', he'd told her. The dress wasn't even short or low cut – not that she had any tits to show off – but it was red, and it was his favourite dress. He had never complained when she wore it when she was with him. Regardless, she obeyed his wishes and swapped it for the plain blue one, which she regretted as soon as she saw Samantha's pals, a bunch of stunners in the latest trendy fashions. She looked like their boring aunt, but she soon forgot about her clothes after her second glass of champagne. Samantha had bought the first two bottles as her birthday gift to Louise; then they all put into a kitty. She didn't know that girls did that; the only time she heard of a kitty was when, just prior to his golf trips, Chris would send her to the bank to withdraw cash or order currency for the golf kitty, depending on whether they were staying in the UK or going abroad. Now Louise knew exactly what they spent it on. She'd naïvely thought that their golf trips were all about golf and a sedate dinner afterwards, but is this what they did, went partying? It appeared that everyone did, except her, but she found that she enjoyed it.

She now knew what she had been missing all these years, and the girls had not stopped telling her all night that 'life begins at forty'. She certainly hoped so.

Life didn't exactly change much, though, at least not at first. Louise soon slipped right back into her dutiful routine as soon as her two-day hangover had subsided. Chris had been unimpressed that she lay comatose on the sofa all weekend, so he'd deliberately left her there suffering whilst he took his parents to the local pub for their obligatory Sunday lunch, not bothering to bring anything home for Louise. She was in the doghouse, and his sulking would outlast her hangover.

She silently seethed about the lack of care he showed her. When he'd attended sportsmen's dinners, another regular activity of the golfing brigade, he always came back worse for wear, staggering out of the minibus, urinating against the garden hedge, then collapsing on the sofa for the night, and not once had she ever complained. The following day, she'd always made him a full English breakfast to soak up the alcohol, and she'd mix a glass of Alka-Seltzer to rehydrate him, nursing him back to normality without any resentment whatsoever, but he clearly had zero intentions of returning the favour. For the first time in twenty years, Louise felt bitter. The tide was turning.

She groaned as she hauled herself up from the sofa and plodded to the fridge. She was sure her brain must be bruised because it hurt so much whenever she moved her body. Pulling open the heavy door, she reached inside desperately to grab a carton of orange juice, from which she frantically swigged to wash down the second dose of paracetamol she'd needed that day.

As she closed the fridge door, she noticed a large, pink carrier bag that had been tossed under the kitchen table. A flashback came to her, and she quickly grabbed the bag, keen to hide it before Chris came home. He most certainly would not approve of the contents. She frantically stuffed the bag inside their cloakroom, burying it deep underneath one of her old winter coats, right at the back. He'd never look there, so it could remain her dirty little secret until she felt well enough to retrieve it again.

As she lay back down on the sofa, she pulled a huge, woollen, cashmere throw over herself, suddenly desperate for an afternoon nap and because her tiredness made her chilly. As she began to doze, further flashbacks began to jump into her head, making her smile and, at one point, giggle to herself. She'd made Samantha promise to never tell

Chris about that night. An Ann Summers party would have been the tackiest, most unclassy thing she could have gone to in his eyes, him being the judgemental prude that he was.

It wasn't the sex toys that had shocked Louise – and the games were rather silly, although she'd found them great fun in her intoxicated state – it was the stories that the others had all divulged that had shocked her. Did normal women all talk like this? She hadn't even imagined these experiences would have even existed, never mind the fact that every single one of the others had all appeared to have enjoyed several of them. She was clearly leading a very sheltered life.

After being grilled about her own sex life, Louise was shocked that they all squealed in horror at her lack of experience. Was she that abnormal? She pondered on the questions of her sexual interrogation. Why didn't Chris ever kiss her on the lips? Why hadn't they tried oral sex? Why hadn't she given herself an orgasm if she didn't get one from her husband?

The more she thought about it, the more unsatisfied she began to feel. Not just regarding the sex but regarding the love. That was what she felt right now. Uncared for. Unappreciated. Undesired. Un-fuckable. Unloved.

What would it be like to have a love affair? The seed was sown.

Louise's little secret began to grow. Pre-forty, Louise would sit in their luxuriant office, in the grand Georgian building on the best road in town, reading interior design magazines or deliberating which flowers to put in the hanging baskets this year, but post-forty, Louise had very different thoughts. As their regular window cleaner Steve swished his

42

silver wiper around the corner of their large shop frontage, she was admiring his. She found herself glancing at his tight jeans and wondering what Steve would be like in bed. He was only in his early thirties, average-looking, but why had she never noticed before what big arms he had? Why had she never noticed other men before? Suddenly, everywhere she looked, she was seeing shoulders, legs, bums and groins, but each time she looked, she found herself preferring what she saw to what she had at home.

By now, she had opened the pink bag. She had deliberately planned an afternoon for the occasion, waiting until they were particularly busy in the office, before announcing that she had a migraine coming on, and just like that, she told Chris that she was going home for a lie-down. She was confident that she would have the whole house to herself for a few hours. This should give her enough time to find out what this was all about. She couldn't admit to Chris that she was now the proud owner of a vibrator. She knew it must remain a secret or he would feel emasculated. Her first experience took a while for her to get the hang of it. The girls had told her that she had to imagine being in bed with a man whilst she used it. She felt too guilty thinking about a man she knew in real life. That would surely be adultery, wouldn't it? Instead, she thought briefly about who she fancied on TV, but only one man came to mind. Oooh yessss! *Martin Kemp!*

That afternoon, Louise not only had the satisfaction of her first-ever orgasm but also her second and third thanks to that silver-haired fox, who, in her daydreams, had licked her out, come over her tits and well and truly shagged her over the end of the bed. After this symbolic turning point,

Louise's fantasies kept her sane. It was her 'naughty but nice' treat, and it sure beat a tub of Häagen-Dazs Cookie Dough ice cream.

Every week, Louise now enjoyed her fantasies. It became her new hobby. She stopped doing Saturday morning viewings and had given the work to their staff instead, informing, rather than asking, a begruntled Chris – after all, he spent his weekends playing golf, so why should she work the extra day? Louise was finally growing a backbone.

By now, she had mentally been though all the shopkeepers in town: Bert from the butchers, Ian from the bank and even Tom the twenty-year-old student who erected their 'For Sale' boards. Steve the window cleaner had it the most though, with him being her favourite due to his rhythmic movements as he went back and forth across their large, glass window. Samantha caught her watching him once, but she was doing the same and she winked at Louise in conspiracy. Afterwards, they shared mischievous smiles which went totally over the head of a stuffy Chris who was sat at his desk bellowing orders down the phone to some unfortunate employee.

Samantha didn't really like Chris, but she was very fond of Louise, and she did love their office. It was the classiest in town, and Samantha was ambitious. She wanted her own agency one day so she was learning everything she could before she struck out on her own. Samantha noticed that Louise had far better ideas about the business than Chris had, but things always had to be done his way. Samantha would never let a man overrule her ideas and opinions like that.

Louise felt guilty that she had also masturbated thinking of all the friends with whom Chris played golf every weekend.

She didn't find any one of them attractive, well OK then, maybe Roger if she was honest. It was his arrogant cockiness, she just couldn't help herself, but she felt that she did it more out of rebellion, to teach Chris a lesson for putting golf before her and their marriage. All the golfers did – she wasn't the only golf widow.

She envied Belinda for being dumped. If Chris dumped her, she would have an excuse to see what it was like to go with another man. She prayed that he would just sod off with one of their staff, but she knew he never would. She also felt guilty for including the golfers in her secret DIY sessions, so she vowed to never repeat that again, primarily out of respect for the other women but also because Roger was an arsehole. She would strike her previous thought of finding him attractive right out of her head.

Now that Louise had fantasised about most of the men she knew, the monster on her shoulder was growing, and she was getting more confident. She yearned to go shopping for a new wardrobe of sexier clothes and matching lacy underwear to replace her Marks & Spencer nude, comfy, boring old bras and big knickers, but she continued to refrain herself in case Chris got suspicious. She knew that if she were ever in a position of sleeping with another man, she would find it very difficult to resist. She was equally frustrated that she'd probably never get the chance, with Chris keeping her on such a tight leash.

Knowing that she would never have any opportunities to find out what it would be like to have sex with someone else, she had even contemplated using a male prostitute. She had googled a male escort agency online and, although it did not state that they provided sex, she believed that *extras* could be purchased at an additional rate. She had thought about hiring one and sending him a script in advance, like the one she had planned with military precision inside her head:

He would make an appointment, then turn up posing as a potential house buyer. She would show him around the show home on the fancy new housing development out in the countryside, and when they walked into the master bedroom and she was giving her best sales speech, he would gently touch her lips with his forefinger, urging her to 'shusssssh'. Then, he would masterly throw her onto the bed and proceed to giving her an experience of afternoon delight.

She chickened out, though. She was far too scared that she might get blackmailed afterwards and ruin the reputation of their business, as well as herself.

She wondered *when*. When and how long it would take her to find out what it was like to go with another man, if ever. She knew that other women moaned about their husbands always wanting sex, and the long list of excuses they made to avoid having to give it to them, but she was the opposite. She was absolutely gagging for it.

She had also heard the horror stories of the menopause, and if that was what was coming for her in a few years' time, she needed to be quick. She needed to find someone new to have sex with soon, and get as much as possible, before her fanny dried up too and before she turned into Belinda and preferred cake instead.

FIVE

JANET

Margaret Thatcher. Lady Muck. Her Royal Highness. These were just a few descriptions of the conservative-looking woman that was Janet Cavendish, wife of the chairman of the golf club, Major Charles.

With his white handlebar moustache, Major Charles was a formidable character. He was an ex-army, old-school gentleman, determined to keep West Seale Golf Club as one of the finest and most exclusive golf clubs in Hampshire. There would be no riff-raff bringing down standards, not on his watch.

Janet was his trusty sidekick. She organised functions and welcomed VIPs with professionalism and diligence. Childless, but not through lack of wanting, and now sixty-one years old, she was the oldest of the Saturday lunchtime golf widows. The others slightly feared her, feeling that they must be on their best behaviour whilst in Her Ladyship's presence.

As well as entertaining the golfers' wives, she was on duty most nights at various charity functions held at the golf club. If she had three nights off each week, then she was lucky. She had thrown herself into charity work when she was unable to have children, keen to busy herself so she didn't think about it too much, otherwise she would have cracked up. Ladies of her ilk didn't crack up; they pulled their shoulders back, held their heads up high and kept that stiff British upper lip. Major Charles would not have stood for anything less. If she ever dared to complain about anything, or whinge as he would describe it, his stern response was always the same: "Man up, Janet." Major Charles thought he was still in the army, and everyone at the golf club, including his wife, were his soldiers.

They were a very traditional couple. They dined each evening at 7pm, meeting for a gin and tonic in the dining room at 6.30pm sharp and always dressed appropriately. They had never grabbed a ready meal, or a eaten a takeaway on the sofa wearing their scruffs, in their whole life.

Janet's marriage had been arranged by her father. She had spent her childhood being homeschooled by her governess and then later sent to a Swiss finishing school. Her childhood was subdued. Her household was formal, calm but very cold. She was summoned to meet with her parents each evening for precisely half an hour, but apart from that, she was brought up by staff. From the day she was born, her parents ensured that she was prepared for one thing in her life, and that was a suitable marriage to a suitable man. Seeing as her father and Charles's father were business partners, it was a done deal before she'd turned eighteen.

She had dreamt of a different life for herself when she had been a young girl. To run away, live in a forest and swim in wild lakes. Janet loved nature, but the only green she ever saw was the golf course, not that she ever got the chance to play on there of course; she was far too busy.

As well as her first lady duties at the golf club, Janet was on many committees. She was secretary at the local WI (Women's Institute); she organised the church choir and helped them with the flower arranging; and she volunteered at the local hospice charity shop every Monday afternoon. She also played bridge on Wednesday evenings, but that was her favourite activity of them all, because unlike everything else she did, this one was through choice. The problem with Janet was that she couldn't say no, especially to her domineering husband.

She knew that she had the nickname of Maggie (Thatcher), based on her always being immaculate, with her lacquered, blonde, bouffant hair, smart Jaeger suits and the obligatory matching handbag, but she lacked Maggie's strength of character. She might look fierce, but it was all a façade. Life was chaotic, and often stressed her out, but one mustn't complain, so like Her Majesty The Queen, she held her head high, put on her nude lipstick and appeared on stage to do her duty. People relied on her. She didn't want to let them, or her husband, down. Janet was in fact a rather shy lady, and despite such a wide and busy social circle, no one really knew the real her. She didn't have a best friend.

Janet couldn't run away even if she had wanted to. She had no money of her own. She'd never had a paying job in her life, passing from the care of her father to the care of her husband. Major Charles was most definitely in charge of the purse strings. She had absolutely no idea how much money they even had. "Don't worry your pretty head with that nonsense," he would reply to her if she ever tried to enquire, or, "Do be quiet. It's crass to discuss money, Janet," he would scold her.

It wasn't as if she went without anything, but she certainly had to stick to what he called her 'allowance', although she felt it was more like her rations. She might have had the luxury of a weekly blow-dry at the local salon every Friday, but that was because Charles wanted his wife groomed and presentable. Appearances were everything to him.

Luckily, a shrewd Janet had worked out a way around his restrictions many years ago. Seeing that her personal allowance was insultingly low, yet the grocery shop was uncontrolled due to her self-indulgent husband's extravagant love of fine foods and top-quality alcohol, she had learnt to buy all her toiletries, make-up, magazines and books in Sainsburys during her weekly shop. He had never been in a supermarket in his entire life – 'women's work' he would claim, so he was ignorant of the fact that you could buy more in there nowadays than just groceries.

Janet's favourite part of her weekly shopping trip was the stand at the end of the aisle that held the gift cards. As she stood in line at the checkout, she would gaze at the rows of credit-card-sized offerings to every store that you could think. She always tossed in a couple of £50 Marks & Spencer cards, they were the absolute best, and this allowed her to buy her underwear, clothing or anything else that she might need for herself, or as gifts for others. If there was a film she fancied seeing, she'd throw in a Cineworld card. If she needed a new hairdryer, the Argos card would leap into her trolley.

Janet didn't even hold her own credit card. She was the second card holder on Charles's account, so the bills were sent to, and thoroughly inspected each month by, His Lordship. All that he saw on her monthly statement was the hairdressers and Sainsbury's. "Why is food so extortionate these days?" he had grumbled to himself.

It wasn't that Janet was a dishonest woman, but she justified herself that it was her right, her wages, for all the unpaid work at the golf club that he constantly piled upon her frail, slim shoulders. Taking what she wanted in return was literally the only bit of control she had over her own life, and she thoroughly enjoyed the feeling of getting one over on her control freak of a husband, far more than the goods that she bought with her proceeds of crime.

As Janet walked outside, she emptied the contents of her trolley into the boot of her seven-year-old silver Honda. She would have loved a sleek, navy Mercedes convertible like Amanda drove, but Charles bought their vehicles, and 'beggars couldn't be choosers' he'd reminded her. Funny how when it came to one for himself, they could afford the latest Jag F-Type, replaced every two years with a brand-new model.

She felt an uncharacteristic wave of resentment come over her as she struggled to retrieve the coin that was stuck in the slot in her trolley, but she soon cheered up when she managed to recover her £1 and pop it into her pocket, because as she did, her fingers brushed against the cool, glass object hidden inside her quilted navy Barbour jacket.

Within the safety and privacy of her own car, she retrieved the object and smiled to herself. A bottle of peach OPI nail varnish was admired by its new owner. Her weekly treat, her gift to herself, for having to run around all week for everyone else. Even better, it came courtesy of Sainsbury's. At their prices, the least they owed her was a freebie every now and again, especially after all the money she spent in their store. But it wasn't every now and again, it was every week. She simply couldn't help herself. It was the most exhilarating thing she did. Her secret hobby. The adrenaline rush she got as she slipped the stolen items into her pocket elated her, and she'd never been caught, had she? Not yet anyway.

Janet was not really that materialistic. Her greatest desire in the world was to swap her big house for a little rustic country cottage and to spend her days pottering around doing her garden, planting lavenders and other beautiful flowers that she might actually have the time to smell. Oh, how she yearned for long lie-ins with a cup of peppermint tea whilst she leisurely read *The Daily Mail* newspaper and not having to get up until 11am. Eating buttery toast in bed and not caring if she dropped crumbs on the sheets. Of course, this had to remain just a fantasy – Major Charles particularly despised people who were not up, showered and dressed by 7.30am sharp.

Janet longed for afternoon walks through the woods, with a nice little dog by her side, something manageable like a little sausage dog, or a miniature poodle, one that she could stroll along with casually to admire the snowdrops, the bluebells, the sunflowers, the autumn leaves and the frosty branches, merely to be outside whatever the season or the weather.

She would love to own a dog, one that she could spoil, who could be her baby, seeing as she never got the chance to have a real child. She had never bothered to beg Charles to allow her to get one though because it wouldn't have been fair on it, seeing as she was out almost every day and most nights.

What Janet craved most was to retire from her duties and to have some time for herself for once. In her daydreams of the perfect life, it was always the same visions – the cottage, the dog, the sun streaming through the rose bushes – but it was strange; Charles was never in her dreams.

SIX

CARRIE

Back to that Saturday afternoon at the West Seale Golf Club in Hampshire.

While the wives waited patiently for their husbands inside the clubhouse restaurant, the golfers were gathered around the eighteenth hole when alerted by Roger to check out something at two o'clock. They didn't even need to turn round to determine what it would be. Roger had always been a ladies' man; they all had been really, except for Andy (too decent) and Chris (more interested in work). The men turned round to see a young, blonde girl in her twenties, clad in skin-tight leopard print Lycra leggings, a black Nike crop top, with a gym bag slung over a perfect, tanned shoulder. Her long, blonde ponytail swung rhythmically from side to side as she strode purposefully towards the gym.

"Yep, I would," exclaimed Roger, suddenly no longer interested in the game.

"Bloody hell, Roger, aren't you busy enough with the teenager you've just traded your wife in for?" berates Andy. "Isn't one enough?"

"Carrie is thirty-one, for God's sake, hardly a kid. Anyway, I can't help it if I've still got it." He smiles arrogantly. "You're just jealous and you know it," teased a smug Roger.

Christopher, envious that he hadn't got a young mistress too, sighed wistfully, patting his pal on the shoulder as if to concur.

Chris jumped to the defence of Roger, telling Andy, "Calm down, goody two shoes. Just because you're under the thumb, doesn't mean us lot can't do what we like," as he raised his eyebrows to the others in jest.

"On the subject of misbehaving," a bemused Christopher enquires to Charles, "Hey, Major, what's the accommodation like for Thailand?"

Charles had organised their trip this time to the villa where he went twice a year. He knew they would love it as much as he did, so he was particularly looking forward to their trip, knowing what decadence and debauchery awaited them all. "Just you wait and see," was all that he would divulge, tapping the side of his nose with his bony finger to tease his audience, adding to the excitement of the group.

Christopher piped up earnestly, "Don't forget, the women think we won this in the South-West Competition. Andy, this means you. Don't go blabbing to Tracey. Amanda would chop my balls off if she found out. I haven't even told her where we are going yet."

A tired-looking Andy replied wearily, "Oh, don't worry about that. I can assure you I won't breathe a word. She's driving me bloody mad right now. I can't wait to get away from her for a fortnight." With that, Andy whacked the ball, then shook his head, frustrated as he shanked his shot.

"Oh, bad luck," laughed Chris. "And with a shot like that, I can't believe the women actually believe that we win all these competitions." Smug guffaws bellowed out from the group, amused at their shared conspiracy of deceiving their wives.

With their game over, the men trooped back towards the clubhouse. Major Charles strutted ahead as usual, thinking he was still in the army with his squadron following obediently behind him but appearing more like a bossy mother duck leading her dopey ducklings. "Time for the nineteenth hole, gentlemen."

The men, fulfilled by their afternoon's activities, strolled contentedly over towards the car park to pack away their expensive, top-of-the-range titanium clubs into the boots of their smart, executive motors. They had the VIP row reserved entirely for themselves, with Major Charles occupying the designated chairman's spot underneath his own carved wooden plaque, 'Chairman'. Janet, as his wife, had secured the one beside his, 'Chairman's Wife', and the four spaces to their right had all been reserved for his cronies.

Their car boots all lifted up in succession, like cabaret dancer's legs. The men carefully wiped clean, then laid down, their beloved golf clubs inside, before slamming their boots closed again. Their cars would now remain parked there until Sunday afternoon so that they could go and sink several pints in the clubhouse. Their obliging wives always drove them home on a Saturday evening and then ferried them all back the next morning in time for their Sunday morning session.

Only Andy's boot now remained open because he had been distracted by something, or someone rather, who was standing across the car park. "Please don't tell me you've brought her here already?" groaned Andy.

The others gaped at what they saw. Waiting nervously two hundred yards away was a very shy Carrie, too timid to approach them but clearly trying to alert Roger's attention.

Roger shouted over to her, "Hang on, honey, I'll be over in a min." Then, he rudely turned his back on her and continued to casually, and without any urgency, talk to his friends. "Why shouldn't I? I'm a paid-up member, and she's my partner now," replied a brazen Roger.

"Oh, Jesus Christ. The women will *flip!*" exclaimed an anxious Andy.

"Partner? Already?" queried an indifferent Chris. "I thought it was just a casual thing."

"Weeeeell, she's super keen on me, so why not?" he shrugged. Roger was never one to turn down an offer or let an opportunity of sex go to waste.

"How do you do it, Roger?" asked an envious Christopher.

"I give them loads of compliments, and I just tell them what they want to hear," bragged Roger.

"Which is?" Christopher pushed him, keen to pick up some tips for himself.

"Well, in her case, she's that age, early thirties. Y'know. Tick-tock, tick-tock," he offered to the group, who were all still confused. "Fertility clock and all that. She's trying for a baby," Roger further elaborated to the now gobsmacked group.

Major Charles shook his head in disbelief and briskly walked off ahead, keen to distance himself from any trouble or scandal at the club. He intended to keep himself busy in the office for the next hour or two, that was for sure.

"Are you *craaaazy*? Back to shitty nappies? At *your* age," gasped an astounded Christopher.

Chris also shuddered at the mere thought of it.

Roger smiled smugly. "Don't be daft – I've had the snip."

The men looked on, perplexed.

Roger now smirked. "But *sheee* doesn't know that, does she?" He laughed out loud arrogantly. "And after all, I am helping her to practise."

"Oh, my good Lord, he is not even joking," groaned a horrified Andy.

With that, Roger turned his back on the men and whistled to her rudely, as though she were his pet dog, and clicked his fingers for her to come and join them.

The others, having lifted their jaws from the floor, scarpered into the clubhouse. They had absolutely no intention of walking in with him and his fancy bit.

Chris, Christopher and Andy, having greeted their wives and bought them all drinks, had now sat down at the adjacent table to the women's, exactly as they did every other week, but this time they were all on tenterhooks, nervously awaiting the reaction of the women when Roger walked in with Belinda's replacement. They hoped that he would at least have the decency to sit far away from them all and not bring Carrie anywhere near the men's table, or they would all be in the doghouse that night.

The occupants of the wives' table were totally oblivious until they were suddenly startled by a low, snarling growl emerging unexpectedly from Amanda as she leant in towards the centre of their table. "I don't *fucking* believe this."

Janet looked up, shocked, on the verge of requesting that she would please refrain from such language in the clubhouse, until she and the others all observed what, or rather whom, Amanda was referring to. "Oh dear, this is most unsavoury," exclaimed Janet. "I must speak to Charles about this." She looked around flustered, but he was nowhere in sight.

Blatantly stood at the bar were Roger and Carrie, him as cocksure as ever as he demanded, "A pint of Guinness, and a white wine for the lady please, squire." Carrie was clearly out of her depth and feeling most uncomfortable, aware of the evil eyes of the wives burning into the back of her pretty little head. "I don't think you should have brought me here, Roger. They are all going to hate me."

With that, Roger crudely slapped her pert backside and laughed. "Don't be daft, gorgeous, how could anyone hate you?" He then tossed a tenner across the bar, telling the young bartender, louder than was necessary, to, "Keep the change." The miffed barman plonked the leftover 10p piece into the recycled jam jar that he had labelled with a yellow faded Post-it note and scrawled 'TIPS' across it with a black sharpie pen.

"They're probably worried though, in case we put ideas into their husbands' heads to trade them in," scoffed Roger. "And if they had any sense, they would all upgrade that miserable bunch. Especially poor Andy, his wife Tracey is a bloody nightmare, just you wait and see."

Tracey, on hearing her name mentioned, glanced up, detecting to her trepidation that the couple were heading straight in their direction. "Oh, Jesus Christ, he's actually bringing her over here. No one look up."

Before the others had the chance to reply, Roger had, without any shame, pulled out Belinda's old chair and prompted a bewildered Carrie to sit down. Unaware of the significance of where he had directed her to sit, she obediently but nervously lowered herself down, then just sat there like a rabbit caught in the headlights. At this point, Roger, much to the distress of the already uncomfortable Carrie, ungallantly plonked down her glass of Pinot Grigio onto the women's table in front of her, and then, without uttering another word, and with zero introductions, he slinked off to join the men on the next table, leaving a cringing Carrie to get on with it.

The men all winced as Roger casually sat down to join them as though nothing was wrong. Christopher cringed and started to fiddle with his beer mat, peeling the paper off the back of it as he attempted to keep his eyes looking downwards, having no intention of catching the eye of his wife Amanda, who he knew for a fact would be raging.

A concerned Chris whispered to Roger, "I cannot believe your nerve," while Andy nervously scarpered to the bathroom.

Meanwhile, over at the ladies table, the deathly silence caused the atmosphere to be even more tense, not to mention excruciatingly awkward. Janet, ever the professional, came into her own as the host of the golf club. "Errrr, are you a fan of golf?" A terrified Carrie spluttered nervously in response to the barrage of polite questions that Janet then continued to fire at her, desperate to be liked but more relieved that she was even being spoken to. The wives, having no option but to endure this farcical situation, soon realised that she wasn't such a bitch, after all. In fact, the women found her to be rather sweet, terribly naïve even, and most definitely far too good for Roger. Every single one of the ladies began to feel sorry for her, although they immediately felt guilty for doing so, out of solidarity for Belinda, whose seat at the table Carrie now occupied. Belinda's chair hadn't even had time to go cold. How would she feel about being replaced? It was bad enough that her husband had replaced her, but her girlfriends allowing this woman into their fold would surely be the ultimate kick in the teeth. They didn't want to replace their friend, but they just couldn't be cruel to this young, timid girl. The general opinion was that Belinda and Carrie, it transpired, were both very similar indeed. It was obvious that the cheating pig Roger certainly had a type. Sweet, kind and naïve. Their conclusion was that Belinda and Carrie were both victims of falling for the wrong man.

SEVEN

THAILAND

Amanda lay motionless in her luxurious Savoir bed just staring at the ceiling. She was deliberating, trying to count how many women she knew who truly had a happy marriage to a lovely, decent husband. How many? As much as she racked her brains, she could only think of two couples she knew who were genuinely content.

She'd made the decision years ago that she was willing to stay put and be bored to death by Christopher, for her daughter's sake, but now that Sophie had grown her wings and was flying, maybe it was acceptable for her to finally leave him.

The closer it got to her fiftieth, the more unsettled Amanda was becoming. She had given her best years to this man. You couldn't turn back the clock, but she knew one thing – she did not want to still be with him on her sixtieth, so she had decided, enough was enough, she really should leave her selfish husband. *I know,* she thought to herself, *I'll give him one last chance to redeem himself.* It would be a test, to determine how much he loved her, or if he even did at all.

With this thought in mind, she leapt of out bed and ran downstairs, keen to catch him before he buggered off to work for the day. Her husband had the most annoying habit of leaving the house without having the decency to say goodbye to her. No matter how often over the years she had told him that it was plain bad manners, he continued doing it, always claiming, "Sorry, I forgot."

Amanda burst enthusiastically into their large and light, minimal bespoke kitchen, presenting herself as cheerful and friendly, with the intention of putting her husband in a good mood. She was draped in a fluffy White Company towelling dressing gown that swamped her slim figure as she whizzed across the room to give him a good morning peck on the cheek. Then, she grabbed two pieces of the granary seeded bread laying nearby and quickly popped them into the four-slot toaster to join her husband's already half-cooked slices so that they could eat together.

"I was thinking..." Amanda proclaimed in an upbeat manner as she affectionately grabbed his hand to hold, but Christopher groaned inwardly, wondering what on earth she was going to nag him for this time. He preferred his toast and marmalade in silence. He liked to ponder on his forthcoming day in peace, and without company, so he didn't respond to her, but she continued anyway. "It's my fiftieth soon and your fifty-eighth a few weeks after mine," she said. "So, why don't we do something really special? A long-haul trip. Something really exciting, like a second honeymoon?"

She looked at him enthusiastically, hopeful of just a simple agreement. A, "Yes. That would be nice, Amanda. Shall I pick up some brochures on my way home?" That's all she wanted. Was it really too much to ask after all these years of marriage?

Christopher spoke without looking up from the letter which he was now aggressively opening with his knife, irritated at his wife for expecting him to deviate from his own plans and activities. *Why can't she just go off and do her own thing?* he thought to himself. *I'm certainly not stopping her.* "How about a joint party at the golf club instead?" he retorted.

Amanda's heart sunk. She was clearly flogging a dead horse. She had been for years if she was honest with herself. "Are you joking? I already spend every Saturday there. You dump me with the other doormats, then we have to sit around waiting for you lot," she argued before snatching the four slices of toast out of the chrome Dualit toaster, then chucking two onto his plate. "And the only reason you all invite us is so we can drive you all home when you've all had a skinful."

"I thought you liked it there?" came his nonchalant reply.

"Like it? When you bore us to death talking about golf?" Amanda threw her hands up in frustration. "I want to do something special for my fiftieth, not what we do every bloody week." Amanda attempted to spread the still-too-cold butter onto the bread without ripping it, furious and taking it out on the stubborn butter. "I want an adventure. It's my fiftieth, for fuck's sake."

"We didn't do anything for my fiftieth," he said, trying to placate her.

"That's because you were away on a golf trip to Portugal, remember," she snapped.

He cringed, having forgotten about that, so he quickly attempted to distract her by offering her some of his marmalade, despite knowing full well that she didn't like it.

She pushed away the jar, irritated by his lack of kindness towards her.

He still tried to sound casual. "Why don't you go and join Sophie? You said you wanted to." He knew he was in the wrong, so he deliberately avoided looking her in the eye.

"I can't do that; she's with her friends. I'm not cramping their style. They're kids on a gap year. They don't want a parent tagging along with them."

He attempted to reason with her calmly, knowing that the conversation was about to take a dramatic turn for the worse. "I've already booked two weeks off for the freebie golf trip we won in the South-West Competition. I'm sorry but I just don't have any more leave from work until Christmas."

She solemnly replaced the toast onto her plate, suddenly no longer hungry. "You didn't tell me this trip was for two weeks. And why so? I thought they were usually four days."

She got no reply, so she demanded, "Well? Where is it?"

"Oh, errm, somewhere in Asia, I think," he mumbled guiltily.

Amanda now felt that she was about to explode. "*Where?*"

Christopher very wisely got up and moved away from her. He rustled about in the fridge under the pretence of looking for juice, making enough distance between them before he dared to mutter his response from the safety of behind the fridge door. "Errrr, I'm not entirely sure, somewhere random like, errrr, Thailand." He said that last word as quietly as he could, anticipating the reaction that it might achieve.

Amanda was unusually quiet now, which worried him even more. She spoke calmly but purposefully. "Please tell me you are fricking kidding me."

Christopher remained standing but grabbed his toast and tried to eat it as quickly as possible, keen to escape and depart for work. "Don't blame me. I didn't book it; I just got given it. I wouldn't stop you if you'd won a free holiday, would I?" he snapped back defensively.

Amanda looked sad now, with the inner acknowledgement that she had been pushed to her limit. "You know how much I want to go there, and you've been promising me for years that we would go." She genuinely didn't know whether she was more angry or more upset. "So, let me get this right… you have used up *all* of your holiday leave for, how many golf trips now? And you have kept *none* whatsoever to do anything at all with your *wife*?"

He looked sheepish and gulped down the last of his coffee to avoid having to respond. He couldn't even justify himself.

Amanda stood up ready to leave the room. "A group of men, without their wives, in Thailand. I don't think so. You go if you want but do so at your own peril." Then, she calmly exited the room and went back upstairs.

Christopher grabbed his jacket and legged it. The door slammed shut behind him.

That Saturday, at their 2pm regular reservation, the wives perused the new menu at the golf club, with Carrie having been forced upon them again but this time for lunch, her first as a golf widow. The women were miffed, having not invited her there themselves, nor even having been given a choice in the matter, which they found to be irritating and rude. They were so angry with Roger for his downright cheek. They knew it wasn't her fault, but her presence had been a total surprise and not a nice one. They had turned up to find her waiting for them and in Belinda's chair again. Sneaky Roger had called ahead to book her in and to make sure the table would still be set for five, but he hadn't had the decency to pre-warn either the women, nor the men, of his intentions, so poor Carrie was just sat there once again, squirming with embarrassment, and praying that it would get easier once they all got used to her.

She desperately wanted to be accepted by Roger's circle of friends, seeing as she saw her future as one with him and their baby or babies rather. Carrie, a homely girl, had always wanted three kids – two girls and a boy – and at thirty-one years old, she was getting very clucky indeed. She needed to hurry up and get a move on.

As the other women sat down to join her, unsure of the protocol and keen to be liked, Carrie offered to go and buy drinks for everyone. Janet placed a caring hand over hers, offering guidance as the elder of the group and as the captain's wife. "No, dear, ladies don't fetch drinks. The waitress will be over shortly."

Carrie blushed at her faux pas, and she was relieved when Amanda distracted everyone with a little cough to get their attention. "No one has mentioned anything, so can I please ask? Is it just me, or is anyone else pissed off about Thailand?" Then, she waited expectantly for a response.

The others looked uncomfortable, never ones to dare

rock the boat or complain, except for Tracey of course, but she was oblivious, only interested in attracting the attention of the waitress as quickly as possible. She was gagging for the pesky girl to hurry up and bring a glass of chilled white wine.

Janet took the lead, unperturbed by the topic. "Thailand is beautiful, Amanda. The food is simply to die for, and oh, the massages, I come home feeling positively ten years younger."

"I don't doubt it is, Janet, I really want to go there myself, but unfortunately, my husband is far too busy to take me anywhere," Amanda snapped frustratedly.

Carrie suddenly finds her voice, to defend Roger, much to the annoyance of Amanda. "I admit I was a little upset at first, but Roger has explained that they won it in a competition."

Amanda glared at Carrie, rattled that this little intruder thought she was one of them now, just because Roger was slipping her one. She replied to the younger girl through gritted teeth. "What I meant, *Carrie*, was five men, in *Thailand*, without their wives?" She raised her eyebrows dramatically and opened out her hands to the others, waiting for them to catch her drift.

Tracey was highly amused. "Ooh I think she means the ladyboys," cackling to herself. She wouldn't give a toss if Andy had a different woman every night.

"Not ladyboys, Tracey. *Ladies*, more to the point, ladies of the night," Amanda retorted back, wondering why no one else seemed to be concerned, or were they all really that gullible?

"I'm not worried; I know Chris won't do anything," chipped in Louise.

"And I trust Roger," squeaked Carrie, who then felt stupid when she was dramatically put down by Tracey who scoffed, "Yeah, but so did Belinda!" Carrie cringed and stayed quiet for the rest of the lunch, upset, and not daring to speak again.

Amanda now discreetly lowered her voice. "What I mean is that I think they will be seeing more ping-pong balls than golf balls."

Tracey chuckled out loud, highly amused, and tipsy from necking her first glass in one go. She craftily gestured for the barman to top up their glasses, although it was actually only her own that needed refilling. She was chuffed. Lunch this week was turning out to be far more entertaining than usual.

Janet, not having a clue what she meant by ping-pong balls but having sensed that Amanda was referring to the men misbehaving, tried to defuse the situation. "I'm sure you don't need to worry, Amanda. Charles and I go to Thailand twice a year, every June and December, always for a fortnight, and always to the same villa. He loves it so much he simply refuses to deviate. Apart from nipping off every afternoon for a game of golf with Johnny, the villa's butler, he would always return home by 6pm, then we would go out for supper. We were usually in bed by 9pm most nights. It really is the most quiet, relaxing destination."

"What, no happy endings?" Tracey said, now having knocked back two wines and guffawing at her own joke.

"Exactly, Tracey" said Amanda, "I don't want to catch some nasty, itchy STD. I think I'll have to go on a sex strike. I don't think I'll ever be able to sleep with him ever again after this trip."

"Well, I must admit, I have had those thoughts too, but I am confident that Chris wouldn't do it. He's just not that way inclined," added Louise.

Amanda rolled her eyes. "He's a *man*. They are *all* that way inclined." After getting no response, she gave in, frustratedly throwing her hands up in defeat. "Well don't say I didn't warn you all."

EIGHT

PREPARING FOR TAKE-OFF

Amanda and Christopher were still not speaking. She sat at their kitchen table with her travel magazine wide open at a page showing glossy images of a giant Buddha temple and colourful wooden longboats floating beside an idyllic beach in Thailand. She studied it again, seething.

Christopher walked in and caught her. "Oh, for God's sake, Amanda, please stop sulking – I'll take you at Christmas. I promise."

She stood up angrily and dramatically flung the magazine across the room, purposely aiming at his head. He somehow managed to duck in time, adding to her annoyance as she screamed hysterically, "I might not be here at Christmas." Then, she stormed out.

***

Chris placed a pay-and-display ticket onto his car's dashboard, then closed the door gently so that it didn't blow it away with a gust of wind. He clicked the electronic key fob to secure his beloved BMW X5 car, before stuffing it into his suit jacket pocket; then he and his wife Louise walked the short journey from the town's main long-stay car park to their estate agency office, just as they did every weekday morning at 8.40am.

"You don't mind me going away for two weeks, do you?" enquired Chris, more concerned about his business than his wife. "You will be able to cope OK, won't you?"

"I've coped every other time you've been away on your golf trips, so what's the difference?" she replied.

"Well, that was always for four days or a week," he replied patronisingly. "I do hope you'll be able to manage for a fortnight."

Louise reassured him not to worry. What her darling husband didn't know was that she couldn't wait to get rid of him. She'd already cancelled her in-laws for the following Sunday's lunch, under the pretence of catching up with paperwork. She wouldn't be able to cook lunch with a raging hangover, and she would certainly have one, because she was hitting the town with Samantha next Saturday night. And she was most definitely going to wear the red dress!

***

It was breakfast time in Janet's Elizabethan manor house. Major Charles put down his silver knife and fork, ready to dictate to Janet the list of jobs that he wanted her to do for him that day.

Janet, exactly as she did every morning, had brought her notepad and pen along with her to their antique mahogany dining table, knowing that she would be given her daily chores. She was more his PA than his wife.

"Collect my navy suit from the cleaners, then fetch me £1000 in Thai Baht please, Janet." He tried to think if there was anything else that he wanted her to do for him, twirling the curly ends of his white moustache as he always did when he was deliberating. Not being able to think of anything else, he informed her, "That's all for today." Then, he picked his cutlery up again and continued to eat his smoked mackerel, as she started on her small bowl of muesli.

He suddenly stopped eating and held up his index finger to indicate that he wanted her to stop eating and pick up her notepad again. She dutifully did so, knowing this routine and his directions so well after all these years. "Oh, and book my Jaguar in for a service while I'm away, would you?"

At home, Charles always ate the same breakfast six days per week, but he made an exception on a Sunday morning when he would meet the men at the golf club, and they would all tuck into a full English fry-up before their game.

Janet watched him eating his smelly dish and then pulling a bone from his mouth. *No wonder his moustache always has the faint aroma of fish*, she thought to herself, *not that it really matters, I don't have to kiss him.* He didn't do kissing. Too sloppy, he had explained to her in their younger days.

"I do hope you've remembered to organise the minibus for Sunday. 10am sharp?" barked Charles coldly, as though Janet was an employee on his payroll.

An ever-patient Janet responded in her usual calm manner, "Yes of course, dear." Then, she added, "And I've kept your usual breakfast reservation, but for the wives. I think a few of them are rather upset about this trip. It might cheer them up."

"Splendid idea, Janet. Can't have trouble in the ranks now, can we?"

***

It was 9.45am on Sunday morning at the golf club, where the large silver minibus that Janet organised for them was now parked, awaiting its five VIP passengers headed for Gatwick Airport. Its back door had been left opened wide to accept five suitcases and five golf bags. The engine chugged out invisible diesel fumes despite not being due to leave for another fifteen minutes. Why did coach drivers do that? Did they not care about the environment?

With everyone parked up, Charles stood with Janet while the men clustered around the bus, cramming in their luggage impatiently. The women stood huddled, chatting amongst themselves, clutching bunches of car keys, their taxi duties complete.

Janet handed Charles the leather folder that she had diligently prepared for him, containing his passport, the flight tickets and the currency. "Do have a wonderful time, Charles. It will do you good to go somewhere different from the same old villa that we always go to. You might find it's a new place for us to visit."

"We'll see, Janet" snapped Charles, meaning 'no'. He was keen to change the subject, knowing that he was going to the exact same place that they go to bi-annually, but they were meant to have won this holiday, so he'd had to pretend that he was going somewhere else. "Goodbye, Janet." he told her formally, turning away without looking at her again. He strode over to the bus and set down his old-fashioned, brown, leather suitcase onto the floor behind the bus, clearly having no intention of lifting it on himself. "Come along then, chaps," he bellowed. "I simply can't abide tardiness."

The men each went to say their goodbyes to their respective spouses.

Tracey held out a passport for Andy. He held onto it but clutched her hand at the same time, not letting go of either. "Please be careful while I'm away, Tracey. Try not to drink too much – it's not good for you – and don't forget to turn the fire off every night," he pleaded.

"Just go will you. Don't think you can bugger off on a boozy boys' holiday and expect me to stay at home sober and miserable."

"I didn't say don't drink." He sighed. "Just don't get completely plastered every single night."

She pushed the passport into his stomach, forcing him to take it from her. "Just go, Andrew."

Andy walked off, deeply concerned. She watched him defiantly and muttered under her breath, "Boring bastard."

***

An angry Amanda and embarrassed Christopher were clearly having an argument.

"I mean it, you can shag whoever, or whatever you like, but I am telling you, if you do, do *not*, under any circumstances, come back and attempt to have sex with me ever again."

"For God's sake, Amanda," he implored her to keep her voice down.

"If you dare to bring any diseases back to me, I will never forgive you. Especially AIDS!"

Christopher now looked around, as he tried to casually laugh it off. His wife slapped his passport into his hand, so he snatched it from her aggressively in retaliation and stormed off angrily. He'd bloody well shag whoever he liked now, seeing as he was getting accused of it, he decided. Mind you, he was going to anyway.

***

Louise gave Chris his passport and a peck on the cheek. "I know you will behave, Chris, but please be careful with that prat Roger. I don't want him getting everyone into trouble."

Chris didn't like to be nagged, nor told what to do by a woman. "I'm a big boy remember, Louise, and I've managed to survive for forty-three years so far, haven't I?" he sneered sarcastically, as though his wife were an idiot.

She shrugged, then left him to get on the bus as she went over to join Janet, not really caring what they did. She was only being polite.

***

The men were assembled, ready to board the minibus, but Charles noticed that he was one soldier short of his squadron. "Where the devil is Roger?" he demanded in irritation.

The others obediently looked around for him, keen not to upset the major who they knew expected everything to run to a tight schedule. Roger and Carrie were behind the bus, hiding for a last-minute kiss goodbye. She clung to him as he tried desperately to extract himself from her octopus-like grip. "Come on, let me go, woman," he laughed. "They're all waiting for me."

"But I don't want to. I'll miss you too much," she bleated through teary eyes. Then she pouted like a sulky schoolgirl. "And it's my fertile day next week and you won't even be here."

"Next month, I'll be here every day, and we'll make up for it then, OK?" he promised, but just to placate her. He lifted her chin up so that she looked him in the eyes. "One month won't make any difference," he assured her, before removing himself from her clutches, giving her a last peck on the cheek, then bolting over to the coach, relieved. *She is really starting to get on my nerves with all this baby talk*, Roger thought to himself. *I thought having a fit bird would be fun. I didn't expect nagging and fertility charts. Belinda would never have acted up like this*. Then he wondered why he was thinking about either of them when he was on his way to Thailand, where there would be plenty of gorgeous young girls at his disposal.

The other men were all already seated on the coach when Roger finally climbed into the bus, grinning like a Cheshire cat. They all cheered jovially and looked up at him in amusement.

"Come on, Casanova, we don't want to miss our flight," shouted an excitable Chris.

"Sorry, guys. She wouldn't let me go," bragged smarmy Roger.

"We're the ones who need to get laid," laughed Christopher. "We don't all have it on tap like you do."

"I wondered how long it would take for Christopher's off-shore rules to start," joined in Andy, determined to try his best to forget about Tracey for once.

Roger remained standing up in the aisle as the now beeping bus began to reverse. He nodded over towards the women. "Look. Don't forget to give them all a nice wave and *pretend* we are going to miss them," he said sarcastically as he waved out of the window in a comical fake manner to Carrie. Then he plonked himself down with a cocky smile. "Anyone got a beer?"

Meanwhile, the ladies waved them off cheerily and prepared to go into the clubhouse, except for Amanda whose arms remained firmly folded across her chest. Her marriage was over as far as she was concerned. Her lips were snarled, and she was absolutely livid. Furious. She felt like she was going to blow a gasket. *Why is life so unfair?* she thought, winding herself up even further. The men got Thailand and the women got toast. Albeit with slices of avocados, but as far as she was concerned, they could shove their brunch where the sun didn't shine. Amanda wanted what the men had. She wanted excitement. She wanted fulfilment.

Janet tottered up the path cheerfully, leading the women into the clubhouse where she had organised breakfast for them all at their husbands' usual Sunday breakfast table. She was very much looking forward to this longer break from Charles, which would give her a well-needed break from her endless list of chores and duties. To her surprise, she found herself pleased that he had gone, excited that she was finally going to have some quality free time to herself. She decided that she would go and pay a visit to Belinda. She had really missed her.

Carrie walked along glumly, trying her best not to cry and embarrass herself. She was devastated, missing her man already. She had hoped that this would be the month that she might finally manage to get pregnant, but now she would have to wait for over another month before she could try again.

Louise saw that she was upset and kindly hooked her arm, walking by her side to give her comfort and support. She was getting rather fond of her, and it was nice to have someone younger join their group. Maybe she could convince her to have a girls' night out while the men were away.

Amanda caught up with them but found Carrie's weakness slightly pathetic. "Oh well, now you're finding out what it's really like to be a golf widow. Still want to be one?"

Carrie burst into tears. Louise consoled her. Amanda rolled her eyes.

Carrie didn't think it would be like this. She thought the golfers would be a refined lot, boring even. She thought with Roger being twenty-five years older than her, that she wouldn't have the same problems that she'd encountered with her last couple of boyfriends who, unfortunately for her, had not been ready for marriage and babies. Her two exes, 'Josh the Cheating Copper' and 'Liar-Liar-Pants-on-Fire Fireman

Dan', had both been party animals who she couldn't trust. They had both turned out to be a pair of fuckboys rather than the husband material that she had been searching for. She didn't know which one was worse as they had both equally messed her about, let her down and played with her emotions, but as bad as they were, neither of them had ever made her feel as insecure as Roger did. Would she ever get her happy ever after?

NINE

BAD NEWS

A flustered Belinda snatched up her trusty old wooden rolling pin and steamrollered over a large sheet of shortcut pastry. She usually made it from scratch and chided herself for lowering her standards and using shop-bought, but she hadn't been given time to prepare. She was swiftly preparing a mushroom and cheddar cheese quiche for Janet, who had invited herself over. She didn't really want to face her, nor any of the other women for that matter, but it had got to the stage where she couldn't avoid her phone calls any longer, and Janet had insisted on coming over to check on her, refusing to take no for an answer. Belinda knew Janet meant well, but she was still wallowing in self-pity and wasn't ready to be dragged out of it just yet.

Janet had not requested nor expected that Belinda would feed her, but ever the perfect hostess, there was no way that anyone ever left Belinda's home without a generous portion of her delicious baking in their tummy. Belinda had made a cheesecake the day before so dessert was already sorted, *not that Janet will eat much anyway, like a frail little sparrow*, Belinda thought, *Major Charles would never tolerate a fat wife.*

Belinda guessed correctly that Janet was coming over because she finally had some free time to herself, what with Charles being away on the Thailand trip. She was fully aware that the men set off earlier today, seeing as it was circled in red pen on the National Trust calendar that was pinned up on her kitchen wall beside the phone. 'Roger away. Golf. 10am coach' it read. Oh well, not her problem anymore. She shrugged. It didn't matter what he got up to. He was Carrie's problem now. She wondered what Carrie would make of his golf trips and his shenanigans. She pondered whether Roger might be different for her. Maybe he would change his ways now that he had got himself a sexy, slim, young stunner, instead of a frumpy, fat old fart.

With the quiche now warming through inside her Aga, Belinda began to dry off her floury hands with a tea towel when the telephone trilled out loud, causing her to jump. Her retro 1950s Bakelite telephone was cream to match her kitchen. She'd always wanted a phone on the kitchen wall, having watched so many American films in her youth and preferring it there rather than in the hallway, where most British people seemed to position theirs. It was also the room where she spent most of her time, so it made perfect sense.

"Hello," she answered cheerfully, masking how she felt inside. Indistinct chatter was heard on the line as a stunned Belinda froze with disbelief. "I think you had better inform

Carrie Carpenter though. Yes, that's correct, she's his partner now," she spoke softly and without any malice.

Belinda replaced the handset as though in slow motion, continuing to stand glued to the spot. She leant over the kitchen island to steady herself as she took deep breaths, in shock. "Oh no, my poor Max. What will I tell him?" She talked to herself out loud. She held her flushed face in her floury hands, and she sobbed, and she sobbed, until she was pulled out of her state by the sudden loud chime of her doorbell.

"*Shit!* It's Janet." A flustered Belinda precariously opened the door, unsure if Janet would have heard the bad news, but when faced with a beaming smile and a large bunch of yellow roses, she realised that she had no choice but to be the bearer of it.

Janet got a real shock when Belinda opened her front door, as she caught sight of the state that her friend was in. She was alarmed to see that Belinda was extremely agitated and flustered; her blotchy face was covered in flour; and her eyes were red raw from crying. Poor Belinda was clearly taking Roger's betrayal a lot worse than she had anticipated. Crikey, the poor woman looked like she needed a doctor!

The two women now sat close together on the sofa, not knowing how long they had been there, and Janet now the most bedraggled-looking of the pair, crumpled in Belinda's arms, having been informed of the recent life-changing phone call.

After a while, Belinda suddenly shot up from the sofa and dashed into and across her kitchen to frantically tug at the Aga door, pulling it open to rescue the black burnt mess, which was once a quiche, then dumping it unceremoniously into her Belfast double sink. She'd sort it out later. Food was the last thing on their minds now. They had to make plans.

***

Amanda relaxed in her Pear & Freesia bubble bath, happy to have the house to herself for a while. At least she didn't need to cook today, seeing that she was still stuffed from her delicious brunch at the club. She'd have a couple of crumpets and a cup of tea later, she decided. She still didn't get how the other women were not bothered by this trip, but she put it out of her mind, fed up of dwelling on it. These two weeks would give her time to think properly. She knew that she should leave him, and more importantly, she really wanted to, but she still felt guilty about the possibility of upsetting Sophie. Would her daughter mind? Maybe she should wait until she saw her so that she could gauge her opinion first.

Her mobile phone started to ring, but she'd left it in her bedroom and she was enjoying her soak far too much to consider moving, so she ignored it. It soon stopped as she disappeared under the cloud of soapy suds. She'd put an oil mask on her hair, she decided, then a face pack. It was Sunday afternoon and she hadn't had a proper pamper for ages. As she squeezed the last contents of the oil sachet onto her head, her phone rang out again. "Sod off," she called out to the empty house. Why did that always happen when you were in the bath or on the loo?

She lay back again, her eyes closed, a disposable sheet mask of hyaluronic acid and ginseng covering her face, with the promise that she would emerge revitalised and replumped. *Bliss*, she thought to herself, exhaling slowly after her stressful week, but she was brought back to earth again by the phone ringing, for the third time.

Her mobile phone tune was set to the Abba song 'Dancing Queen'. It reminded her of her Sophie. It was insane how many times they had watched the film *Mamma Mia* together, always their first choice of film for their girls' duvet days, but more importantly, it was 'their film'. They watched it together and pretended that Amanda was Donna, and Sophie was Sophie. She also loved it because of the feel-good factor. Watching any film that was set in sunny climates, or foreign shores, took her to where she wished she could be.

With the sudden realisation that it could actually be her Sophie calling from abroad, she frantically clambered out of the tub, now not wanting to risk missing it. *If this is a sales call, I will not be responsible for my language*, she thought to herself as she now rushed to locate, then answer, the device and managed to do so just in time to hear a male stranger's deep voice greet her, rather than the sweet, feminine one of her own daughter. She sighed disappointedly.

Two soaking wet puddles began to form on the lux carpet that laid beneath Amanda's bare feet and adjacent to her bed. She stood there, transfixed to the spot, water continuing to drip freely from her naked body but her not caring in the slightest. It was the least of her worries. "But what will I tell my daughter?" she cried out to the voice on the other end of the line. She received no advice in return. The man's job was just to inform her.

***

Tracey lay on her sofa watching a catch-up episode of *Britain's Got Talent* from the night before. Andy would never watch anything that he described as trash, so two weeks of being able to do whatever she wanted to do was going to be brilliant, she decided, so much so that a celebration had been in order. After the couple of glasses that she'd knocked back over brunch, she had come home and opened a bottle of cava, but now the second bottle was practically empty, and the two bottles stood on her glass coffee table, surrounded by a mass of chocolate wrappers. This was a good day, she concluded. She was well and truly hammered.

She began to nod off but was interrupted by the ring of her mobile phone. She patted around the top of the rustic oak coffee table, hearing it but having no idea where it was. She missed the call, but not caring, she didn't bother to continue to look for it to establish who it had been, and she began to doze once more, until again, it started to ring out for a second time. She half sat up, her head spinning, but she noticed it this time, laying discarded nearby on the carpet.

Snatching it out of curiosity, she answered, "Who? Who is it?" she slurred.

A male voice she didn't recognise talks seriously down the phone. Tracey laughed out loud, objecting to the stranger's bizarre information. "Noooo, he isn't. I know for a *fact*, he's on his way to *Thailand*."

The concerned voice tried again to reason with her that it was a genuine call, but she slurred back at him, "He's gone off golfing. *Again!*" Then, she slugged the last drop of the wine directly from the bottle and rolled over on the sofa, telling the bewildered caller, "Don't be so *silly*," before cutting him off and collapsing into a deep slumber.

***

Carrie Carpenter strutted energetically into the smart, trendy gym, the one where she had met Roger. He had only just joined when he met her, knowing straight away that she was exactly what he desired. He had been a good boy for well over two years now, but enough was enough. He was bored again. He'd chosen 'Pure Fit' with the intention of meeting a woman, or a girl rather. He thought most women turned boring and frumpy once they got over forty and they stopped wearing tight dresses and high heels.

Having been through most of the available women he met through work, he'd needed a new hunting ground, and he liked the calibre of customers at this establishment very much indeed. He'd observed them all going into the building when he nipped out at lunchtimes to fetch his daily chicken-and-stuffing sandwich and packet of crisps, but best of all, he didn't know anyone there, so his naughty secret would be safe.

He hadn't planned to leave Belinda, never had done, but there was something about this one that was different. Maybe it was that, unlike all the others, she wasn't willing to be a bit on the side. "All or nothing," she had told him. She was decent, he liked that, and she had refused to sleep with him unless he was definitely single, with him having tricked her into believing that his marriage had been over years ago.

Carrie swiped to sign in at the desk, having pre-booked the Pilates class on her phone via their app. She was already dressed for her class. After walking into the changing room, she opened the nearest locker to keep her bag, keys and phone safe, which just happened to ring as she was about to lock the door. *Better answer,* she thought, *maybe it's Roger; his flight might have been delayed.*

"*Arrrrggghhhhh, noooo,*" she screamed hysterically, collapsing onto a low wooden bench, gasping for breath and swiftly being surrounded by a circle of half-naked women who rushed to console her.

***

A distraught Belinda sat on her kitchen floor, her back pressed against the wall, the spiralling corkscrew of wire from the telephone stretched down to reach her low position. Hugo, sensing her sadness, rested his fat, loyal head on her lap, and she gratefully held onto him for comfort while she spoke to her only son. She gave him the latest news. "We just don't know yet." She sighed. "All they told us is that their plane is missing." She cried again at the thought. "They are going to update us again at ten."

"Please don't cry, Mum," her son pleaded, wishing he was there with her right now. The earliest he could get a flight was at 7am the next day, but he'd be home by the following afternoon, he promised her. Thank goodness he was in Germany right now instead of Japan where he'd been the week before. Belinda shuddered at the thought of her precious son now having to board an aeroplane for a flight.

***

Last to hear the bad news was Louise. Blissfully unaware, she sung cheerfully to herself as she sorted out her wardrobe. She was ruthlessly throwing out all the frumpy garments that she had accumulated over the years as a boring, loyal wife to make space for a new, sassier, more modern look that she planned to buy herself this week when she went clothes shopping with Samantha, who had promised to come with her on the condition that they had lunch out too. She knew Chris would go mad if both her and Sam had the same day off together, but he wasn't here was he, so he wouldn't know, and as Sam pointed out firmly, "If it's OK for him to go to Thailand for a fortnight, then it's OK for you to have a day off and buy a few dresses." *She was spot on*, thought Louise.

She had filled four bin liners so far, surprising herself at exactly how old some of her clothes were. This sort-out was well overdue. She planned to take the bags over to the Heart Foundation charity shop when she went to work tomorrow, already looking forward to her coming week much more than usual.

She acknowledged the fact that the atmosphere in their office was always far more harmonious when Chris was away. If she was in charge, she knew she could make the office more relaxed, more stylish, just better, for both the staff and their customers. She had sketched designs in a notebook of how they could improve their branding and 'For Sale' signs, but when she had proudly showed them to Chris, he had pooh-poohed her ideas, insisting that everything was fine as it was. "If it ain't broke, don't fix it," Chris had argued, but

Louise thought they should keep moving with the times. She knew that the other agents in town were upping their game. She was wise enough to see that they couldn't afford to sit still, or they might be overtaken by their competition, but her husband wouldn't listen, assuming that he knew best as usual.

Louise stopped herself thinking about work and put her mind back to the job in hand. She carried two of the bulging, heavy bags to her car, ready for the following morning, cramming them into the boot but realising that she would have to use the back seats too, as there was so much stuff to get rid of.

Her thoughts were interrupted by her mobile phone vibrating in the back pocket of her jeans. After casually answering it, Louise gasped out loud, then slumped to her knees on her manicured front lawn. Her head bowed down, her forehead resting on the cold damp grass. She didn't move.

Half an hour later, she finally managed to find the strength to get up without her legs giving way again. Once inside, she turned on the cold tap in her kitchen, leaning over to drink directly from the spout, feeling light-headed, nauseous and dehydrated. In her hand was her phone. She dialled Chris's parents. This was the first Sunday ever that she desperately wanted them to come over. *Now!*

***

The following evening, Belinda clutched her son Max's hand as they sat side by side on her sofa, solemnly watch the evening news together. His other arm was wrapped protectively around her to comfort her, having only just discovered that his father had already left his mother a month earlier and had moved out to be with some young tart.

"Why didn't you call me, Mum? I'd have come straight home."

"Exactly," she explains, "why should your life be disrupted too?"

He pulled his mum close and kissed the top of her head, furious with his father for putting his mother through that.

"I don't know what to feel right now," he exclaimed in confusion. "I am so angry with him, but how can I be when he isn't going to be coming home to any of us ever again?"

"Do you think we should call Carrie, to see if she is OK?" Belinda queried.

"No way! Stop being so nice, Mum. She hasn't called you to check on you, has she? And she's the one who stole him from you."

Belinda shrugged. "She was besotted with him apparently. Janet said she's a decent girl, just a bit daft and naïve. And she is grieving, after all."

"Well, so are we. Just forget about her. She'll have her own family to look after her."

They were interrupted by the news headlines that they had been waiting anxiously for. A frosty-looking female news reporter informed the general public, in a matter-of-fact manner, that, "This evening, at seven o'clock UK time, wreckage was found of the missing passenger jet that set off from Gatwick Airport yesterday afternoon at two-thirty, bound for Thailand. There were 416 passengers and fifteen crew onboard. They are not expecting to find any survivors."

Max grabbed the remote and switched off the TV. A tear rolled down Belinda's face as they clung to each other in their grief.

TEN

THE FUNERAL

In the largest function room at the now solemn West Seale Golf Club, five wooden easels stood together in a row, lined up in a regimented fashion that Major Charles would wholly approve of. Each one held a large photograph of the individual deceased men.

Charles was first of course, being the chairman of the club, but they had been placed in order of age, so he would have been first regardless. The golf club had generously paid for the men's funerals, which the wives had chosen to hold in one service. Seeing as the men spent every weekend together, and had died together, it seemed only fitting that they had a joint funeral, otherwise the poor wives, the club staff and members and their friends and families would have had to attend five separate funerals, one after the other.

Janet was holding it together very well, knowing that it was the very last time that she would be doing an official duty for her husband, so she was determined to do him proud. He was the only one who was going to be buried afterwards, in his family tomb, the others all opting for cremations.

Although it was a written rule that ashes were not allowed to be scattered on the golf course, Charles and the club committee had always turned a blind eye to such activities, with many of their old members' final resting places ending up at their favourite spots or little bits of their remains spread over the full eighteen holes.

The wives had all planned to go and walk the course to do the honours together but when the club would be closed, and the time was right. Janet intended to join them, even though Charles wouldn't be sent off in the same fashion. As she stood there in her elegant black dress and Akoya pearls, handed down to her from her own late mother, she felt anxious, unsure of how she would cope after today when all the formalities were over and she went back to her home, alone and with no purpose in her life.

Janet surveyed the room and saw that the other wives were all pulling their weight, milling around to assist her, mingling with the mourners, despite it being the last thing they all felt like doing.

Max stood and observed too. He watched Belinda, concerned that his mother looked exhausted. She had been through double heartache, mourning her husband twice, albeit for totally different reasons. He went over to join her, handing her a glass of sherry and urging her to sit down for a rest. He thought he might stay home for a while – she needed him now, and he was not going to abandon her in her hour of need. He was a good man. He might have inherited his father's handsome looks, but he had his mother's kind heart, decent morals and soft nature. He had certainly been blessed with the best parts of both of his parents.

"Why don't you go and check if Carrie is OK? She looks a bit lost." Belinda nodded towards Carrie, who was sat down all by herself, clearly not coping.

"Oh, Mum, what do I say to her? It'll be awkward. She'll start talking about Dad."

"You can still talk about him, you know. It might do her good, and maybe you too."

A reluctant Max obeyed his mother's wishes and went over to speak to Carrie, but the sight of him, so similar in looks to his father, set her off again, causing her to dramatically burst into tears.

Amanda came up behind Belinda, witnessing the kind act that she'd persuaded Max to do. "You are simply too kind, Belinda."

Belinda smiled and hugged her friend. She had missed them all so much. "We've all just got to get through the day as best we can," she sighed to Amanda who clung onto her arm, for her own comfort as well as her friend's.

They were soon joined by Sophie, suntanned and glowing from her round-the-world travels but looking forlorn and lost. They made room for her in the middle, fussing over her, aware that she was the youngest victim of them all, losing her father at the age of just twenty-three years old.

Louise was sat down on the comfy sofas between her in-laws. They hadn't left her side since that fateful day, and she wouldn't have had it any other way. Her mother-in-law, having fetched her a plate of food from the buffet, was now insisting that she eat it. They were fussing over her and treating her like a child, but she didn't mind, finding it refreshingly comforting, especially as she had no parents of her own to look out for her, and after all, she was the only child that they had left now, so looking after her was giving them something to focus on.

A flustered Janet suddenly appeared in front of them and requested that she please borrow Louise for a moment. "Would you help please, dear?" she asked, nodding towards a table in the corner. "Look at Tracey – she's getting too drunk. We don't want a scene. Not today."

Louise jumped into action. "Oh crikey, I'll find her a job to do."

With everything running smoothly again, Janet walked over to Belinda, Amanda and Sophie to find them amused at the look of horror on Max's face, with Carrie dramatically draped over his shoulder and still sobbing dramatically.

"He's such a handsome boy," observed Janet. "You must be so relieved to have him home."

"I am," agreed Belinda. "And he's promised to stay a while." She smiled happily, secretly thinking that at least one good thing had come from all this.

"Go and help Max out, will you, Sophie?" laughed Amanda, which her daughter obediently did, willing to go and sit down with the only other young people at the funeral, even if Carrie was rather hysterical.

"I was just telling Amanda how much I miss you all," Belinda told Janet. "In fact, I missed you all more than I missed Roger." She whispered it discreetly, keen to avoid sounding disrespectful to her dead husband. The women all smiled at each other knowingly.

Amanda announced a decision that she had arrived at. "I think we are going to need each other more than ever now, so I propose that you all come to mine for lunch on Sunday. Let's have a good catch-up where we can all talk properly."

"That would be delightful, dear, but what about Carrie?" Janet enquired, still observing and feeling desperately sorry for the young girl. "She seems to be taking it the worst."

Amanda looked awkwardly at Belinda and replied, "It's not a competition, you know, Janet, who is the most grieving widow." She had totally forgotten about Carrie now officially being one of the men's partners. She wasn't intentionally being spiteful to Carrie, nor leaving her out on purpose, but Belinda came first in her eyes.

Any awkwardness about the situation was quickly resolved by Belinda. "It's fine by me," said a charitable Belinda. "I genuinely don't mind at all."

"Really? Are you sure?" checked Amanda. "Because you come first, you know, she's just an intruder!" She said it in jest, but she meant it sincerely.

Janet gave Amanda a scolding look, but she was joking too. They both cared very much for Belinda, and she did deserve their support, even more than Carrie did.

Feeling reassured that she still had the support of her friends, but keen to change the subject, Belinda insisted, "I'm in then, but as long as I can bring the desserts. It'll be nice to have something to bake for."

"Deal. That's settled then," smiled Amanda. "Our new club is now officially open." She raised her glass as an offering to the others. "The Sunday Lunch Club."

The three women chinked their glasses in agreement.

ELEVEN

THE SUNDAY
LUNCH CLUB

It was the first Sunday since the funeral and the first that they met for the Sunday Lunch Club. It was a welcome relief to them all, otherwise the weekends would have been the time when they felt the most lost and most lonely. None of them felt like going out, and where would they go, and what would they do? But staying home alone was not good for their mental health. Meeting weekly in the privacy of their own homes was the perfect antidote for their shared grief. Other friends didn't really understand, or they acted weird around them, not knowing what to do or say for the best, but at least with each other, they had all shared the same terrible experience.

Despite none of them having been entirely happy in their marriages, it was different when they'd found themselves completely alone. Grief tended to have a habit of making people just remember the best bits of their deceased partners. The cruel manner in which the men's lives had been cut dramatically short created immediate forgiveness and seemed to erase any bad memories. It certainly made their secret resentments disappear. The thought of starting over again, once a fantasy, was now a reality, and it was a scary one for most of them.

Belinda was not scared though, having been already left, dumped rather, and having already been forced to adjust to living alone. She had also discovered that the disaster had turned out to be a huge advantage to her, seeing as she was no longer being forced to sell her house in order to give Roger half the proceeds of the sale. The relief of not losing her beloved home had lifted Belinda's spirits and taken away all the stress that she had previously been suffering. Seeing as he had not long left her, and no divorce lawyers had been instructed, the house automatically became one hundred per cent hers. Not only could she now stay put, but it appeared that Roger had never got round to cancelling the life insurance policy that he had taken out many years ago to secure the now paid off mortgage, meaning that a lump sum would also be due, so she would be OK for the foreseeable future. Carrie, as mistress, received nothing.

Belinda had discussed with Max whether she should give some of the insurance money to Carrie, but he was horrified at his mother's misguided generosity, reminding her that she would need that money to last her for the remainder of her days. He pointed out that Carrie was still young, held a good job and had only been his dad's girlfriend of a few months, whereas Belinda had been a wife of over thirty years, so it was her money as much as it was his father's. Max didn't want anything for himself, and he was just being protective. His only concern was that his mother would be OK. She was still only fifty-five, but she hadn't worked for years, having always been the homemaker. Regardless, the money wasn't a huge amount, and it had to last her. She would still probably have to start doing some sort of part-time work at some point, but he felt that it would do her good and get her out of the house. She was far too lovely to rot away in suburbia. He wanted her to lead a full life again.

Only Carrie, having not had enough time to get to know the real Roger, and naïvely thinking he had been the ideal man, was of the belief that her life would never be as perfect ever again. The others had already spent many years with their men, but she hadn't spent long with him, so she felt that she was being robbed of her future. She was pleased, though, that she had been included in the Sunday Lunch Club. She really liked the other ladies and appreciated that they were all looking out for her, even Belinda, which astounded her and made her feel incredibly guilty. She was nothing like Roger had described. He had told her that his wife was boring, miserable and never wanted to do anything. She found the opposite to be true, finding her to be bubbly, cheerful and very kind indeed. She did notice, though, that Belinda was totally unaware of how lovely she really was, and she wondered what had happened to cause her to have such low confidence.

In fact, although she was still slightly apprehensive around Belinda, she'd decided that she was her favourite of all the women. She wished that her own mother was like Belinda, but unfortunately, hers was the opposite. A cold career woman who saw children as a nuisance, and who had told Carrie many times when she was a child that 'having kids ruins your life'. Her mother had been absent a lot, always working long hours or staying away from home in her high-level sales job.

She had mostly had to fend for herself when she was a schoolgirl, coming home to an empty house and making herself some toast or a bowl of cereal for her dinner. She had often craved a warm, loving home like the one that Belinda had provided for her family. One that she could come home to that would be welcoming, with lights on as she approached, and where she would smell a cooked dinner as she opened the door. One with people inside instead of the dark, empty house that she had faced daily. It might not have been as bad if she had had a sibling, or two, but her mother claimed that having Carrie had been 'more than enough thank you very much'.

Carrie thought that Belinda's son was very lucky indeed to have a mother like her. Max had been very kind to her at the funeral, which made her feel worse, knowing that the baby boy that she had hoped for wouldn't happen at all now. She had got her period that morning, causing her to grieve all over again. She'd already worked out the dates and knew that Roger had left over a week before the small slot in her fertility calendar, but deep down, she had hoped and prayed for a miracle, for her very last chance of motherhood. Her hopes were dashed though, by the dreaded red announcement that had turned up early, probably brought on by her grief. All she wanted was a warm, loving family of her own, with a few children that she could look after, love and adore. *Why is life so unfair?* she thought.

With the six women now seated at Amanda's dining table and having devoured the roast lamb dinner expertly cooked by the host, Louise and Belinda emerged from the kitchen carrying two plates of desserts. Belinda spoke proudly to inform them of their options. "Strawberry cheesecake or banoffee pie."

"I've never tried banoffee pie," admitted Janet, having had to always stick to traditional food. Charles had refused to try anything that he would refer to as 'American junk' or 'foreign muck'.

"Then you must have a bit of both," insisted Belinda, with Amanda and Louise chipping in that they wanted both too. All the women ended up having both puddings, despite being full. Belinda's desserts were legendary and not to be resisted.

"Mmmm, you really should make these for a living," suggested Louise. "You'd make a fortune. You could sell them to restaurants."

"I used to really want my own café or cake shop," Belinda informed them. "But Roger wanted me to stay at home, so I..." She stopped talking, aware that Carrie was there. "Oh, sorry, Carrie, I shouldn't really talk about Roger."

"Noooo, not at all," insisted Carrie. "Don't be silly; it's fine." She was aware that Belinda had more rights than she did to talk about him, him having belonged to her first, and for much longer, but it had thrown Carrie and she was feeling fragile enough in her menstrual state.

Tracey was insisting that they made a toast, even

though she'd already done so three times since they'd sat down, finding an excuse for each one but making it sound fun. Her real intention was to get them all drinking more, keen that they would keep up with her. She hated drinking alone. "Cheers to Belinda's delicious pudding," shouted a merry Tracey, knocking back her wine and being joined uncharacteristically by Carrie, who had been keeping up with Tracey and slowly getting pissed due to a combination of nervousness about the lunch and being distraught at getting her period. None of the others had realised exactly how drunk she was.

Tracey was herself half-cut and far more emotional than usual. She was usually a happy and boisterous drunk, but with what had happened to them all, she was in a more contemplative mood. Through watery eyes, she addressed the group. "We are going to have to help each other to get through this," she said, bringing down the mood of the room and reminding everyone why they were all there together. "We're gonna have our good days, but we're gonna have our *baaaad* days," she slurred.

Janet, always one to restore balance and order, spoke out in agreement. "Tracey's right. We only have two children between the six of us, and Max and Sophie will be off abroad again soon, so we need to stick together more than ever." She looked around at the others earnestly. "The men were a team, so we should be too."

Suddenly, a loud wail erupted from Carrie, as she burst into tears. "We were trying for a *baaaby*. I'll never have one now."

Louise, sat beside her, immediately reached over to

console her but was aware that it was an extremely awkward topic with Belinda also at the table. Keen to avoid an atmosphere, she diplomatically jumped up enthusiastically and dragged Carrie to her feet. "Come on, Carrie, let's go and get some fresh air."

As the two women exited the room, Louise considerately pulled the door shut behind them, after which the others all spun round towards Belinda to check that the news had not devastated her. Amanda immediately grabbed Belinda's hand, concerned, and enquiring, but furious at Roger for planning a new family when he could have, should have, been at home with his beautiful wife. "Did you even know about this?"

"No, I didn't," replied Belinda, calmer than the worried group had anticipated. "And *no*, they weren't."

Tracey piped up, "But you heard what she said?"

"I heard what she said, but I know that he wasn't trying."

The others waited with bated breath for her explanation. Belinda checked that Carrie was out of hearing range before she provided it. "Roger has had a vasectomy!" The others look confused, uncertain that Belinda had her facts correct. "I know this because I had to take him to the hospital for the operation. He booked himself in when our Max was only three months old."

"I don't understand, dear." Janet didn't know anything about vasectomies, Charles clearly not requiring one himself.

Belinda continued sadly, "I desperately wanted more children after Max, but Roger was adamant that one child was enough. Typical *selfish* Roger." Belinda was angry, the bad points of her late husband being firmly reinstated back into her head. "So, he got his own way as usual, and I cried all the way home for the baby, or babies rather, that could never exist." Belinda now slammed her napkin down angrily, in surprising defence of her replacement. "But he clearly hasn't had the decency to inform that poor girl about it, has he?"

"Oh my God. What an utter prick," shrieked Amanda, quickly putting her hand over her mouth, then apologising profusely to Belinda for her outburst. "Oh, I am so sorry, Belinda, I shouldn't have said that."

Belinda held her hands up. "No need. Please don't apologise for telling the truth, Amanda. Roger was no angel in life, so let's not pretend he is an angel in death." She spoke quieter now. "Look, ladies, we are all widows now, and let's face it, were any of us truly happy before the men died?"

The others were shocked by Belinda saying what they all thought deep down, but they were also relieved that someone had come out and admitted it.

"I think Carrie was." Janet sighed.

"Yeah, in her own naïve little world," snorted Tracey. "But even she would have realised it one day."

Belinda was on a roll now, the stress of her past few months being released and her confidence finally emerging. "The men are gone now, and we are left behind. Let's not make them saints when we all know that they weren't."

Amanda agreed, "You're right. What's important now is the kids and each other, but let's not tell Carrie about the vasectomy, OK? She's so fragile, I really don't think she could handle it," finally having some sympathy with her.

A chorus of 'agreed' went around the table like a downhearted Mexican wave.

Tracey held up her glass in agreement and slugged the lot. "And now that I am allowed to drink what I want, when I want, without being monitored, cheers, ladies. To us."

"Oh my God," gasped Amanda with a sudden realisation. "We really are golf widows now, aren't we?"

TWELVE

MAKING PLANS

Belinda was at her best. She was entertaining. It was the third week that they had met for the Sunday Lunch Club, and to her delight, it was her turn to host for lunch. She was going to present her guests with a perfectly cooked fillet of beef, dauphinoise potatoes and green beans. Her desserts, as usual, would be the icing on the cake, literally. She had made a strawberry Eton mess, but she had also made, especially for Carrie, a raspberry Bakewell tart, because she had mentioned last week that it was her favourite cake. Being the intuitive and kind-hearted person that she was, Belinda anticipated that Carrie might feel uncomfortable coming to the house where Roger had lived for over thirty years with his wife and son. She didn't want her to feel intimidated, so she thought if she pointed out she had made her favourite dessert, especially for her, then she would realise that she was welcome, and wanted, in her home. At least she hoped she hadn't been there before. She suddenly froze at her own thoughts, suddenly feeling queasy at the possibility that she was being naïve. Surely Roger wouldn't have brought her to their house, in their bed. Maybe he had brought others back over the years too.

She shook herself out of her bad thoughts, remembering that Carrie had pulled her to one side shortly after the funeral and assured her that she had not slept with her husband until he had convinced her his marriage was definitely over. Belinda felt relieved. She totally believed Carrie and was rather fond of the girl these days. She didn't blame her or even Roger anymore. He had wanted to go out and party, and she wanted to stay home, so she got what she wanted, and she was now content. She sincerely hoped that Roger found what he was looking for before he died.

The doorbell rang and in poured Louise and Tracey, soon followed by Janet and Amanda, and last of all, Carrie. Belinda had been right – the poor girl looked both nervous and anxious, despite her efforts to hide it; she was clearly thinking about Roger.

Belinda had prepared a tray of champagne glasses and bustled around, handing one to each woman enthusiastically, determined to lighten the mood for Carrie, as well as the others who were fully aware of the absurdity of the situation. The proud host tinkled her glass with a spoon to make her announcement. "We need to make a toast."

Tracey's eyes lit up – whatever the occasion, she highly approved.

"We have a birthday girl in the room," Belinda gleefully informed the others.

Amanda groaned in jest. "Arrghhh, it's not until Friday."

"Yes, but you are going to turn fifty, Amanda," berated Belinda. "You must celebrate it. You can't just let it pass by."

Tracey jumped in at the possibility of a party. "Right then, I'll organise a party."

Amanda attempted to object, "I haven't felt that a party was appropriate, with… you know," referring to the fact that their husbands had not long passed away. She paused. "And with Sophie having gone back abroad, and my family all up in the Midlands, I just didn't fancy the idea."

"What about just a nice quiet meal at the local wine bar then?" suggested Carrie. "My friend Charlotte is the manager. I could sort out a good table for us." She looked to the others for confirmation.

"Yep, I'm in," declared Tracey gladly.

"Perfect," concurred Louise. "But, Carrie, please let me help you to plan it. I work in town too. We could meet up on Monday lunchtime to make arrangements?"

"Yes, ok" agreed a relieved Carrie.

"What is the dress code for a, errrr, wine bar?" enquired Janet, having never been to one.

Tracey smiled. "Wear whatever you like, Janet. It'll be fun." Then, she added mischievously, "But no black, I think we have all been in mourning long enough."

"Well, alright then, if I must," laughed Amanda. "But just a quiet meal, OK?"

"That's settled then, and lunch is almost ready if you'd like to take your seats." Belinda directed them towards her dining room.

Amanda hung back to help Belinda to serve the food, whilst Carrie, Louise Tracey and Janet huddled over the dining table, whispering ideas for the forthcoming Friday night out for Amanda's fiftieth.

The ladies, having thoroughly enjoyed their meal, were conscious that they must leave room for dessert, knowing that Belinda would not give them a choice, not that they wanted to miss out on her delights anyway. She was what's known as a 'feeder'.

Janet absolutely loved being introduced to new tastes, seeing as Charles had previously always chosen for her, and without fail, it had always been either apple pie, treacle pudding, spotted dick or some other old-fashioned traditional dessert. He had always ordered just one portion for them both to share, always asking for two spoons, but after she had just a couple of mouthfuls, he would selfishly pull the dish away, then scoff the rest himself, telling her, "We don't want you getting fat now, do we, Janet?" Her very first Eton mess went down a treat.

"Bakewell tart?" asked Belinda but already holding out the plate towards her.

"Charles never let me eat a whole dessert," admitted Janet.

"That's terrible," exclaimed a now tipsy Tracey. "Imagine now if he could see you eating two!"

Janet sniggered and took the plate in defiance. "I always wanted to play golf too," she admitted, now getting braver by the day. "But Charles didn't approve of women playing golf."

The others gasped in horror. Amanda was gobsmacked. "*What?* The chairman of the golf club and with all those lady golfers admiring him so much. Oomph, if only they knew."

"Oh, please don't tell anyone, Amanda. I really couldn't face any scandal, and I don't want people to think poorly of Charles. I think I should attempt to preserve his legacy at the club."

"OK then, but on one condition," teased Amanda. "As long as you book yourself in for a golf lesson." The others all joined in and urged her to do so, keen for her to not miss out on doing things that she had always wanted to do. Janet smiled in agreement, the women's enthusiasm and support spurring her on and giving her a new-found confidence.

"And you too, Belinda," slurred Tracey. "You're as bad."

Belinda looks confused. "But I don't want to play golf."

"Not golf!" laughed Tracey. "Cakes! You wanted to bake for a living, well, what's stopping you now?"

Belinda protests, "Oh, I'm not sure I am good enough, not to do it professionally."

"Oh yes you are!" rang out a unanimous chorus from the others. Belinda blushed but enjoyed the compliments.

After their delicious meal, and with bellies full of Belinda's scrummy desserts, the ladies relaxed over coffee in Belinda's cream-and-green-coloured cosy lounge, sharing stories of the frustrating issues they had been encountering, having to sort out their late husbands' estates.

Louise, having been fortunate that Chris's parents had taken care of everything for her, and being aware that Carrie had nothing to organise, seeing as she was merely a mistress and not a wife, dragged Carrie off to the kitchen so that they could avoid this topic of conversation. They cleared away the plates and loaded the dishwasher for Belinda after all her hard work. Carrie covered the remainder of the desserts with clingfilm and opened the door of the gigantic American fridge freezer. As she popped them inside, she marvelled at the array of homemade quiches and scotch eggs, delicious sauces and fine foods that were encased in the most organised fridge she had ever seen. Roger had been a lucky man. Why hadn't he appreciated it? "Do you think Belinda secretly hates me?" she asked Louise.

"No! No way. Why would you even think that? Belinda is the most kind-hearted woman I know, and she most definitely isn't two-faced." Louise stroked Carrie's arm to reassure her. "There is no way she would be able to even socialise with you if she did, and she just made your favourite cake especially for you."

"Ahh OK, I just feel bad, that's all; I feel so guilty for what I did to her."

"You didn't do it, Roger did. She knows that. We all do."

Carrie smiles gratefully at Louise, thankful for her support.

"And I'm sorry to say this, but I think you had a lucky escape." Louise glanced at Carrie to check that she wasn't overstepping the mark. "What you need is a nice boy. One your own age. One who you can have a family with."

Carrie nodded in glum acknowledgement. "I really loved him, you know." She sighed, then smiled. "But now I love Belinda too."

THIRTEEN

CONFESSIONS IN A
WINE BAR

Baileys Wine Bar was *the* meeting place in town for the over thirties. 'Gastro Food and Fine Wines in a Sophisticated Setting' was what they advertised in the *Hampshire Life* glossy magazine, but it was known more locally as the 'Champers Bar' for its wide selection of champagnes and the extravagance of their customers, who regularly featured within the pages of the upmarket publication at various launches or special events.

It was 5.45pm, and with the cool lunchtime crowd having vacated, and the venue having been cleaned, the waiters now bustled around preparing tables for their 7pm evening opening time. They were all uniformly tall, male, dark and handsome, with a Latino look. The young men were all dressed the same in smart black trousers with designer black shirts, with the top few buttons undone, looking like they had all just stepped out of a Dolce & Gabbana aftershave commercial. The manager, though, was female, the queen bee who commanded the respect of her workers. Her name was Charlotte, and she excitedly dashed across the restaurant as soon as she spotted Carrie walking through the wide, glass door.

Tall, elegant and suntanned, more resembling a supermodel on the runway than a wine bar manager, her long balayage hair was blow-dried to perfection, her cream trouser suit classy but on trend. She rushed to greet Carrie warmly as Carrie and Louise arrived laden with props for the night ahead.

Louise surveyed the place in awe and wondered again why on earth she had previously allowed herself to lead such a sheltered life. After witnessing the glamorous creature that was Charlotte, she was extremely relieved that she had finally updated her wardrobe, thanks to the assistance of her best salesgirl, and now her good friend, Samantha.

Carrie squealed in excitement upon the sight of her friend, suddenly feeling more alive, having not been out since the death of Roger. She had stayed in and cried for weeks, only venturing out to go to work and to join the others for the Sunday Lunch Club.

Charlotte had tried desperately to get Carrie out to cheer her up but to no avail, so she'd been very relieved to receive the call from her to book a table for six, although she did think it was weird that she seemed to be spending all her time with all these older women. Mind you, she had been horrified when she'd turned up there a few months prior with Roger. Carrie was her prettiest friend, not to mention the sweetest, so when she had introduced Roger to her, she was perturbed to say the least. She encountered his type in the wine bar all the time. Lounge lizards. Arrogant, pot-bellied men who thought they were a good catch because they had a bob or two. Despite having wives and families at home, they came in on the roam, usually straight from work, so they could pretend to be working late in the office. Their appearances were timed to perfection as they were guaranteed to catch the groups of young women popping in for their after-work catch-ups and Prosecco with their pals. These chancers would park their Porsches as near to the door as they could, keen to show off and to appear a good catch, then, once inside, they would do their hunting at the bar, positioning themselves where they would get the most attention. They would deliberately check the time whenever a pretty girl happened to stand next to them, giving them the opportunity to flash their Rolex watches. Charlotte had disliked Roger immediately, but being the good friend she was, she had smiled politely, despite making a mental note to introduce her friend to some more suitable, and younger, men.

After greetings and introductions had been exchanged, Charlotte showed them to where she had reserved the very best table for them, and Carrie and Louise set to work, decorating it with streamers and balloons. "Don't worry, Charlotte, we've only brought silver and white," joked Carrie, knowing that Charlotte despised it when they had to host the odd hen party, which would proceed to lower the tone of the establishment with garish bright pink balloons, silly hats and male blow-up dolls with inflated willies and painted-on curly, black pubes and even curlier chest hair.

Louise tied two large, silver helium balloons in the shape of the numbers five and zero to Amanda's chair at the circular table. She approved of their designated table, preferring round ones to rectangular because you could talk to everyone equally and not be restricted to chatting to whoever you were sat near to.

With the table respectably and conservatively adorned for the birthday girl, it wasn't worth Carrie and Louise going all the way back home again, seeing as the others were due to arrive at 7pm, so they sat and waited for them at a bistro table in the bar area. They were joined by Charlotte, who kindly provided them with a complimentary bottle of champagne, chuffed to see her heartbroken friend finally out and about again. Secretly, she was celebrating the fact that her adorable, beautiful friend was no longer in the clutches of that selfish old man, but then she felt awful for even thinking such thoughts when he had only just popped his clogs.

At 6.45pm, Charlotte excused herself, informing them that she would have to leave them to it so that she could go and welcome her evening customers. She gave Carrie the biggest hug before she disappeared but made her promise that she would come back again very soon.

Carrie and Louise had managed to polish off the champagne already, so they ordered another two bottles, which now stood proudly in vintage silver ice buckets, awaiting the arrival of the others. They were already both rather tipsy, seeing as Charlotte hadn't shared any of the bottle with them, sticking to water as she was on duty, so when Tracey arrived first, she was gutted to see that she had missed out and swiftly made amends to catch up as quickly as possible. The party was clearly starting early.

Amanda, Belinda and Janet arrived five minutes later, and did so altogether, courtesy of a driver arranged by the latter. Since Charles's death, Janet had discovered, to her astonishment, just how much money they held in various bank accounts, savings, property and investments. Her husband had always controlled the finances, and she'd never been given access to his account, nor did they hold a joint account. Instead, he'd set up a standing order, from his current account to hers, providing her with her monthly allowance, which was just about enough for what she needed. Not wanted, just needed. She had never bothered to open a savings account for herself, seeing as there was never anything left over to save at the end of each month.

Having made these discoveries, Janet was initially both furious and hurt at the frugal allowance that her stingy husband had made her live off for all these years when they were clearly very well off, but once it had actually sunk in just how rich she now was, she was elated. Consequently, she made a decision that going forward, she could afford, and therefore intended, to indulge herself in whatever she desired. She finally felt liberated.

With the night in full swing, the two helium-filled, age-announcing balloons bobbed about above Amanda's head. She batted them away, laughing at the others and thoroughly enjoying herself, glad that she was talked into doing this by her friends. "Thank you to whoever put these decorations up," she laughed. "And the balloons too, even though they are advertising the fact that I am now officially old!"

Tracey nodded towards the younger two of the group. "It was all done by Carrie and Louise, the smug pre-fifty-year-olds."

"Well, thank you, everyone, I was not looking forward to my birthday at all, but now that I am here with you all, I certainly am."

"I've heard fifty is the new forty," chirped a more-outgoing-than-normal Carrie, the champagne giving her Dutch courage.

"Says the girl who isn't even forty," groaned Amanda.

"It could be worse; you could be sixty," laughed Janet, the oldest of the group, with raised eyebrows.

"Well, I'm not far behind you, Janet," piped up Belinda.

"Nonsense, you're still only fifty-five, still a mere youngster," Janet retorted, keen to make Belinda realise that she still had so much life in front of her.

"They do say that life begins at fifty," piped up Louise.

"Says the forty-year-old," laughed Amanda. "Just wait until it's your turn, madam."

Tracey, never one to miss an excuse for a toast, held up her glass to encourage the others to toast her. "Cheers to the birthday girl."

"To Amanda," they chorused in unison.

It was good for them all to have something to celebrate after what had happened recently, and on that note, "More champagne please," demanded an excitable Tracey to the waiter. *At last, they are finally starting to have fun*, she thought to herself.

On Charlotte's recommendation they had pre-ordered the party platters of tapas for which the wine bar was renowned. That way, there would be something for everyone. The selection of Catalan dishes went down extremely well, with everyone thoroughly enjoying them, especially Janet, who was again getting to experience something different to the usual meat and two veg suppers she had eaten all her life, and who declared herself a calamari virgin.

"At least you aren't an actual virgin, though," snorted a now sloshed Tracey.

An embarrassed Janet didn't know how to answer but whispered to Belinda, "I do hope she isn't going to get too drunk."

But Tracey was on a roll. "Fifty is the new forty," she hollered to Amanda, and half the restaurant, followed by, "And champagne is the new… champagne," as she knocked back the glass, proudly holding it empty in the air. Then she looked around, unimpressed. "Oh, come on, you lot, it's Amanda's fiftieth, and we all need to have some fun for once. Don't we?" The first few glasses had already relaxed everyone, and instead of being annoyed with a boisterous Tracey and her bossiness in trying to force everyone to drink, they individually but collectively obediently relented. For the first time since the dreaded day that changed all their lives, they had finally exhaled. It turned out that the night out was well and truly needed, with all six women having a proper drink and chilling out. Even Janet.

With the food cleared away and the alcohol abundantly flowing, the women were tipsier than any of them had ever seen each other. Apart from Tracey, of course, but she was on good form and was behaving herself.

"Y'know, I think I am going to like being fifty," declared Amanda. "It's like a chance to draw a line under the past. A fresh start. You're right – life should begin at fifty."

Carrie and Louise were now so merry that they were almost in Tracey's league as they 'whoop whooped' loudly in agreement with Amanda's statement.

Amanda wasn't far behind them and laughed in appreciation, but then she turned more serious when she had a realisation. "I know I shouldn't speak ill of the dead, but our men…" she paused and the others suddenly went quiet in anticipation of what she was about to say, "…they were all *selfish*. They did what they wanted, when they wanted, and they thoroughly enjoyed their lives. Why shouldn't we all do the same?"

"Exactly," enthused Tracey, drunkenly raising her arm in salute.

Amanda continued, "And I should probably shut up now because I am rather drunk… but me and Christopher… we weren't really happy. We just stayed together for Sophie's sake, for the nice house, the security, and because…" she shrugged nonchalantly, "basically, I couldn't be bothered to go out and find myself a better, less selfish one. Better the devil you know, hey?"

The table went quiet, the conversation about to turn more heartfelt and honest. Finally, the women started to open up to each other, the formalities of the golf club and the Sunday Lunch Club about to be overcome and their friendships deepened.

Louise was the first to question Amanda, keen to understand more about what she experienced with her own husband. "What about the sex? Did you have a good sex life?"

"Nah, don't be daft, two pumps and a squirt was my Christopher," replied a past-caring, drunken Amanda, who was clearly in the mood to spill the beans. Her thirty years of frustrations were about to be well and truly poured all over the trendy, ceramic table.

Janet was visibly shocked. "Please, ladies, have some decorum," she pleaded, having never in her life encountered anyone who had discussed their sex lives so blatantly.

Totally ignoring her, Amanda continued. The combination of the night out and the flowing alcohol was like therapy to her, and she clearly needed to vent. "Then he would roll off and say, 'Ooh we are so good together, aren't we?'" She sighed. "I don't think he had ever heard of the word foreplay, but for some reason, he thought he was bloody brilliant." She let out a scornful laugh, but it echoed as a snort around the table. "He was a typical public-school boy," she continued, on a roll. "Selfish *out* of bed and selfish *in* bed." She sighed again. "No wonder my sex drive has completely vanished." Amanda looked around before admitting her next revelation. "I am now literally *dead* from the waist down." The tipsy birthday girl comically pointed down to her own vagina, then indicated its death by making a slitting throat action.

Tracey, absolutely loving this new, relaxed group of women, comically slurred, "I always thought he was an *arrogant* prick."

Belinda totally understood where Amanda was coming from. "Isn't that normal, though? I thought that was just age. Mine's been dead for years."

Janet squirmed. She did not want to join in this conversation, having little experience in such matters.

Louise suddenly decided that she also had something to get off her chest. "OK, if it's confession time, then me too. My marriage was as dull as dishwater... and I have a secret." She paused, appearing embarrassed at what she was about to divulge. "Chris and I... we only had sex twice a year."

Carrie was visibly shocked. "*Noooo!*"

Louise explained, "Chris was impotent. He could never get it up."

Amanda, surprised but amused, chokes on her drink. "Oh, I am sorry, Louise, but please carry on."

"He would take a Viagra but just on my birthday and at Christmas, as though he was doing me a favour," Louise explained.

Janet gulped, finding the conversation excruciatingly embarrassing.

"Oh, that's awful," exclaimed Carrie, clearly a woman who thoroughly enjoyed sex.

Louise continued to elaborate. "He didn't have one romantic bone in his body. Everything was always about him. He thought he was the prize because he went to a posh boarding school and had a good business. And probably because his parents told him he was." Louise now looked around before making her final confession. She whispered to her friends, "It was far lonelier being married to him than it is now that I am a *widow*!"

The others didn't look as shocked as she thought they might have. They looked at her instead with empathy and understanding.

Tracey comically slurred, "I always thought he was a *pompous* prick."

Belinda surprised the others by also joining in with confessions. "I have to admit, I don't blame Roger for leaving me. We had fizzled out years ago. It was the family unit that I wanted more than I wanted him. I did still find him handsome, but I didn't want to sleep with him anymore." She continued, forgetting about Carrie... "He wanted to go out and party, and I wanted to stay home, watch movies and do my baking." She paused and looked sad. "I couldn't wait to have grandchildren, but he was absolutely dreading it." As soon as the words were out of Belinda's mouth, she realised she had mentioned Roger not wanting kids, and she cringed at the thought of upsetting Carrie, but luckily, it went straight over the girl's very tipsy head. Relieved that Carrie had failed to put two and two together to make 'Roger is a twat', she continued, "Not that my Max is in a hurry to give me any, mind." She sighed. "Oh, I wish he would flippin' get on with it." Belinda then turned to Carrie and smiled kindly at her. "So, I don't blame you, Carrie. Roger needed someone younger to socialise with. He always was Peter Pan."

Tracey slurred her opinion as usual, "I always thought he was a *flash* prick."

Carrie knew they were right, but she still felt enough loyalty to attempt to defend him. "He wasn't all bad, you know."

Amanda couldn't help herself, not being a fan of Roger. "Ohhh, he *was* sweetheart, you just hadn't been around long enough to find out."

Everyone looked at Carrie, expecting her to burst into tears as usual, but this time, she just shrugged it off, deciding it was best not to discuss Roger with the others.

To the group's astonishment, Janet contributed to the conversation. "I feel very disrespectful speaking of Charles like this, but we didn't really go in for that sort of thing." She whispered the next word, unable to speak it out loud. "*Intercourse*. And I refuse to divulge any further because I was brought up to believe that it is vulgar to talk about such matters."

Carrie and Louise looked at each other and stifled a giggle. "Janet, you are not in the olden days now. You need to open up and *chill out*," said a normally nervous Carrie but with the fizz now loosening her tongue.

Tracey, as usual, offered a direct verdict. "I thought the major would be a right *goer*."

They all laughed now at the sheer thought of the major in that way, all having feared him slightly.

"Most certainly not, Tracey, quite the opposite actually." Janet sighed sadly. "Maybe that's why we never had children; I would have loved to have a family, but Charles wasn't interested."

"Well, Andrew was a *nag*," stated Tracey, very matter-of-fact. "Always trying to stop me from having fun. But apart from that, he was OK, I suppose."

The others looked knowingly at each other, all fully aware that Andy was the good guy, and one that had his hands full with Tracey. They had all felt utterly sorry for him at times.

"Oh well," said Amanda, "now that we have all aired our marital disappointments… to the men." She raised her glass, and the others all joined her to remember their late partners. The birthday girl still held her glass high. "We loved you all, but now it's *our* turn to do what we want for once."

Janet added the final words, "To *us*."

FOURTEEN

THE WORMS TURN

It had now been six weeks since the golfers' tragic accident. After opening up to each other at Amanda's fiftieth, the women had become much closer and were a huge support to one another. They had even set up their own WhatsApp group 'The Golf Widows', so they were all intrigued, but concerned, when they received a message from Amanda, sent at 6am on a Saturday morning:

URGENT!!!! Meet me today for coffee. 11am. Golf Club.

Followed by another message sent immediately after:

If you have plans, please cancel them. This is VERY important.

It is followed by a further message of two emojis: the praying hands and a crying face.

Janet was the first to receive it, being an early bird. The rules of being up and dressed by 7.30am, dictated by Charles for years, was a habit her body was now used to. She immediately called Amanda, concerned for her friend.

"Please, Janet, I don't want to say anything until we are all together," responded Amanda.

"But are you alright, dear?" queried her worried friend.

"I'm fine honestly, but this isn't about me. It concerns us all."

Janet hung up baffled, wondering what on earth it could be. The worst had already happened, and the men were all dead, so it couldn't be that bad, she concluded.

Phone calls followed from all the others except for Tracey, but they all received the same response: "You'll have to wait until we are all together." So, they all hung up baffled, their next hours spent wondering what on earth could be wrong.

By 10am and with no call from Tracey, Amanda called her, deciding that she must still be sleeping, or have a hangover, so might not get the message until the afternoon. She was proved correct when a tired- and confused-sounding Tracey spoke hoarsely down the phone, "Hello?"

"Tracey, did you see my message?" shrieked Amanda frantically.

"What message? I'm in bed. You woke me up," she retorted nonchalantly.

"Get up *now!*" shouted Amanda. "It's an *emergency*. Golf club, eleven o'clock. Read your message!" Then, she hung up, not wanting to waste any more time and needing to get there herself to arrange a table, aware that this would be the first time she had ever had it to arrange it for six women. Luckily, most of the golfers would already be out on the course by then, so they should not be disturbed nor, more importantly, overheard.

The ladies turned up one by one at the golf club, with

none of them having been there since the day of the funeral and all feeling rather strange, uncomfortable even, as though they shouldn't really be there. The golf club had been such a major part of their lives for so many years, yet now they felt like they didn't belong there anymore. It was especially the case for Janet, and although several of the staff greeted her warmly, she could tell that they didn't really know what to say to her. Death tended to do that. People never knew whether to commiserate and mention the circumstances or cheerfully talk about the weather instead, fearing that any mention of their late partners would be awkward or upsetting.

Amanda had managed to book their old table and was now sat down, having already ordered herself an orange juice and a cappuccino. She used the OJ to gulp down a couple of paracetamol, attempting to alleviate her sore throat and swollen glands caused by the sleepless night that she had just endured.

Janet and Belinda had pulled up at the same time, so they walked in together discussing what it could possibly be. "I've just had to reschedule my hair appointment for this," complained Janet. "So, I hope it is nothing trivial."

"It must be serious. We're meeting for lunch at Louise's tomorrow, so what could be so important that it couldn't wait for one more day?" replied Belinda. "And I wonder why she's asked us to meet here?"

The pair joined the sombre Amanda who was sat anxiously waiting for them. Belinda thought that she would feel sad and nostalgic coming back to the club, but she was surprised to find that all she felt was relief. Sheer relief that she didn't have to spend every Saturday here like she did for years.

Janet, too, had thought the same as she arrived and drove up towards the clubhouse. She had still parked in her old spot in the chairman's wife space, because she had phoned ahead to see if it would be free, having heard that the new chairman's wife never frequented the club at all.

The ladies were choosing their coffees as Louise joined them just in time to add her skinny salted-caramel latte to the order. She was soon followed by a nervous Carrie, sincerely hoping that this was not going to be about Roger.

Then they waited, all of them feeling a mixture of anxiousness and curiosity, a million thoughts running through their heads but still completely baffled as to what it could possibly be.

"I do hope Tracey isn't still in bed. I don't want to be kept waiting all day, and I could only postpone my hairdresser for three hours," complained Janet, clearly miffed at being summoned at such short notice.

"Don't worry, Janet, I did call her to make sure that she got up," reassured Amanda, who then sincerely hoped that Tracey did indeed get up and not fall straight back to sleep again. Her fears were alleviated when she looked up, at hearing the door being barged open, to see that the last person had finally arrived. A red-faced Tracey came rushing across the room puffing and panting. She pulled off her Burberry mac, sweating profusely in her menopausal state, then strewed it across the back of her chair, dumping her Louis Vuitton bag onto the stripey carpeted floor; then, she flopped down ungraciously into her chair. "Well? What's so important that you've dragged us all out of bed on a Saturday morning?" She caught her breath then, confidently but impatiently, clicked her fingers to signal to the waiter to come and take her order. As he approached, she looked at her watch, contemplating whether to order a large white wine, but then, observing the other's coffee cups, she decided against it, not wanting to be judged.

"A large cappuccino, please," she gasped.

"Errrr, I'll have the same as well," piped up Carrie, having been overlooked by the waiter but not having the nerve, nor the bad manners, to demand immediate attention in the way that Tracey did.

There was a cocktail of emotions as five fidgety women nurse five frothy coffees, all awaiting Amanda's announcement, until they were put out of their misery when she finally gave a nervous cough to indicate that she was ready to speak and divulge her news.

"So, ladies…" She stopped, glaring at Tracey, who had her head down slurping her coffee, trying to drink the hot beverage without getting a white, milky moustache. Amanda clasped her hands seriously until Tracey put the cup down. She needed their full and proper attention.

"I have called you all here today with some rather *unsavoury* and upsetting news." She scanned the room to make sure she was not overheard. "I'm not sure if any of you will want to hear this or even acknowledge it. Especially you, Janet, so please forgive me."

Janet had just picked up her coffee to take a sip, but she put it down abruptly.

"But it is my duty as your friend to enlighten you all," she inhaled, "about the devious activities of our dear departed husbands."

"Oh, er, I don't think I want to hear th—" Carrie begins to protest.

"*Tough!* You need to wake up and smell the coffee, Carrie," snapped an exhausted Amanda. "He didn't deserve you and the sooner you get over him the better."

Carrie now looked scared to death, stayed silent and squirmed in her seat.

Tracey's eyebrows rose. She looked amused, but she was the only one who was enjoying this. "Bloody hell, this must be *baaadddd*," she said, trying not to snigger.

Amanda continued to explain. "Yesterday, I received a letter. Well, actually, Christopher received a letter, but seeing as he isn't here to open it, and us ladies have been left with the *crappy* job of sorting out the men's affairs…" The other women nodded in agreement and understanding. "…I obviously opened it…"

Louise leant in, intrigued and eager to hear more. "Oh no. What was it?"

"I expected to find the usual – a credit card bill or one of those bloody fancy booklets getting him to buy yet another cashmere golf jumper or a crate of overpriced wine – but no, it wasn't." Amanda paused to take a deep breath. "It was tickets. Holiday tickets to be exact. For all of our wonderful husbands to go to Majorca on yet another golf holiday."

The others look puzzled, unsure why was she making a fuss about this, so Janet interrupted her, "But we already know about that trip, dear. It's the one that's coming up soon. It's the one that they won in the Saunderson Cup."

"No, it isn't, Janet. They all *lied* to us. It turns out that my husband, who told me that he didn't have any spare leave to take me away, had actually *bid*, and *paid*, for the holiday himself in a charity auction at one of the sportsmen's dinners that they went to."

The others looked baffled, but Amanda continued. "Furthermore, I then checked his bank statements from around the same dates, and it transpires that he received the same exact sum of money from all of your husbands for their share. They all paid a fifth each."

The others still looked confused. The penny still hadn't dropped yet.

"So, I dug deeper," continued Amanda like a detective. "There is *no* Saunderson Cup." Amanda bent down and retrieved a notebook from her bag. On the page was a list of all the competitions that the men claimed to have won over the last few years. She gestured for the others to look at all the names on the list. "Look! They have been pretending to win all these competitions to justify why they took so many golf trips. *None* of these competitions even exist. They just tricked us so that they had excuses to go away so often. They all booked and paid for the trips themselves. They didn't actually win anything."

The women looked at each other, too stunned to speak, confused by the reality of what it means.

Amanda now spoke quietly and urged the others to lean closer so she could whisper, "And that includes... the *Thailand* trip!"

Janet gasped in shock.

Amanda offered further proof. "I have been up all night investigating. There is no South-West Competition either."

The others looked distraught.

"I have googled every single competition that they claimed to have won over the past three years." She then tossed the notepad onto the table for them all to see. After each name on the list, she had written a big fat cross. "Nada! They. Won. Nothing," Amanda confirmed, sitting back righteously with her arms crossed whilst the others all leant forward to scrutinise her list.

The table was deadly silent.

Tracey broke the silence first. "I'd always wondered how they managed to be so successful in these competitions when I didn't think that they were that brilliant at golf. So, I just thought the other teams must have been even worse."

Carrie spoke but immediately regretted it, realising how pathetic she sounded. "Roger was good. Well, he said he was."

Louise snapped, "He was good, Carrie. Good at bragging and cheating and *lying*." Then she paused and looked disappointed. "They obviously all were."

Janet suddenly shot upright in a manner that would put Margaret Thatcher to shame. She snatched up the list and with it her smart Basler jacket and navy patent handbag. "Righto. Leave this with me, ladies. I intend to go and further investigate this matter immediately." She pushed her chair back in under the table, but before she left, she added, "I'll report back when I see you all for lunch at Louise's tomorrow. Is that OK?"

Louise nodded in agreement to confirm that she was still going to make lunch for everyone the following day as planned. The others muttered in despondent agreement. With that, Janet turned on her heel and marched off on a mission towards to the club's offices in which Charles spent so much of his time.

FIFTEEN

THE BOMBSHELL

Sunday lunchtime could not have come a moment sooner for all the women. None of them had managed to get much sleep the night before, after Amanda had dropped her devastating bombshell. The women had each been dealing with their grief in their own ways and had individually made peace with their husbands, because whatever their marriage problems were, and despite the fact that the men weren't perfect, they were gone now. Therefore, the ladies had chosen to hang onto the good memories and to forgive and forget anything else, because it didn't really matter now, did it, seeing as they were dead.

Or did it?

Because last night's revelation had totally changed things. It had made them all feel that their marriages had been one big fat lie. A joke. A *fraud*. Had they even known their own husbands at all? Fibbing about one trip wouldn't have really mattered. It might have even been funny, like a schoolboy prank, but to lie so consistently, about all their trips, over so many years, then that was a different matter altogether.

The ladies had each missed out on so many holidays and opportunities of their own due to the men going away so often, not to mention the financial deceit. Their family money being abused in this way was not only unfair, but it was downright fraudulent and totally unforgivable. Some of them were hoping that maybe Amanda might have made a mistake, so they were desperate to hear what Janet had to say after she had been to the golf club offices to double check her claims and to establish the facts for herself.

The flabbergasted and exhausted group sat around Louise's dining table, far more interested in hearing an update from Janet than what they were going to be having for lunch, which was just as well. Louise apologised profusely for not having cooked a proper Sunday lunch, serving up Marks & Spencer lasagnes instead, but in her defence, they were steak ones from their *Best Ever* range and cooked properly in the oven, so they were far superior to Asda's three-for-a-fiver cheapo microwave meals. She had used the excuse of feeling too tired and being far too stressed, but the reality was she had always hated cooking, especially roasts, and after being expected to cook Sunday lunch every week for her in-laws in her previous life, she had made a promise to herself that she was never going to have to do it ever again. If one Sunday she ever fancied eating one, she would simply go to the pub; the price of a carvery was so reasonable, it was crazy to even bother cooking it yourself, never mind all the dirty dishes and pans to wash afterwards. In fact, she had already planned that when it was her turn to host, she would just take everyone to the local pub and pick up the tab, but seeing as the conversation today might be upsetting, she didn't feel that a public venue would be appropriate, so the privacy of her own home was most definitely called for.

Anyway, she had also provided an Italian rocket salad and a selection of rustic garlic breads to accompany the main course, as well as a generous portion of roasted mushroom paté for their starter. Actually, it was good old reliable Mr Marks and Mr Spencer that had supplied the whole meal, but their Tiramisu dessert was 'as delicious as you will find in any restaurant' she informed everyone. "But not as good as yours though, Belinda," added Louise kindly but truthfully.

"I would have made one if you'd said you needed help," replied her kind friend.

"I know you would have, Belinda, but it'll be your turn to cook again soon, and I am sure you've had as little sleep as I have."

Mutterings of agreement rumbled around their table, with the weary ladies all subdued. Even Carrie looked like she had finally 'got it'. Janet filled everyone in on her findings from the golf club. It transpired that Amanda was a hundred per cent correct in her findings. Charles's young secretary Katie admitted to Janet that she already knew all about their deceitful behaviour, having often organised the trips for the men herself. She confessed that she had been sworn to secrecy but had never felt comfortable with it and had only done so because she was a single mother, so she desperately needed her job.

She had explained to Janet that it was so difficult to find

a job that fitted in with the school run, so when Charles had kindly allowed her to choose her own hours, she had been extremely grateful, and he had reminded her on many occasions that she 'owed him a favour'.

"Poor girl, how dare he put her in that position!" Amanda exclaimed.

"My thoughts exactly," Janet agreed, informing them all that the young girl had apparently burst into tears as soon as Janet requested to see the details of the competitions that they held in their files and had promptly spilled the beans, followed by her begging the older lady for forgiveness. Katie had even elaborated, admitting that on one occasion, when they had indulged in more trips than usual, Charles had instructed her go to the local trophy shop to purchase some mini silver cups. She was ordered to get them engraved, purely to ensure that none of the wives would get suspicious when they had won yet another golfing holiday.

"What a sneaky old sod," said an irritated Tracey, for once not amused by the drama.

Janet's discoveries compounded the raw emotions that the group were already feeling. They were numb, not knowing what they thought anymore. They all needed time to process this ultimate betrayal.

Carrie surprised everyone when she announced, "I can see now that Roger told lies. I am so disappointed in him."

"Not half as much as I am," said Belinda disdainfully. "Thank God my Max is nothing like him."

Tracey shrugged. "I wouldn't have even minded, so I don't know why Andy just didn't admit it."

"He was probably worried you would drop them all in it," countered Louise.

"S'pose so," shrugged Tracey, then she carried on enjoying her wine. It clearly hadn't caused her a sleepless night, so her tiredness must be due to a hangover.

"Well, I am absolutely disgusted," announced a very disappointed Janet. "I don't think I will ever think the same about Charles again." She was flustered, and the others had never seen Janet this emotive, so she shocked them further when she said, "What utter deceitful *bastards* they all were."

Louise and Carrie glanced at each other, amused that Janet had actually swore.

Janet then resumed her graciousness to enquire, "Amanda you are awfully quiet – are you OK, dear?"

Amanda had appeared quiet but was in fact seething, bottling up her furious thoughts until, suddenly, they erupted. "He said he had no leave left to take me away for my fiftieth." She sighs angrily. "Not even a normal birthday but my bloody fiftieth. And all the thousands of pounds he was squandering on golf and their boys' holidays, while I stayed home and worked my guts out to pay for everything for Sophie." She looked around the table like a deranged woman about to tip the table upside down. "I fucking hate him, and I'm glad he's dead, because I would bloody kill him if I could get my hands on him right now."

The others sat quietly, still in shock. They were all upset, but Amanda was clearly deeply resentful for all the things she had missed out on over the years due to Christopher's selfish actions. You could hear a pin drop as everyone observed Belinda stroking Amanda's back to comfort the woman who was on the verge of bursting into tears out of sheer frustration. "I just wanted to travel too," explained a now subdued, but clearly upset, Amanda.

Everyone was upset to see their friend crying, except for Tracey, who was half-cut and staring at the ceiling pondering. The others ignored her until she had an excitable outburst. "I *know*!" They all turned to stare at her, dreading what she was going to come out with next. "Why don't we all go instead?"

The others looked at her puzzled.

"Go where?" asked Louise.

"*Majorca!* The golfing holiday," shouted an excited Tracey, thinking primarily of herself and cocktails by the sea.

No one spoke at first, until Amanda stated sarcastically, "I suppose we did technically pay for it."

Louise then joined in to support Tracey's idea. "Tracey is right. Why don't we? It's only for four nights, and what have we got to lose?" She opened out her palms to the others, daring anyone to think of a good reason not to. "You didn't get a big party for your fiftieth, Amanda, so let's go for you, for your birthday," she added.

Carrie mentioned something that they hadn't thought of. "There are only five places though, so you go, Belinda. I have to work anyway."

Amanda had suddenly cheered up. "It is still two weeks away, so I am sure we have time to add an extra flight. I doubt it will be fully booked."

Louise added, "Yep, we're a team now remember. Everyone comes, and that's final."

Belinda looked anxious; she had never been on a girls' holiday. She reminded herself that she was old, and more importantly, she was *fat*. The thought of being in the embarrassing position of having to wear beachwear in front of people filled her with sheer horror. "I really don't think I am that bothered, Carrie, you go instead."

"Nonsense," exclaimed Amanda. "I am not going if you don't come too."

"I will if you do, Belinda," chirped Janet, keen to start having adventures after being so controlled all her life.

Belinda sighed, looking unsure and unconvinced, until Amanda clinched the deal. "Look, would the men stay at home, all alone and miserable, or would they go off and have fun?"

The thought of Roger enjoying himself on holidays clinched it, so Belinda grinned in agreement.

Amanda further convinced them. "The booking is for three twin rooms. Charles was having a room to himself, so the six hotel places are already confirmed. We just need to check which flight it is and add another seat to the booking."

"I'll sort that out, ladies. Just leave it to me," demanded Janet, glad that she had something to organise again, but this time not for her husband. "I'll call you this evening for the info," she told Amanda. Janet looked mischievous. She was up to something.

"Well, that's sorted then," concurred an elated Tracey, raising her glass. "Cheers, ladies. To our holiday."

SIXTEEN

THE JET SET

It was 6am on a clear but crisp morning, as the engine of a smart minibus purred patiently outside Janet's house. The others had all been picked up first, so she was the last stop en route to the airport.

"How come I had to be picked up first?" complained Tracey.

"Because you are the one most likely to sleep through your alarm," teased Louise.

"And how come she's the last pick up, when she's actually the furthest from the airport?" retorted an observant but grumbling Tracey.

"She is the oldest, so have some respect and stop moaning, woman," laughed Amanda. "And look what a lovely vehicle she has arranged for us." And she had. It was a black Mercedes with tinted windows, the type that normally shuttles rock stars around when they need to travel incognito. Their driver looked more like a pilot in his smart, gold-trimmed cap. Not only had he personally helped each lady into his vehicle, but he'd also handed them chilled bottles of Evian water, informing them that he had blankets available should they get cold on the journey. He had left them momentarily whilst he went out to Janet's front door to pick up the brown leather luggage she had left outside on her doormat. After placing the last of the luggage in the boot, he returned to the house to escort Janet down her path and into his vehicle. She surprised everyone by getting into the front with the driver rather than in the back with the others.

"Good morning, ladies," chirped a bright and breezy Janet. "Are we all ready? Do you all have your passports?"

Belinda waved hers excitedly in response. "I'm so glad I came now. I've never been on a girls-only trip before."

"Neither have I, dear, it wasn't exactly the done thing in my day. However, I have decided to start accepting every invitation and to try every new experience." And with that resolution, Janet ordered the driver, "Step on it, James," sitting back and smiling to herself.

The journey to Gatwick would only be forty-five minutes long but, still being early, each of them relaxed back into their seats to grab a last bit of shut-eye before their flight. With the women's eyes all closed, they were unaware that they had driven into the private terminal entrance until the vehicle stopped and parked adjacent to a private lounge. The women woke up confused, expecting to have been dumped at the drop off zone outside the main terminal like most of the travellers.

"Where are we?" asked Amanda. "I thought we were going from Gatwick?"

"We are, dear. Just a better lounge," said Janet casually, not giving the game away just yet, but as the women climbed out of the vehicle, they were guided by their driver towards the entrance of a private lounge, where he invited them to go in and take a seat and informed them that someone would be with them shortly to check their documents. The enthusiastic bunch trooped into the smart executive lounge and immediately realised that they were in first class.

Carrie was beyond excited, but she resisted jumping up and down, opting to play it cool after spotting a few very smartly dressed businessmen reading *The Times* or shuffling through important documents from their expensive-looking leather briefcases. In the waiting lounge area, they were offered comfy leather sofas and passed menus, all with no prices due to the offerings being complimentary.

Four of them delighted in sipping the freshly brewed Italian coffee, whilst Belinda and Janet deliberated over their choice of tea with every imaginable option available. They would be served from expensive cups and saucers, whilst they devoured delicious pastries from fine bone china plates.

A smartly dressed young man conferred with Janet, who had already collected the passports from the others and was now handing them over to be checked, along with their flight documents. The others could see out of the window that the nearby planes were all private jets. They chattered excitedly amongst themselves, keen to get onboard, the extravagant journey ahead being a new adventure in itself.

"Is one of those really for us?" Belinda asked Janet.

"It certainly is," smiled Janet, happy to be able to treat her friends and being more than able to afford it thanks to the recent improvement in her financial situation. "The men didn't feel guilty spending our money, so neither do I," she quipped. "And now that Charles isn't here to spend it all on golf, I can decide how to spend it for a change." And with that, she picked up a Danish pastry and took a huge bite in defiance of her husband's previous restrictions over her diet.

Amanda was the first to thank her. "Thank you so much, Janet. I can't believe that you've gone and booked us a private plane. This is going to be my best birthday ever."

Louise agreed, "I feel like it's mine too! This is just what we all needed."

Their gratitude was interrupted by an extremely handsome pilot approaching them. Louise nudged Carrie, meaning that she too should also check him out, just like she was doing with enthusiasm. "Your plane is ready for boarding, ladies," he announced to the whole party.

Tracey shot up first. "Let me on there. I'm gagging for a glass of champagne." With that, she snatched up her bag and rushed over towards the exit, like a kid running towards a sweet shop.

The women gathered at the foot of the plane's steps waiting for the airport ground staff to give them permission to board. Tracey bustled her way to the front and bounded up the stairs like a crazy puppy. Belinda and Amanda followed, giggling in anticipation. Below, Carrie stalled Louise and Janet. "*Wait!*" she ordered, as she took out her phone. "We must get a photo." She held her phone up high to squeeze herself and the other two in a selfie. "I feel like a Kardashian," shrieked an excitable Carrie.

"What's a Kardashian?" asked a perplexed Janet.

"Come on, I'll tell you on board," laughed Louise, politely gesturing for Janet to go first, then following her up the stairs. Carrie lingered below for a moment longer to take a few more selfies alone with the jet gleaming in the background, before herself galloping up the stairs to join the others.

A young male steward was stood in the doorway of the plane awaiting the final girl's entrance, then, no sooner was she on board, he switched duties to offer everyone a glass of champagne as soon as they had all taken their seats. With everyone settled, he pulled the door shut and locked it with a large lever. Tracey flirted with him but only for the drinks that he distributed. "Oh, I do like you... Marcus," she teased after reading his name badge, then offering up her empty glass and winking to indicate that a replacement was required. Marcus was used to a variety of passengers in his job. He often had to calm down wild parties, but he could see that this gig was going to be an easy one. He couldn't imagine this lot getting up to any shenanigans.

With everyone buckled up and holding a drink, Janet addressed the group. "We've all had a tough few months, so let's put it all behind us now and start to do what the men did. Let's finally start to enjoy ourselves." She raised her glass. "And more importantly, here's to a proper happy fiftieth birthday to Amanda."

"To Amanda," they chorused as the plane began to taxi down the runway and ascend gracefully up into the clear morning sky.

Up above in a cloud-free sky, the women decadently reclined into the sumptuous ivory leather individual armchairs. Classical music from Chopin could be heard discreetly in the background, as each of the six passengers relaxed and gazed out of the window, deep in their own individual thoughts.

Janet made a mental note to do this more often. She daydreamed about which countries she would like to visit. Venice and the Italian lakes were on the top of her wish list, then maybe Portugal, to one of those intensive 'learn to play golf' holidays. Most of the women her age who played had done so for years, so she could do with catching them up.

The day before, she had been online to look for women's golf attire. She knew she could just nip and buy them from the club, and still be given a generous staff discount, but she didn't want to make a fuss; besides, her plans to take up golf were still a secret. She had ordered them from the internet and treated herself to the full monty. On its way to her were two pairs of spiked shoes, checked trousers, Bermuda shorts and a variety of polo shirts, gilets and waterproof jackets to suit every possible weather, as well as a set of ladies' golf clubs with the matching bag and trolley.

Luckily, she already knew what the best brands were, having had to wash Charles's kit for years. Even better, by the time she got home, it would all be waiting for her. She smiled to herself, contemplating her new hobby. She was excited, an emotion that she hadn't felt for many years.

Belinda thought about her son Max. He was now back abroad and currently in Copenhagen in the middle of his Scandinavia tour. She missed him so much, but she was pleased that he was having fun. Maybe he had it right after all, travelling the world with his friends instead of settling down and getting married. *I should be brave and go and visit him*, she thought but then decided against it – she didn't want to impose, and if she was honest, his music wasn't really her cup of tea. Why on earth didn't she send him for piano lessons instead of the drums?!

She put her thoughts of Max out of her head, not wanting to feel sad and instead wondered what the food would be like in Majorca. She hoped she might pick up some new recipes. She already made a mean frittata but was sure there would be versions in Spain that would inspire her. She also planned to go into a Spanish bakery to get new ideas for her baking obsession. *The Europeans make such very beautiful and elegant cakes*, she thought, wishing she could be more experimental, but there were only so many cakes that one woman could bake, especially when she ended up eating them all by herself.

Amanda stared out of the window and across the pale blue sky. As she watched the lines of vapour trails following other aeroplanes that shared this vast open space with their own little jet, she contemplated her future. She was thinking about just how small the world really was. You could get absolutely anywhere in the world in a day. The world was her oyster.

Sophie had been as far as Australia and New Zealand, which she envied, but herself, she particularly wanted to visit South America. She wanted to experience the colourful carnivals of Brazil, to learn the tango in Argentina with a tall, dark, handsome man with shoulder length hair and to climb Machu Picchu in Peru, something she had dreamed of since she was a teenager. She yearned to drink coffee in Columbia and red wine in Chile. She wanted to see all of it.

She thought about her life so far and realised that she was at the end of an era. She was standing at a crossroads. She not only had an empty nest, but she was no longer trapped by having a partner whose job he couldn't leave and whose golf trips he wouldn't give up. No ties. What was the point of staying in her big house if it was just her rattling around in it by herself? If she sold up and downsized, she could take some time out, travel the world, write that book. She deliberated whether she should pack in her job and sell the house as soon as she got home, then she would really be free. Free to fly across as many blue skies as her heart desired.

Carrie thought about Roger. She still missed him. She thought so anyway. Or did she just miss what she *thought* she was going to have with him? The promise of a future of a family, with a baby of her own. She wondered again if he thought about her when he knew, *if* he knew, that his plane was going to crash. The thought of his final moments had given her many a sleepless night and bad dreams. She hoped that he hadn't known. That he had drunk too much champagne on the flight and was fast asleep snoring his head off. She had believed that it was just her that had these morbid thoughts, until she had broken down in tears over one Sunday lunch and had been forced to confess what was wrong by the others. It turned out that they had all suffered with these intrusive thoughts too, and it was normal apparently. She quickly put the terrible thought out of her head and tried to think of something nice instead. She stared out of the window at the fluffy white clouds which floated beneath them like giant marshmallows. *Is there such a thing as heaven?* she ponders. *If so, are the men up there right now, in those clouds?* She smiled fondly to herself, imagining the five golfers floating around in white togas with gold halos, like overgrown funny, fat, hairy angels, swinging golf clubs and putting golf balls to each other, from one cloud to another. Then she frowned at herself for being daft. How could they be? They weren't angels; they were all devils. And if there was such a thing as heaven, she didn't think they would be allowed in. Especially not her Roger!

Louise thought about sex. She had been watching Marcus in his tight trousers, showing off his pert little bottom. She decided he must be gay to be that cute. The most handsome men always were. Life was so unfair. He also smelt so good that he was giving her a twinge every time he passed by. She decided she had waited long enough to have sex with a new man. It was just a fantasy when Chris was still alive, but now that he was dead, it was officially and legally allowed. Surely, no one would judge her now, she hoped, but she bet that they still would if she didn't wait for at least, like, eighteen months or some other ridiculous mourning period.

She thought about the fact that there wasn't an official legal, nor moral, time in which it was deemed acceptable until widows and widowers could move on, but it was funny how the men never seemed to wait about for too long, and neither did they get judged for it. Just look at Paul McCartney. He was all *Linda this* and *Linda that*, but then the poor woman died, and before you could say *bouncy tits,* he had shacked up with that sexy blonde bird with one leg, Heather whatshername. Why was it OK for men and not for women?

She knew she was a widow now, but she hated that word. It made her feel old, which she wasn't, and it made her seem sad, which she most certainly was not. She planned to not admit to anyone that she met that she was one. If any suitable men should happen to enquire about her status, then she would simply reply that she was single. She liked that word. Single. Single and ready to mingle. She smiled to herself. She was going to get laid on this trip if it killed her.

Tracey didn't think about anything. She had knocked back as many glasses of champers as she could, and after the very early start that morning, she now slept, mouth wide open, snoring her head off.

Marcus watched her in amusement. *Thank God she is finally asleep*, he thought, *the bloody pisshead.* He hadn't had time to grab breakfast yet, so wanted to sit down in peace, have a cup of tea and a biscuit and check his Facebook account so he could stalk his butch, bitch of an ex-boyfriend to see what he had been up to since they had split up. He glanced at Tracey again. She had been a right pain, getting him up every two seconds to top her bubbles up. He made a mental note to get her smashed as soon as possible on their return flight.

SEVENTEEN

MAJORCA

The atmosphere was exuberant as the widows descended the steps of the plane, all of them on top of the world after their jet-set experience. The Majorcan heat belted down on them as a prepared Amanda transferred her designer Burberry sunglasses from the top of her head to the top of her nose, very much looking the part of the executive traveller.

Belinda was not so prepared, mistakenly wearing a jumper and jeans and having to shield her eyes from the sun, not even owning a pair of sunglasses yet. She never had been a sunbathing type.

"Do we get to fly home in this too?" asked a childlike Carrie, clearly beyond excited at the thought of being a Kardashian on the way home too.

"Of course," laughed Janet, pleased to see her looking happy for the first time in months.

Carrie squealed at the thought of it and gave Janet a huge hug. The older woman simply adored the young girl's naïvety and innocence. She felt all warm inside, feeling very maternal towards her. She dearly wished that she had been lucky enough to have a daughter, but lately she had thoroughly enjoyed looking after her group of girls. They were starting to feel like family, and she hoped that these trips would now become a regular thing. She wanted to do more travelling, but she certainly did not want to travel alone.

Carrie found that she loved being with this group of women. Her friends thought it was odd for her to hang around with these older women when she could be out partying with them, but she had never been a party girl, preferring to stay at home or go out to the cinema or for quiet meals. She just wanted to settle down and start a family. Maybe it was because her parents had never been the nurturing types, always having been busy in their careers, and of the belief that kids had to fit in with you and not the other way around. She was an only child and had been a latchkey one at that for most her life, but she was determined that when she had her babies, she would do things differently. She would just be a proper mum, like Belinda, she decided, except she couldn't bake! That was why she had gone for Roger. She had initially felt safer with him being an older man, a father figure, until he had got her where he wanted her, then made her feel even more insecure than the lads her own age had done. She accepted now that the others were right about him all along. It was the widows, rather than Roger, who made her feel safe now.

Tracey embraced the baking sun on her skin and raised her face up towards the giant yellow sphere in the sky, keen to grab just a few moments of that burning feeling before they got into the awaiting transfer vehicle, again another VIP minibus courtesy of Janet. She had yearned to live in Spain for so many years, so she had secret plans to check out the property prices while they were there, as well as the bars of course.

Without Andy here to stop her, she realised that it was finally possible to follow her dream. She decided that she might stay on longer and not come back with the others at all. Maybe she could rent a villa for a month, to get a feel for the island and take a proper look around. There was nothing to rush back home for. No kids, no pets and no husband. She decided to do whatever the hell she damn well pleased from now on.

As they all clambered into their air-conditioned ride to the hotel, Belinda gasped in relief, glad to be out of the sun. She fanned herself with her jumbo crossword puzzle book, her cheeks as red as Tracey's bloodshot eyes were after her blatant abuse of the complimentary bar on board. *I will have no choice but to strip off this holiday if it is going to be this bloomin' hot all week*, she thought, absolutely dreading getting her flabby white flesh out and praying that she would look acceptable on the beach. She must remember to grab the lounger next to Janet, or preferably on the end, away from everyone, but certainly not next to Carrie.

"Pool as soon as we arrive?" offered Amanda to the others. "We may as well catch the afternoon sun whilst we can."

"And lunch too, I'm famished," interjected Tracey, but they all knew the Majorcan rosé wine was what she really wanted, after going on about it for half the flight.

"I've already reserved us a table for a late lunch in the patio restaurant," informed Amanda.

"Oh, you are a star," replied a thankful Belinda, her belly rumbling as they spoke.

Louise couldn't wait to get to the hotel, dump her case in the room, strip off and get into the swimming pool. She had purchased several new bikinis, all with matching kaftans, especially for this trip. This was going to be her very best chance to pull, but with the glamorous Carrie now in their group, she had had to up her game and pull out all the stops.

Surely to God she would manage to meet a man now, she hoped, especially seeing as they were staying in a hotel used primarily by men on golfing trips, and now knowing exactly what they were like. It would be sheer bad luck if she returned home still with the body count of one. That was what the youngsters called it nowadays. They didn't ask how many people you had slept with, they asked each other, "What's your body count?" Well, she intended to increase her count to as many as possible. Some women lied about theirs and would have been proud to be on one, but she wanted to get into double figures – the more the merrier. She wanted to try out all types of men, in all shapes and sizes. All ages and all nationalities. She wanted to experiment. She had even endured her first waxing experience. Samantha had roared with laughter to discover that she still had a 1970s bush, having never been to a salon for anything other than getting her nails done, and that had been only on very special occasions such as going to a wedding. She had obeyed her friend's advice, though, and had it done a few days prior to the holiday so that the redness had now subsided. The excruciating ordeal now meant that she was the proud owner of a landing strip, and if she said so herself, it looked rather sexy, if vaginas ever could be described as such. Samantha had suggested she go the whole hog and get a Brazilian, but Louise was worried she'd look like a plucked chicken, so instead she had opted for the landing strip. Maybe she would go further next time, although after the pain of it, she thought she might just shave it off herself in future.

She had been watching *Naked Attraction* on TV a lot lately, mainly to check out the variety of men and their penises, but she'd been surprised to see that the women came in all shapes and sizes too and were not always pleasant to observe. She watched with interest at the same sex couples. She thought it might be interesting to try sex with a woman, but although she could appreciate a pretty face, and possibly take pleasure in a nice pair of boobs, she knew that she could never ever eat in the downstairs garden. The thought of her mouth going anywhere near one of those ugly vaginas made her want to retch, so she deduced that she must not have an ounce of bisexuality in her bones whatsoever. She definitely planned to stick to experimenting with men.

Louise was brought out of her thoughts as they pulled up at the hotel. It wasn't the fanciest place they could have stayed in, but it was booked as a golfing holiday, and the women didn't care, just happy to be away doing something fun for once.

Janet had sorted the flights, but Amanda was in control of the hotel arrangements seeing as it was initially booked by Christopher and therefore the information had arrived at her home. They trooped into the foyer and all flopped onto the large, comfy sofas whilst Amanda checked them all in at reception.

A water machine was stood in the corner dispensing a choice of either room temperature or chilled H2O into paper cones. Louise filled them with the cooler option, handing them out to her flustered friends, supplying Janet and Belinda first seeing as they were the oldest and the ones who looked like they needed cooling down. By the time she had handed one to each of the women, she started again, refilling them, as the cones were so tiny that one or two gulps completely emptied them. After all of the others had been satisfactorily replenished, she stood at the machine and knocked back three in a row herself.

Louise then saw Amanda approaching, so she got a drink ready for her after witnessing her frustrated attempts to discuss their booking with a grumpy concierge who appeared to speak little English. Amanda thankfully grabbed the paper receptible and then handed it back to her friend with an unimpressed look at the quantity that she received. Louise laughed and returned it to the machine to refill it for her. Amanda quickly gulped the second drink, then announced the arrangements to everyone. "So, I have put you in the following rooms together: Janet and Belinda; Carrie and Louise; and Tracey, you're with me. Is that OK for everyone?"

The older two women were extremely relieved to be together, as were the younger two. Tracey couldn't care less who she went with, so that only left Amanda, who was fully aware that she had given herself the short straw, but she did so feeling that it was the right thing to do. *What the hell have I let myself in for?* she fretted. Amanda distributed the room keys, and they all agreed to meet down by the pool in half an hour to get in a couple of hours' sunbathing before their late-lunch reservation.

Up in Belinda's and Janet's room, Belinda watched through the open ensuite door as Janet lined up tubs of various potions and creams onto their bathroom shelf. Crikey, she only possessed one tub of Astral cream. Maybe she would have to start making more of an effort now that she was single again. As she began to unpack her suitcase, she held up a large, plain, black swimsuit, shouting out to Janet for advice. "Have you brought a bikini? I only brought swimsuits. I wasn't sure if we should wear bikinis at our age."

"There are no rules, dear. Only the rules that your body sets."

Belinda looked down at her swollen tummy and looked downhearted. "Well, my stomach definitely says swimsuit only." She wobbled her belly fat to gauge how disgusting she would look. "Oh, why do I love baking so much?" she said disparagingly of herself.

Janet told her off. "Belinda, we are here to have fun, so please stop worrying." Janet walked back into the bedroom and picked up a glamorous kaftan and chic straw hat. Holding the garment up in front of her, she told her friend, "Just throw on a kaftan and a hat." She then popped the hat onto her head in jest. "And own it, darling." Janet effortlessly looked every inch the rich widow that she now was.

"Joan Collins, eat your heart out," laughed Belinda approvingly, admiring how Janet always managed to look so classy without even trying. She must take some tips from her friend because she was rubbish at putting outfits together.

When Janet disappeared into the bathroom, Belinda quickly and discreetly grabbed the kaftan and sun hat that Janet had left lying on her bed. She held the kaftan up against herself and she put the hat on. Standing in front of the full-length mirrored wardrobe doors, she looked at herself and sighed in despair. In her mind, she still looked frumpy and mumsy. She wondered how come, even in the same garments, Janet managed to look so upmarket, whilst she looked more market stall. *It must be my chubby body and fat face*, she deduced sadly.

Meanwhile, in the room next door, Louise flicked the switch on a tiny plastic kettle and ripped open a yellow sachet of Lipton's tea. "Cup of tea, coffee?" she offered Carrie, who was busy unpacking a selection of little summery dresses to hang up before they creased.

"No thanks, it's far too hot. I think I'll wait for a cold drink by the pool." Carrie began to hang her clothes up in the left of the wardrobe, having counted exactly how many coat hangers they had been given and shared them equally, pushing Louise's fifty per cent over to the right.

"I hope they all want to do some partying this week," stated Louise. "Cus I need some action, if you know what I mean," she said cheekily, with a wink.

"Well, I am happy to. Party that is, not the other. If the others won't mind." She lifted up a gorgeous red bandage dress to hang up.

"Wow! It would be criminal to bring a dress like that and not show it off," proclaimed Louise, primarily trying to convince her room-mate to come out and play but also genuinely meaning it.

Carrie held it against herself and twirled happily. "Do you think so?" Then she remembered something and looked sad. "Roger bought me this."

Louise took another look at the dress again, this time with new eyes. It was tight, very tight. Red. Verging on slutty. Yep, just what Roger would have chosen. Suddenly, she had gone off it. "Oh, don't mention that to Belinda then," Louise warned, knowing that it would make her older friend feel like shit. "She's insecure enough about her weight as it is."

Carrie looked concerned, then hung up the dress. It definitely wouldn't be leaving the wardrobe that trip. She would never do anything ever again to upset the wonderful, beautiful woman that she now saw as her friend.

Across the corridor and a little further away from the others was Amanda and Tracey's room. *Maybe for the best*, thought Amanda, anticipating that Tracey might come home singing at the top of her voice or whatever other rowdy behaviour she might get up to this week.

Amanda dumped her case onto her bed, deciding that she would leave her unpacking until later that evening. All she needed to do was pull out her bikini, sarong and flip-flops, then she would be ready. She flung off her clothes in a hot fluster but noticed that her armpits were a tad whiffy from travelling. "Would you mind if I quickly jump in the shower?" she asked Tracey, who had somehow managed to get changed in two seconds flat.

"Be my guest," replied Tracey cheerfully, knowing that as soon as the bathroom door closed, she would sneak out and check out the pool bar while she waited for the others to faff about.

Forty minutes later, Belinda and Janet apprehensively arrived down at the pool, unsure where to go, but to their relief, Amanda was there waiting for them, having already organised six sunbeds, along with six large yellow-and-white stripey towels for their arrival. They excitedly set themselves down, got comfortable, then began to relax and enjoy the novelty of the balmy Spanish sun.

Amanda was already stretched out on her bed, having sprayed and lavishly smothered her whole body with factor thirty oil that now filled the air with the aroma of coconuts. It was her absolute favourite smell, one that instantly reminded her of holidays. As she offered some oil to Belinda and Janet, she snitched to them that Tracey had already sneaked off before she got out of the shower. "She'll be in the bar no doubt," Amanda accused, dreading the few days ahead if Tracey was going to go wild.

"There she is," exclaimed Belinda pointing, and there she was, sat at the pool bar, chatting to a stocky, bald golfer who had rushed over to buy her a drink.

"I bet that was what Roger was like," began Belinda, but she was quickly interrupted by Amanda.

"Shush, here comes Carrie, you'll set her off again if you talk about Roger."

As the women looked up and glanced across the pool, Carrie came strutting into view. Louise was with her.

"Oh my God, just look at her. She's like a goddess. A supermodel," exclaimed a despondent Belinda. "I'll look like a hippo next to little Miss Perfect." Belinda looked traumatised.

Louise also looked good, but all eyes around the pool were firmly on Carrie. There were several individual groups of men sat around the pool in their packs, each of between four and eight in quantity. There were the Lexus car salesmen from Leicestershire, the financial advisors from Folkstone and the bathroom fitters from Birmingham, but the loudest and most flashy of them all were the stock dealers from Essex. They had all played golf that morning but were now ridding themselves of their golfers tans, the T-shirt lines across their upper arms from being out on the course dressed in the obligatory polo shirts under the sweltering Spanish sun.

Sat upright on their loungers, knocking back chilled bottles of Estrella beer, the men had been bantering amongst themselves about their earlier game, but they soon stopped talking about the golf, and suddenly, their eyes were now firmly fixed upon a new prize. Carrie.

Tracey, too, had spotted Carrie and Louise, so she yelled out loud to call them over to join her at the bar, where she promptly introduced them to her new friend, Barry from Basildon. The two girls were unimpressed, but they chatted to him for a moment out of politeness, yet in less than a minute, they were suddenly joined by the golfer's three pals, all keen for an introduction to Tracey's two hotter friends.

The trio on the sunloungers observed the scene and carried on discussing Carrie. "No wonder Roger was happy with his upgrade," Belinda continued, feeling more insecure than ever.

Amanda scolded her. "Listen to me. She is certainly *no* upgrade. I admit, I do like her now, but you are the loveliest, most decent and classy lady I know, Belinda Morris, so stop that nonsense right now."

"Here, here," echoed Janet.

Belinda was unconvinced but she smiled in appreciation, then adjusted her kaftan to hide her fat as Louise and Carrie escaped from the vultures and began to walk over towards them. The two new arrivals dragged their loungers around to form a circle, keen to be nearer and more intimate with their friends.

"What's the plan for this week then?" Louise asked Amanda, who was clearly the designated organiser.

"Well, today we relax and settle in, but tomorrow we all have massages. I couldn't get a refund for the golf, but I've managed to swap the golf vouchers for spa credits."

"Oh, clever girl," exclaimed Janet. "I do love a good massage."

"Well, get ready for quite a few then. I didn't realise golf was so expensive," Amanda added.

"Humph, I did. We had many arguments about it," interjected Belinda.

"It's not a foot massage, is it?" queried Carrie, not particularly liking her feet being touched.

"Not ticklish, are you, Carrie?" laughed Amanda, grabbing the girl and tickling her in the ribs in jest. She certainly was ticklish and let out an ear-piercing squeal, but at the same time, she accidentally let go of a loud squeaky fart. Louise and Amanda roared with laughter as Belinda and Janet stifled their giggles. Carrie apologised, "Oh, excuse me. How embarrassing. I am mortified."

Amanda leant over to Belinda and whispered, "See, not so perfect after all." Belinda smiled and suddenly cheered up.

"Get used to it, dear, because by the time you are my age, you will be doing it all the time," Janet admitted kindly to ease Carrie's discomfort.

Belinda nodded in agreement. "Unfortunately, that is true," she laughed. "These days when I walk down the aisle in Sainsbury's, sometimes I sound like Donald Duck." From her lounger, she mimicked a waddle. "Quack, quaaaack."

The widows all roared with laughter. At that moment, a nonplussed Tracey appeared. "Did I miss something?"

"We'll tell you over lunch," said a still chuckling Janet.

EIGHTEEN

LADIES WHO LUNCH

A patio dining table, laid out for six guests, was protected from the scorching Mediterranean sun by a stunning pergola, its roof smothered with trailing pink bougainvillea flowers that shaded the diners below. The women gasped in awe at the exquisite setting. The tablecloth was crisp white, the napkins precisely folded, and the two ice buckets that stood beside were topped up with large uniform square cubes awaiting their choice of Spanish vino.

Five of the six women took their seats and began to peruse the menus, all of it delicious, making their decisions even more difficult. "I think I will have the calamari again," announced Janet, pleased that she was introduced to this delicacy on Amanda's birthday night out.

Miguel, their waiter, arrived to take their wine order, then went off to fetch the bottle of Spanish rosé ordered by Tracey, and a jug of sangria preferred by the others. They informed him that they would wait until the sixth guest joined them before ordering food. Carrie had nipped off to the ladies, and as she casually made her way back from the bathroom to the restaurant, the ladies watched as she had to pass through the pool area to get back to their table. Janet shook her head disapprovingly as they observed a group of golfers wolf-whistling her and making filthy, crude gestures behind her back. "Just look at them. And all old enough to be her father," she said, annoyed at what she saw.

"I bet that's exactly what our men were like on their golf trips," sneered Louise.

"Well, Roger would have been for sure," scoffed Tracey.

Belinda, very aggressively, shook out her napkin and placed it across her lap. "Bloody tossers! I think I have been very naïve in my previous life."

With Carrie now safely back in their fold, and the men forgotten, they began to relax and enjoy the moment. Between them, they placed orders of garlic and chilli prawns, more calamari and a family-sized paella to share. As they awaited their food, they sipped their wine and casually chatted in the warmth of the Majorcan sun. A gentle breeze blew which kept them comfortable, and the stresses of the past few months began to melt away.

"Tell me, why didn't we do this before?" asked Belinda, thoroughly enjoying the girls-only break that she had previously dreaded.

"Because we were all at home, holding the fort," replied a miffed Louise, "while the men had all the fun." She dwelled briefly on how much harder than Chris she'd worked for their business.

"Well, not anymore…" Janet put down her fork to explain. "I've decided to do the one thing that I was forbidden to do. I'm going to take up golf so that I can join the senior team." She sat back, looking satisfied that she had finally been brave enough to confirm her decision, one that she had wrestled with due to a lack of confidence.

"You might even win some competitions!" joked Carrie. The others all burst out laughing at the irony of it.

"I feel like rebelling," Janet continued, the sunshine and the sangria certainly agreeing with her, much to the delight of the others.

"Bravo, Janet. Good for you," exclaimed Belinda. "Who else has any new resolutions?"

"*Me!*" bragged Louise, raising her hand as though she were still at school. "I've decided that I have been sex-starved for too long… and it's about to change… starting this week."

"*What? How?*" spluttered an intrigued Tracey, even putting down her wine glass to hear the juicy details.

"I am going to get laid," explained Louise, shrugging. "Tonight or tomorrow, but definitely before we leave." Then, she calmly picked up her glass and took a sip in celebration.

The others stared, open-mouthed.

"Chris only got it up once in a blue moon. If that had been the other way around, he would have certainly cheated on me, but I never did. I stayed faithful, like a loyal lap dog. So, I've got twenty years of catching up to do." She winked.

Amanda queried, "Could he really not get it up? Christopher said he was always bragging that you pair were always at it."

"Errrr *no!* Definitely not," confirmed Louise. "The couple of times each year that he took Viagra and we actually had sex, he would look at me as though he was some big stud. He'd pull back the sheets to show me the very average erection that his little blue pill had managed to give him, then he would always say," she used her napkin and a knife to demonstrate and mimicked his very posh voice, "could you cope, Mummy?"

Carrie spat out her drink, almost choking; her and Amanda both expressed their revulsion out loud in unison, "Urgghhhhh."

"Exactly," explained Louise. "Then, for the rest of the day, he would strut around like a ram that had impregnated a hundred ewes, very pleased with himself."

"Crikey, I thought mine was bad." Amanda grinned.

"I wasn't truly happy." Louise was on a roll. "But I just didn't dislike him enough to leave." She took a big gulp of wine. "So, after putting up with that, I think I *deserve* a treat." She raised her glass, hoping for support.

Tracey was the first to respond. "You sure do; I'll drink to that."

Then, far too loudly, Louise added, "Cus if I don't get an *orgasm* soon, I'll explode."

At this point, the waiter refilling their water glasses spilt it all over the table in his flabbergasted state. An embarrassed Janet took the bottle from him and reassured him that they could manage, keen to send him away and mortified by such rude talk in public. "We can pour that, thank you, Miguel." She smiled as though nothing had happened. She then looked around to check no one had heard and then comically fanned herself.

An amused Amanda, who loved it that her friends were finally more open with each other, said, "Well, I don't blame you, Louise, but I won't be joining you. I told you, I'm now officially dead from the waist down. My vagina has been in hibernation for years. I don't think anything could make it come back to life now."

Belinda nodded in empathy. "Join the club," she said knowingly.

Amanda elaborated, "I think it was a combination of the menopause and Christopher's lack of attention and romance in the bedroom, if you know what I mean."

Tracey was keen for more gossip. "Noooo, we don't, explain please, missus."

Amanda looked from side to side to check she couldn't be overheard by the neighbouring tables. "Christopher always had the same old routine. I think most men do, to be honest. When he was randy, his leg would stroke my leg. That was his foreplay! I think he thought my G spot must have been above my knee. In fact, he must have never heard of it, but anyway, after a few moments of this strange ritual, he would climb on top for a quick hokey cokey, and that was it."

Carrie looked horrified. "Why didn't you just tell him what to do?"

"Because you can't teach an old dog new tricks," Amanda clarified. "Anyway, when I merely asked for a back massage, he would say, 'Oh, I'm no good at that, get one from the spa tomorrow.'" She took a big slug of wine before continuing. "So, I wouldn't have bothered wasting my time asking him for cunnilingus. He wouldn't have a clue." She opened her hands out in frustration. "So, I had zero foreplay and no affection, and he wondered why I was never interested. I bet he told the boys that I was boring or that I hardly gave him any sex, but what he didn't get was that I wasn't interested because I got absolutely *nothing* out of it."

The waiter turned up with their lunch, so to save Janet's embarrassment, Amanda stopped talking about sex and sat back. After giving each woman their starter of garlic prawns and calamari, he returned to place the big dish of paella in the centre of the table. With all seriousness, and certainly not at all quietly, Janet enquired, "Amanda, what is *cunnilingus*?"

Poor Miguel dropped the plate in shock, half the paella spilling onto the pristine tablecloth, splodging orange-coloured saffron stains all over their table. The ladies erupted into raucous laughter as Janet looked on perplexed.

Belinda excused herself to go to the toilet, fearing she had half wet her pants. She had never laughed so much in her life. Belly laughs with good friends certainly were a tonic that she was long overdue. "Want to come with me, Janet?" she offered kindly, deciding that her friend's question deserved a private answer and a rather delicate one too. The two women left for the bathroom whilst an apologetic Miguel took away the old paella and cleared up the mess. The others reassured him that they didn't mind, aware that it was not his fault. He placed a new, smaller cloth down to cover up the stain, and he informed them that a fresh dish would be along very soon.

The others carried on their conversation. "That was so funny," sniggered Carrie. "I hope she isn't disgusted when Belinda explains to her what it is."

Tracey was having to wipe her eyes with her napkin after laughing so much. "I am surprised that Belinda even knows herself."

Louise added, "Well, I didn't either until Samantha and her pals told me." They all laughed again.

"Janet might have to go and lie down with some smelling salts," added a tickled Tracey.

Amanda wanted to laugh too, but only about the situation, she did not want to laugh at Janet. "Let's not tease her," she pleaded. "She came from a different era remember."

Carrie agreed, so she changed the subject. "Your stories are so sad, girls. Maybe it will be different for you all when you meet someone else one day."

"I doubt it. I think my days in that department are well and truly over." Amanda sighed. "Plus, I have no urge whatsoever."

"I'll let you know at the end of the week!" laughed Louise mischievously.

Belinda and Janet rejoined the table, and as they did, a new plate of the famous Spanish dish was brought over to them, this time by a young, female waitress. "Oh dear, I think we must have traumatised Miguel," said Belinda, still chuckling to herself about the situation.

"You've definitely all traumatised me," laughed Janet, thankfully not in the stuffy, disapproving mood that they had all feared.

They calmed down to eat the delicious meal. It had been a long day and they were all finally de-stressing. Their relaxing late lunch had now gone on past 5pm, and they were so relaxed and comfortable, they decided to stay where they were, have a few more drinks, then later they could order dessert and coffee. That way, they would all get a good night's sleep after their very early start and day of travelling.

Belinda had started telling everyone all about Spanish desserts, so a bored Tracey decided to get the conversation back onto a more amusing topic. She would rather talk about blowjobs than *buñuelos* any day. "I can't say anything bad about Andy in the bedroom," she stated.

"What's that got to with *Tarta de Santiago*?" Belinda questioned in jest, realising that her research into popular Spanish dishes was clearly not being appreciated.

Tracey totally ignored her and continued, the drink now taking effect, seeing as she had consumed the whole bottle of rosé to herself, as well most of the large jug of sangria that the others had ordered to share. "The only thing wrong with Andy was that he nagged me too much."

The others didn't say a word, knowing he had very good cause to do so.

"I think he secretly hated me," she continued, "because he never tried it on with me first. I always had to make the first move. In fact, to get *sex*, I used to have to almost *rape* him."

The waitress who was busy placing down dessert menus heard but looked confused, doubting her understanding of the English language and believing her translating skills must not be as good as she thought.

Janet spluttered in shock, "Oh, please have some decorum, Tracey."

"Well, that's what he told me I did," she excused herself. "But I can't believe that. Can you?"

The others looked awkward, knowing full well what she was capable of, suddenly looking at the dessert menus to avoid answering her.

"Ooh look, Belinda, they have it. Your *Tarta de Santiago!*" shrieked Amanda, not knowing why she was so excited, but it did the trick, and the conversation was back onto puddings. They all ordered a different one, agreeing to share and try them all, more to satisfy Belinda's curiosity rather than their stomachs which were so full by now.

"We may as well have dessert," she had said to convince them, "or you'll be hungry later if we go up for an early night."

At the end of their first day, they now sat and enjoyed the early evening lull. The loud, boisterous men from around the pool had all gone up to their rooms to get showered and dressed up for their boozy night out. Tracey wished she was going with them. She couldn't believe her friends all wanted to have an early night. *We are only here for four nights, so why can't they just rest when they get home?* she thought.

"I've had a really lovely day," Belinda said, and she meant it.

"I totally agree," enthused Janet. "We should make this a regular thing." She was super keen to start travelling and enjoying herself.

"I hope we didn't upset you earlier, Janet, with all the rude talk. I know you don't like it," said Louise, feeling a tad guilty.

"Not at all," responded Janet. "It's not that I don't like it, I am just not used to it, that's all."

Amanda was keen for her to open up more to them. She saw a lady who had led a very sheltered life, with a highly controlling man, and she knew that she could be far happier if she started living a little and shedding some of her inhibitions. "I know you think it's vulgar to talk about rude stuff, but can I ask, did you and the major have a good sex life?"

Janet surprised them by responding without embarrassment, "In my day, nice girls simply did not enjoy sex. It was more a case of 'pull my nightie down when you have finished.'"

"What, you wore a nightie when you were doing it?" asked Tracey bluntly.

"Yes, of course," replied Janet. "What was I meant to wear in bed?" The possibility of being naked in bed with her husband was clearly going over her head.

Tracey stifled a giggle. "I had imagined Major Charles to be a randy old goat."

"No, not at all. Charles said he preferred to take his exercise on the golf course," said Janet, now wondering exactly why that was.

A tipsy Tracey demanded of Carrie, "Well, what about *randy* Roger, then?"

Carrie replied, feeling awkward with Belinda sat next to her, "Err, OK, I suppose."

In response, Belinda kindly and genuinely leant over and touched her arm in a protective manner and she suggested, "How about me and you don't join this conversation?", which Carrie appreciated, smiling in relief and in solidarity with her good friend Belinda.

NINETEEN

EARLY NIGHT

It was 8.45pm on the island of Majorca. The echo of six pairs of flip-flops could be heard flip-flop-flapping in harmony on the tiled floor as the group of friends came traipsing back from the pool area and into the hotel foyer.

They looked sun-kissed but with the slightly red tint that you get on the first day of your holiday, before your skin has managed to turn into a better shade of tan. They were weary but elated, and more importantly, they were relaxed and happy.

Other guests exited the lifts, coming down all dressed up for their night out, just as the widows were going up to finish unpacking and get an early night. Whiffs of expensive aftershave floated around, causing Tracey to wish they were going out too. The others were all exhausted, but she never was. Her energy was boundless.

Amanda suggested that they all meet downstairs for

breakfast in the morning and enquired if 9am was an acceptable time for everyone.

"Jesus Christ. That early?" queried Tracey.

"We're having an early night so you should manage it," Belinda said, feeling sorry for Amanda having to share a room with her. Having got up at the crack of dawn, and having enjoyed an eventful day of jets, jesting and jugs of sangria, they were all keen to unpack properly and get a good night's sleep. They would go out the following night when they were fully rested.

As they lazily strolled towards the lift, Tracey eyed the bar. She went to suggest that they had just one nightcap but anticipated the others wouldn't want to, and might judge her, so she reluctantly followed them all, the six ladies cramming themselves into the same lift to save waiting for another. The lift door closed.

In their bedroom, Amanda flicked on the kettle to make a cup of tea as she unpacked her case. Tracey flopped on top of the bed and picked up her phone. She checked her Facebook, aimlessly scrolling through posts of people that she didn't really know, liking the odd photo, especially if it was people on crazy nights out enjoying themselves or funny memes with jokes about consuming vast quantities of wine or gin.

"Aren't you going to unpack? Amanda asked her. "Your clothes will be all creased if you don't."

"Yeah, in a min," replied Tracey, sounding more like a petulant teenager than a fifty-two-year-old grown woman.

Amanda had finished tidying her clothes and took her toiletry bag into the bathroom, where she neatly organised various bottles of expensive shampoo, conditioner and aftersun lotion; then she popped her toothbrush and toothpaste into a glass meant for drinking. She shouted out to let Tracey know that she was welcome to share any of her products, explaining that she wasn't going to bother carrying home half-empty bottles.

Having showered to wash off the sweaty suntan lotion, Amanda emerged from their bathroom, her body wrapped in a towel and her head wrapped in a turban. She plonked herself on her bed and sat up against her pillows. As she sipped her tea, she informed Tracey that the bathroom was all hers before asking, "Why does flying always dry out your skin?" It was not really a question, and she was just making conversation. She tried again. "Want a face pack? I've brought a few."

"Nah, too messy," Tracey replied, then she questioned, "Are you really going to go to sleep this early?"

"I'm shattered, aren't you?" Amanda questioned but got no reply, her friend deeply engrossed in her phone again.

After Amanda had patted a ghost-like sheet gel-mask onto her face, she placed two cotton pads soaked in water over her eyes, then she relaxed back, daydreaming about what an eventful day they had all had. She continued to try to converse with Tracey. "We've got a couple of massages booked. Which ones do you prefer?"

Tracey didn't reply. Amanda turned her head to the right, lifting up her right eye pad, about to scold her room-mate for being so rude. There was no one there. *She must be in the bathroom*, thought Amanda, replacing the pad to wait the required twenty minutes for the saturated sheet to do its magic.

Meanwhile, a fifty-two-year-old teenager scarpered frantically down the hotel hallway. Upon reaching the lift door, Tracey's forefinger, fast and furiously, continued to press the lift button, expecting her hotel room door to open any second and an irate Amanda to lean out and demand that she returned immediately, like a naughty child.

Louise and Carrie giggled in their room about the events of the day. They had become good friends. They drank hot chocolate and dunk the complimentary biscuits into their mugs like they were kids on a school trip. Carrie confided in Louise about her dire dating history, and in return, Louise confessed her lack of such and her plans to ensure that she made up for lost time. She persuaded Carrie to come clubbing with her, even if the others wouldn't. She was desperate to sample all that the resort of Puerto Portals has to offer and to make the most of being in a place where she could finally do as she wished.

After her discoveries about Roger, and the realisation that he was not who she thought he was, Carrie knew that she ought to join in with Louise and have some fun herself, but she couldn't. She knew it would take her a long time to get over him. She was a one-man woman. She had only slept with a few men and never in her life had she had a one-night stand, nor did she plan to start doing so anytime soon. She knew that she was pretty, and could easily attract a string of admirers, but she despaired at why it was so difficult to find just one decent chap to settle down with.

Belinda and Janet had unpacked, drank tea and found out things about each other that they had never realised in all the years that they frequented the golf club. They already knew that they were both Virgos after their birthdays had been celebrated at the club just one week apart, but they were surprised at the many other similarities. They were heartened to discover they had both owned Persian cats when they were children, had both spent their summer holidays in Rock in Cornwall and had both owned a Mini as their first car. Coincidentally, they were also massive fans of Tom Jones, Marmite and Agatha Christie novels. In that order.

Janet was the happiest that she had been in a long time. Using her used *outward* plane boarding card as a bookmark, she closed her detective novel and leant over to switch off the reading lamp on her side of the room, as Belinda lay in the adjacent single bed, in the dark, wearing a white satin sleep eye mask. "Goodnight, Belinda," she whispered contentedly. No reply came back, just a rumbling snoring sound.

It was after midnight in the lounge bar at the Sol Marques hotel. The barman wanted to close up and go home to his family, but there was one guest remaining. A very drunken woman sat, or draped rather, over the polished wooden bar. Perched on a high stool, she still wore her kaftan and flip-flops that she had been in all day. She was two-thirds of her way through her second bottle of cava that she had been knocking back all by herself. The barman was concerned that she looked very unsteady, worried that she might fall off the stool onto the rock-hard floor. "Are you OK, señora?" he enquired.

"*Sí... sí*," she replied, sticking up her thumb to confirm that she was.

"Sorry, but we close very soon," he told her, hoping that she would not attempt to order more alcohol and wanting her to hurry the hell up.

She sighed out loud frustratedly. "Mi amigos," she slurred, pointing upstairs, "boring bastards."

TWENTY

TENA LADIES

The following day, five of the women had made it down for breakfast. Over their fruit and yoghurts, Amanda, Carrie, Louise and Janet discussed their plans for the day. Belinda was still in the hot counter queue for a full English breakfast, having to jostle amongst the golfers, clearly the breakfast of choice for them all. She finally gave in and switched to the 'egg bar' where there was only one very tall German lady waiting. She was clearly dressed for golf too and had a very athletic physique. Belinda admired the woman's lean, strong body, acknowledging she really ought to do some form of exercise herself. Janet had invited her to learn to play golf with her, but she couldn't think of anything worse.

Having been served, she walked off with her mushroom, onion and extra cheese omelette to join the others, considerately checking with everyone, "Do you think we should take something down to the pool for Tracey? If she doesn't get here by ten, she'll miss breakfast altogether."

"It might teach her a lesson to get up on time," replied Janet, not unkindly but fearing that the girl clearly needed to sort herself out.

Belinda concurred, "I hope that she doesn't turn to the bottle too much now that Andy isn't here to look out for her. I think he was the good guy out of all the men."

"We all know who the worst one was." Carrie gobsmacked them with her statement.

Belinda nodded in agreement, relieved that Carrie had finally woken up and smelt the coffee.

"I feel awful snitching on her and talking about her behind her back, but she went out last night." Amanda enlightened them all about the non-appearance of Tracey.

"Where?" gasped Louise.

"No idea. I didn't ask," Amanda replied. "I had a face pack and eye pads on so I couldn't see, and she must have sneaked out. I thought she was in the bathroom, but when I went to clean my teeth, I realised she had gone out."

"What time did she get in?" asked Carrie.

"I think about one. She woke me up bashing into everything when she came in, but I was so tired I fell straight back to sleep."

At 9.55am, as they were leaving the restaurant, a red-faced Tracey came rushing in.

"Quickly. You'll miss it," Belinda told her helpfully.

"It's OK, I just need a juice. You lot carry on to the pool. I'll catch you up," Tracey gasped breathlessly before dashing over to the juice machine where she proceeded to glug back three glasses of apple juice in a row. With the others gone, she helped herself to a cappuccino and a couple of pastries, which she took to a table and ate alone. She thoroughly enjoyed people watching, so she scanned the room to entertain herself while she attempted to calm her throbbing head with a couple of ibuprofen.

The groups of male golfers devoured their fry-ups, loudly and jovially cracking jokes about the day ahead, ribbing each other about their performances the previous day. They really did live and breathe for golf, she deduced. Obsessed more like.

She looked at the men's content, smiling faces. *Was Andy this happy when he was away?* she wondered, *because he was never any fun at home, and he hadn't been for years.* He had been particularly grumpy and miserable in the few months prior to his death, but she hadn't taken much notice, nor bothered to enquire why. She felt a strange emotion come over her. She missed him.

Then, she watched a middle-aged couple on holiday. Clearly married. They sat and didn't speak, both looking bored to death. Maybe it was unrealistic to be happy in a long-term relationship? After all, these men certainly looked happy, and she had experienced more laughs with the girls lately than she had with Andy over the past few years. The group were finally starting to let their hair down and have fun. They might not be that bad, after all.

With the breakfast hall staff preparing to clear away and close the restaurant, she jumped up to grab a boiled egg and an apple before they packed them away, discreetly wrapping them in paper serviettes to take them away with her to the pool. She was still ravenous. She acted like a shoplifter trying not to get caught, then walked out trying to convey her most innocent look.

On her way to the pool, Tracey made a detour to the bathroom, then she felt much better. Why did a wine poo manage to do that? Feeling lighter, in body and head, she then sauntered round the pool to locate the others. Louise spotted her first and waved to grab her attention. Tracey decided that she liked Louise the best. She seemed up for some fun and was her best option for a good drinking partner. Carrie should be, being the youngest, but nah, far too much of a goody two shoes for her liking.

By the time Tracey joined them, the widows had established the perfect spot by the pool, with four loungers in the sun and two positioned under the trendy square umbrella for Janet and Belinda, who preferred to read their paperbacks in the shade. Carrie and Amanda had brought magazines instead. Amanda had brought *Hello*, *Times Travel* and *Woman and Home*. Carrie's contribution was *Grazia* and *Vogue* as well as a multipack containing *Closer* and *Heat*. "I like a bit of trashy gossip to read on holiday," she offered as an excuse and in case she was considered dumb. She had a slight inferiority complex that the others might think she was a bimbo after being Roger's 'bit on the side'. Tracey and Louise had brought nothing to read. They intended to make their own entertainment.

After a morning sunbathing, they had discussed in detail every part of their bodies that they disliked, as women always tended to do. Why did women do that to themselves? Across the pool, the men's moobs and beer bellies were out and proud, with no insecurity whatsoever, all clearly thinking that they were gods.

Despite their various shapes and sizes, not one of them had mentioned anything that they did like about themselves. Carrie had plenty to like about herself, but she was far too modest to admit them, and despite her gorgeousness, she was still as insecure as the next girl. Amanda hated her sticky-out tummy and her big ears. Janet complained about her bony décolletage and her skinny, veiny legs. Louise jiggled her 'fat arse', as she called it, to show them her worst asset, despairing also at her lack of boobs. Tracey moaned about her overall chunkiness, as well as her fat feet, complete with sausage toes, which appeared to have become even more so in the Majorcan heat. Carrie claimed to have sticky-out ribs, but they all scoffed in jest, knowing that the girl was stunning.

Belinda looked dejected, hating, "All of it," she declared. "Fat all over." She told them about herself as a chubby child and how, apart from the few years when she was obsessed with Weight Watchers, she had always been a big girl. The others felt sorry for her, having noticed that she comfort-ate, exacerbating her problem.

Luckily for her, the subject was changed by a surprising admission from Louise. "If it makes you feel better, Belinda, at least you don't wet yourself."

The others all looked shocked, especially seeing as she was only forty years old. They might have not been so surprised if Janet had this problem, being in her sixties, but Louise was still relatively young.

"Do you mean a bit of wee comes out when you laugh? Because we all do that," laughed Belinda, not realising the severity of the girl's condition. "When my Max was young, I used to do it all the time when he made me bounce on his trampoline with him."

Amanda laughed too. "Yes, we all do that."

Carrie looked confused. "I don't."

"That's because you haven't given birth yet; it's a mum thing," Amanda explained but immediately regretted mentioning giving birth to Carrie, with babies being a sensitive subject for her.

"No, you don't understand," Louise continued. "I don't just have a weak pelvic floor, and I haven't had kids either. I have a proper incontinence problem."

They all looked alarmed. "What, like wearing a nappy?" said Tracey rather too bluntly and unsympathetically.

"Not exactly, but I do sometimes have to wear pads if I am somewhere where I can't get to the toilet in two seconds flat."

Janet came to the rescue, placing a sympathetic hand on her leg. "Don't worry; it's very common, dear, especially amongst women my age. Most of the women at the WI have something similar."

"What does the doctor say? Can't they do anything?" asked a caring Carrie.

Louise admitted that she had been too embarrassed to go and get it treated, seeing as her doctor was a member at the golf club. "I just couldn't face him," she admitted.

Janet insisted that Louise would allow her to book her in as soon as they got home, with the private doctor that she and Charles had used for years. "Dr Taylor is a genius. He'll sort you out."

Louise smiled, relieved to have got it off her chest and confided in someone, adding, "I wish someone would 'sort me out,'" she laughed, raising her eyebrows to indicate she meant sexually.

TWENTY-ONE

HAPPY ENDINGS

After a light lunch, the ladies relaxed again around the pool on their sunloungers. They were due to have massages that afternoon, so they hadn't wanted to eat or drink too much beforehand. They had consumed a filling breakfast and they would be going out for dinner that evening, so a pizza slice and a glass of sangria had been opted for, which they ate sat on high stools at the snack bar, keen to escape the midday sun at its hottest hour.

Tracey had drunk four glasses of the fruity sangria, to the others' single glasses, and was now flat out asleep with her mouth wide open, causing Carrie and Louise to giggle, desperate to pop something inside but being far too kind to do so.

Suddenly, a tall, handsome, but hirsute, Spanish man appeared in front of them, his shadow blocking out the sun. He was thinking the same, amused at the state of her.

He looked very suave in his uniform of khaki cargo shorts, teamed with a tight-fit white T-shirt. The spa logo on his chest advertised where he was from, his dark chest hair sprouting generously from the V-neck of his top. He looked about forty-five, but he clearly worked out and looked after himself. An excited Amanda shouted to wake up her dozing friend, "Wakey-wakey, Tracey. Massage time, everyone!"

The masseur smiled and pointed to his name badge. "*Fernando*," he offered, in a croaky but manly voice, to introduce himself to the group. "You are all having back massages. *Sí?*"

"*Yes!* All of us, please," confirmed Amanda, holding up six fingers and pointing to everyone, as though he were stupid and couldn't understand English.

Belinda, slightly shy at the sight of such a virile, handsome man, suddenly felt self-conscious. "Janet, you go first," she panicked, wanting to see how he did it first. She was worried her rolls of fat would wobble around too much. She wasn't the only one to notice that Fernando had many attractive attributes.

Louise watched him intently. He was the best Spanish sight that she had seen so far.

Janet happily volunteered to go first, being a massage connoisseur. She hoped that he would be as good as the Thai women who used to pummel her twice a year in Thailand. She also wondered if she would ever go back there now that she didn't have a husband. She would certainly love to, as long as someone would accompany her. When her half hour was up, she gave the others a thumbs up to indicate that it was satisfactory.

Belinda went next, deciding that the more she worried, the worse it would be. She wanted to get it over and done with. She also didn't want the hunk to have to do her after he had done all the others, in particular, Carrie.

It was Carrie's turn after Belinda. She wriggled and giggled, then squeaked and squirmed, finding it excruciatingly ticklish. She had never felt entirely comfortable getting massages, but she tried to relax and enjoy it, appreciating the effort Amanda had gone to.

Tracey was next, but Fernando had such a magic touch with the rhythmic strokes of his firm, strong hands that he sent her straight back to sleep. She carried on sleeping even when he walked away to his next customer, whilst he chuckled to himself at the funny, snoring lady.

Finally! Louise thought to herself as Fernando crouched down near to her lounger in preparation of doing her next. She had been watching him work, his strong, masterful hands turning her on immensely. She hoped that he hadn't lost his strength by the time he got to her, because she wanted a firm going over. Oblivious to her thoughts, he calmly organised and wiped down his bottles of oil as she continued to admire him, greatly appreciating his forearms.

She had concluded, after inspecting many men recently, that forearms were most definitely underrated. His strong, tanned arms certainly aroused her. She looked at his hairy chest and legs, finding them so manly. He was turning her on so badly that she couldn't wait for him to put his hands onto her body.

Amanda had clocked that Louise was perving over him and caught her friend's eye to give her a knowing smile and share in her secret. Louise took great pleasure in her massage. When his oily hands were sliding downwards, reaching her lower back, she yearned for his hands to go even lower, unaware that she was slightly raising her bum higher towards him. She totally forgot that she thought she had a fat bottom, as all she could think about was her burning desire. As his tanned, powerful hands worked on her, the fantasies in her mind were raunchier than any she had ever had about the men back in her local town. She thought Fernando was the sexiest man she had ever seen. She was absolutely smitten. As she got up, she thanked him profusely and gave him a look to let him know that she *really* did appreciate it. He was clearly a man of the world, and he understood her completely.

Amanda was the last one to be massaged, but he had been working for two and a half hours, so he excused himself so that he could go and take a short break to get a drink of water from the bar before he started on her. As he walked away, Louise couldn't wait to share her thoughts with Amanda. "Oh my God, I think I am going to have to finish myself off after this."

After fifteen minutes, their masseur returned. Amanda requested that she could have a foot massage instead. She had pulled a muscle in her lower leg, not used to wearing flip-flops so much. She told him that she would have her back massage the following day. As she lay back and relaxed, he raised her left leg and began the most relaxing massage that she had ever experienced. She closed her eyes in sheer bliss.

Louise could see how much Amanda was enjoying it and she couldn't believe that it was possible to have zero urges, wondering how her friend could lie there and not get turned on by the scrumptious Fernando. As Amanda's massage was nearing the end, she signalled to Fernando to let him in on Amanda's secret that her friend had zero sex drive. She did this by copying Amanda's previous action of a slit throat gesture, followed by pointing at her private parts. She mimicked doing a sexy massage, urging him to step it up a gear. Fernando understood, chuckled quietly, then nodded and winked at her. He was a master of women, having been a seducer for most of his adult life. With his knowledge of the female form, from both a professional and a personal perspective, he knew women and their bodies, more than they did themselves, having had more than enough practice.

For Amanda's final treat, he gently took her foot, pressing down expertly on each pressure point; then, to even Louise's surprise, he held her foot next to his face and discreetly sucked on her big toe. Amanda's eyes jolted wide open. She experienced a surge of energy fire shoot through her foot and through her entire lower body.

"Relax please, señora, this is ancient Spanish reflexology," he told her.

She looked at Louise in alarm, but Louise just gave her a thumbs up to indicate all was good, so a baffled Amanda closed her eyes again and allowed him to continue.

The others had either been reading or snoozing, oblivious to what was happening, but Louise had alerted them all by poking each one so that they could all witness it. Carrie used her sarong to cover up her mouth to stifle her giggles. Janet blushed and buried her head in her book, hardly daring to look. Belinda was gobsmacked but also intrigued at how seductive he was. Spanish men were very fanciable, she decided, lusting after him herself, much to her surprise. Tracey couldn't be woken, so they left her to it.

After seductively sucking both of her big toes, he wrapped her feet securely in a towel and gently laid them down onto her lounger; then he got up as though nothing had happened and packed away his kit. A flustered and blushing Amanda opened her eyes, spluttering to thank him. Janet generously handed him €30 tip on behalf of the group.

As he walked off, an astounded Amanda turned to Louise. "Crikey, I didn't think Spanish foot massages were like that."

"They aren't," laughed Louise, letting her know that it was not entirely professional, and the others all joined in, falling about laughing until they cried at Amanda's faux pas.

"What was it like?" asked an intrigued Belinda.

"My vagina is *throbbing*!" Amanda cried out. "I'm *alive*!" The others were highly amused. "Now I get why Fergie loved it so much," she squealed. "You have all got to try it." No one spoke. They didn't look so sure.

Louise couldn't take any more. She saw Fernando disappearing across the other side of the pool, so she jumped up. This was one chance she was *not* going to waste. "That's it, I can't wait any longer," she exclaimed, jumping up enthusiastically. She grabbed her wicker beach bag, then started to run after him, much to the disbelief of the others. "Fernando! Oh, *Fernando*. Wait for me."

They watched open-mouthed as she caught up with him, then pointed up towards the hotel. Then, they walked off together.

"She didn't really just do that, did she?" said an astounded Belinda.

"I think she actually did," said a bemused, but still flustered, Amanda.

TWENTY-TWO

NIGHT OUT

It was a balmy early evening in the chic harbour of Puerto Portals. The tranquil Mediterranean Sea glistened beneath the million-pound yachts, the proud owners posing on their decks, sipping gin and tonics as they scrutinised the evening crowd strolling past, who, in return, checked them out, wishing they could win the lottery and get themselves a posh boat too.

The smell of extravagant perfumes and colognes wafted along the promenade, the widows getting hit by alternating aromas. One minute they got a whiff of citrus and musky fragrances, suddenly changing to a mouth-watering tang of garlic, grilled steak and delicious seafood dishes being freshly cooked in the high-end restaurants along the main strip.

The widows walked in pairs, arm in arm, so they could manoeuvre through the early summer crowd and locals. Luckily, the schools hadn't broken up yet, so it remained grown-up and sophisticated, seeing as the families with children and the day-tripper rabble from Magaluf wouldn't be descending on the resort until mid-July.

The wealthy crowd were out in full. The men, having swapped their daytime uniform of Vilebrequin shorts and Hugo Boss polo shirts, all now look the same with Bermuda shorts, Ralph Lauren shirts and suede loafers being their choice of evening attire. Their wives were divided into two categories: the preserved posse and the au naturels. They did all have one thing in common though: they were all skinny.

In Spain and its surrounding islands, the more upmarket the resort, the thinner the women tended to be, compared to the cheaper package-holiday resorts, where the women certainly didn't starve themselves, their evening wardrobe consisting of XL leggings and vest tops, their chunky arms covered in tattoos, their swollen feet strapped into faux-leather studded roman sandals that they bagged for £4.99 in Primark, as they traipsed around the bars knocking back toffee vodka shots. Mind you, they always seemed to have more fun!

In the upmarket resort of Puerto Portals, the new-money wives were the Botox Brigade, with luminous bleached teeth, fillers in their lips and silicon in their tits. The old-money wives had thin lips, flat chests, and if they were having fun, they needed to tell their faces as you would never tell. They kept their look classic, in plain linen trousers, simple tops and would never dream of leaving their private villa without a pashmina draped strategically around their bony shoulders as they looked down on the former, whose attire was anything feminine, sexy and which showed off a bit of cleavage.

Roberto Cavalli-inspired flashy dresses, in bright summer colours, was the uniform of the more stylish Europeans, who strutted and posed like vain peacocks, showing off their deep mahogany tans and designer handbags.

Every now and again, the widows would pass elderly men with leathered crocodile skin from enjoying too many holidays in far-flung places. They dressed ostentatiously in coloured chino trousers or flashy patterned shirts and swaggered along arrogantly with much younger girls from foreign lands hanging off their arms. And you would have thought there was an all-white party going on somewhere with the amount of people dressed completely head-to-toe in blanc.

The widows stopped outside a restaurant that Amanda had been wise enough to pre-book the week before due to its reputation and popularity. 'Wellies' it was called, the name not at all suiting its location, seeing as there were no muddy fields around for miles, but they later discovered that it was in fact named after the owner's dog, whose picture was all over the menus. It was superbly positioned on the main drag, the ideal spot for people watching, and its customers wore sandals, loafers or high heels but never anything made of rubber! Amanda had done her research well, ensuring they had secured tables at all the best places.

The atmosphere was sophisticated but casual, the tables laid out classy but not too stuffy. The diners were a mixture of a young glamorous crowd, laid-back couples, Germans with choppy haircuts and Dutch tourists wearing eccentric clothing with added bling that would ensure they would not get run over in the dark.

The widows were greeted by a waiter called Juan who led them to their fabulously positioned table in the centre of the restaurant but at the front, so they had a superb sea view for when the sun went down.

After seating them, he took no time at all in supplying them with a basket of still-warm bread and bowls of plump, green olives. They were all hungry, the smells of fire-grilled food making them even more so. They ordered a bottle of Barbazul white wine and a bottle of Velorose rosé, whilst deciding what to choose from the tempting menu.

Whilst they waited to order supper, they people-watched and quaffed their wine, relaxed after their lazy day, all of them euphoric from the ambience of their location. Their view was to die for, right on the waterfront. The music chilled. Agapanthus flowers everywhere added to its Majorcan charm.

"What are you all having?" Belinda enquired, not being able to make up her mind and wanting to try all of it.

Tracey was in a particularly playful mood and had something on her mind. "I'll have what she's had!" she said, nodding towards Louise.

Louise just smiled, secretly and smugly, but didn't reply. Since she had disappeared from the pool earlier that day, she had not uttered a word about it. They had all been curious, waiting for her to spill the beans, but she had not mentioned it, so they didn't want to ask, fearing that she might have been rejected by him and might be embarrassed. She was suddenly aware that five sets of eyes were on her, waiting for her to elaborate. "What?" She laughs, more coy than usual.

"We are waiting," Amanda pushed her.

"Oh sorry, give me five minutes; I can't decide" replied Louise.

"Not the food, dingbat! Fernando. Remember him? Spill the beans then." Amanda was not letting this go.

An inpatient Tracey suddenly blurted out loudly, "Oh, for God's sake, Louise. DID YOU FUCK FERNANDO?"

Half the restaurant heard her and turn around. Janet nearly died of embarrassment. "Oh, bloody hell," she exclaimed, holding her menu in front of her face so she could hide behind it.

Louise just sat there and grinned, then she leant in, beckoning the others to do the same if they wanted to hear all the juicy details. Which they most certainly did. Even Janet! "Yes, I did. And before you ask, no, I don't feel guilty, and was it was amazing? Yes, it most definitely was." Then, she sat back, very proud of herself and still buzzing from an afternoon of everything she had been hoping for and more.

Carrie whispered, "But what about the incontinence? I hope you managed to avoid an accident."

Louise grinned again. "Nope, I pissed all over his bed!" She looked extremely pleased with herself, but the others were baffled, not to mention horrified.

Janet covered her ears. She couldn't bear to hear any more.

"Weren't you mortified?" asked Carrie, secretly appalled.

"Nah I just pretended I was a squirter," Louise laughed, proud of herself for her quick thinking.

It was so blatantly shocking that the others had no choice but to laugh out loud. Janet fanned herself with the menu in shock, but really, she was having so much fun.

They managed to calm down and stop laughing as Juan returned to take their order, removing his little notebook from his shirt's breast pocket and snatching the tiny pencil from behind his ear. As he scribbled down Belinda's choice of salt-crust seabass, he turned to Janet, but she was distracted. She innocently called across to Louise, "Louise, what's a *squirter?*"

Raucous laughter echoed around the table as the astonished waiter snapped the lead off his pencil.

"I'll tell you later, Janet," Amanda offered through her giggles.

With them all having calmed down, three of them decided to go for the same as Belinda, with Tracey and Carrie choosing 'Wellies' famous burger'. The food was scrumptious, the wine divine, but it was the company that was the highlight of the night.

Post-supper, they strolled slowly but happily back towards their hotel in their pairs. On the journey back, Carrie and Louise admired the luxurious, sleek boats in the harbour. Belinda and Janet admired the beautiful flower blossoms that hung bountifully over garden walls. Trailing behind them, Tracey asked Amanda to accompany her so she could buy herself a nightcap. Amanda agreed, feeling that it would be far safer for her to drink in their room rather than sneaking out alone again where anything could happen to her. She called ahead to the others to let them know they are just nipping to the shops and would catch them up. The two women diverted down a side street towards the local minimart, but when they arrived, they discovered that they'd literally just missed its closing time, meaning they must venture further into the town than they anticipated to the late-night supermarket.

With their mission complete, and Tracey content now that she possessed a carrier bag containing two bottles of cava, they turned back to join the others. "We've been so long the others will think you've dragged me out drinking tonight," laughed Amanda.

"I would if I thought you'd actually come," retorted a miffed Tracey.

Realising they had walked the long way round, they took a shortcut home, turning down an old passageway, where, to their surprise, they saw a shop lit up only by a single fluorescent sign: 'TIENDA SEXO'. Out of curiosity, Tracey poked her head inside to discover that it meant 'sex shop'. She grabbed Amanda, pulling her to peek too, and joked, "It's a good job Janet isn't here!"

Amanda had an idea. "She doesn't even know what an orgasm is. Let's buy her something to give her one!" She continued, "Can you believe that women get to her age without ever having one?"

"Well, in her day they only slept with their husband, and if he was crap then that's all they knew," consoled Tracey. "Poor Janet."

They entered the shop sniggering in their conspiracy, heading straight for the section where the vibrators were displayed. Tracey picked up a large, black one and waved it childishly in Amanda's face.

"Let's start her off gently, Tracey. We don't want to kill her," she said, spotting a more discreet silver bullet. "This'll do – come on, let's get the hell out of here."

The hotel foyer was still lively upon their return. To their surprise, the others were drinking coffee in the lounge, awaiting their return. "We were worried about you two," explained Janet.

"What kept you?" enquired Belinda.

"Just stocking up on refreshments seeing as you boring lot won't drink with me," laughed Tracey, holding up her purchase, the bottles clinking together loudly.

Amanda discreetly passed the small paper bag to Janet. "Here's a small gift for you. He's called Bertie, by the way."

Janet took the bag and looked puzzled, about to look inside. Amanda stopped her. "Only open it when you are alone, and you will get the answer to your question." Janet looked more confused. "Bit of advice," Amanda offered, knowing that Tom Jones was her secret crush, having heard her and Belinda going on about his thick, curly hair and manly hairy chest, "when you use it, just think of Tom and his sexy chest. That should do the trick."

TWENTY-THREE

THE AWAKENINGS

Over breakfast the next morning, guffaws of unnecessarily loud laughter drowned out the morning conversation of Amanda, Louise, Belinda and Carrie as they attempted to discuss their plans for the day. The golfing brigade were showing off as usual, their bragging and boasting to each other irritating the unimpressed spectators.

Carrie was coming more out of her shell each day and gaining more confidence thanks to the supportive guidance of her five new friends. "Noisy twats," she complained. Golfers were now clearly on her no-go list. She knew her friends from back home all had such lists. Charlotte refused to date posers who drove Porsches, solicitors and footballers. Her other friend Becky wouldn't touch anyone in uniform with a barge pole. So, policemen and firemen, but army blokes in particular, were a definite no-no for her. Bossy bullies, she had explained. Carrie had never had a no-go list, but she was starting one now: no married men, and most definitely *no* golfers!

They had discussed this topic the previous day by the pool, with the results being as follows: Amanda, no selfish or mean men; Janet, no controlling types; Belinda, no golfers or socialites; Louise, no public-school boys or mummy's boys; and finally, Tracey, no men at all – she just wasn't interested, she claimed, too much trouble, and besides, she never met anyone she actually fancied.

"Where's Janet? It's not like her to be late down for breakfast," Amanda said to Belinda, who attempted to swallow her mouthful of sausage before responding.

"She said she'd catch me up." Still with half a mouth full, "Where's Tracey?" she asked in response.

"The usual. Sleeping off her hangover," Amanda replied with raised eyebrows. "She drank the whole bottle of cava for her nightcap. I just don't know how she does it." She sipped her orange juice, then added, "She'll join us in time for lunch no doubt."

"What treatments do we have today then?" asked Belinda, having enjoyed her back massage in the end.

"Foot massages today, although after yesterday, I am sticking to a back massage," said a now embarrassed Amanda, remembering what happened the day before. "And at least I won't have to look him in the face after what he did to me."

"You seemed to enjoy it from what I saw," chuckled Louise.

"I bet he calls in sick after what you did to him," retorted Amanda in jest. "You probably traumatised the poor man."

"I did not traumatise him at all, and he must have liked

it because he gave me his number to meet him for a drink. Anyway, he said he isn't working here for the rest of the week."

"Thank God for that," uttered Belinda in humorous relief.

They all laughed again, thinking of the adventures from the day before, until Carrie alerted them to the entrance of Janet. She was sauntering over to the breakfast buffet with a broad smile on her face, wishing a 'good morning' to all the golfers and staff, in an exceptionally jolly mood.

"She looks remarkably happy today," noticed Carrie.

"She does indeed," agreed Louise.

Janet had grabbed herself a pineapple juice and sauntered over to put it down on their table. "Well? Did you meet Bertie?" asked Amanda before Janet disappeared to choose her breakfast.

Janet bent down to whisper to Amanda, "Yes, and my eyes have been truly opened." Then, she jokingly fanned herself before walking off. She was a new woman. Her uncharacteristic behaviour left Belinda and Carrie gobsmacked and baffled.

"Who is Bertie?" Belinda asked, wondering how on earth Janet could have managed to go on a date without her noticing.

"Bertie the bullet," jumped in Amanda, eager to tell. "We bought Janet a bullet last night so that she could find out what an orgasm was!"

Belinda was truly shocked, then had a disturbing realisation. "Is that what that buzzing noise was coming from our bathroom this morning?" she asked in disbelief. "I thought she was cleaning her teeth for a rather long time."

Janet overheard her as she returned from the buffet carrying her platter of Spanish chorizo and slices of stinky cheese, and without an ounce of embarrassment, she astounded her room-mate. "Well, you'd better get used to it, Belinda, especially now that I know what I have been missing all these years."

Carrie almost choked on her toast. "What on earth happened to the old prudish Janet?"

"She *chilled out*," beamed Janet to the astonishment of Carrie but with the approval of them all.

"I definitely prefer the new Janet," encouraged Amanda.

"Oh, so do I, dear. She's much more fun," laughed Janet.

"What did I miss?" said the shadow suddenly looming over them that was the arrival of Tracey.

"We'll tell you by the pool," said Carrie, still laughing.

They decided to sunbathe by the pool again, seeing as they had more massages booked in for later, but with plans that they would try out the beach the following, and their last full, day. As they reclined on their loungers, soaking up the sun and improving their nicely developing tans, they observed a group of golfers messing around in the pool. The noisy men ruined their peace by bombing into the water and with rowdy, immature horseplay.

"Look! They're just like big, daft kids," commented Belinda. She had found herself getting highly irritated with anything to do with golf and golfers.

Louise wasn't miffed, though. A new group of men had arrived, and she was thoroughly enjoying the parade of lean, tanned bodies, some of them not too shabby-looking either. She preferred the youngest one, early thirties, six-pack and clearly a gym member. He must be the son of one of them, she deduced, unless they were work colleagues.

After her experience with Fernando, she was as randy as ever and couldn't wait to try out another one. Saying that, she had arranged to meet up with him on her last night, but she had chosen not to tell the others, honourably not wanting to desert her friends for a man, so she had arranged to meet him in one of the late bars after the others had all gone up to bed. With dirty thoughts on her mind, she asked the others, "What's the youngest any of you would go?"

"Oh, good God, she's off again," laughed Amanda.

"I couldn't even think about it," winced Belinda.

"Me neither, dear," added Janet.

"Lock up your sons!" jested Tracey.

"I've always preferred them older than me," said Carrie.

"You can say that again," teased Tracey. "But I hope you have learnt your lesson, madam."

Carrie sighed. "Sure have."

Tracey supported Louise's efforts to make up for lost time. "Get 'em young while you can, I say." She pulls a face. "I would if I could, but the young and the good-looking ones never seem to fancy me." She shrugged. "The only ones I get are the old, ugly and bald ones. That's why I would rather go without."

"I think we just want a nice companion at our age, don't we, Janet?" said Belinda, turning to Janet, expecting her to agree.

"You speak for yourself," said the new, improved Janet. "I think I would welcome the chance to have a little romance in my life. I'm in the last chance saloon now, and after finding out what I have been missing all these years, I'd actually like to know what it is like to sleep with a new partner."

Amanda teased her. "But you have a new one now. Bertie!"

"He will do for now, but I would love to find myself a nice gentleman friend," Janet enthused. "Someone to take me out for supper, weekends away and to the cinema and the theatre."

"Oh, I could cope with that," Belinda piped up. "Without the weekends away, though." She was still not confident enough to even think of undressing in front of another man.

"You'll find another one you want to be with one day. When you're ready," Carrie assured her, having in mind the lovely, kind widower who lived next door to her. He would be perfect for her friend, so she planned to introduce them when the time was right. She so badly wanted Belinda to be happy and meet someone who would care for her and look after her, even though she had no desire to try and find a new man for herself.

"Hello, ladieeez." They were interrupted by their new masseur who had turned up to give them all foot massages, except for Amanda and Carrie who were going to get their backs done. Carrie because she was too ticklish to allow anyone near her feet and Amanda because she didn't get her back done the day before.

To their surprise, this one was not male. "I am Elena," she introduced herself chirpily.

Louise sighed, unimpressed and rather put out, much to the amusement of the others, not to mention their relief. Although Elena didn't have Fernando's strong hands and magic touch, it was a perfectly acceptable massage. Five of the women had all taken their turn, but when it finally came to Louise's, she had still not returned from the bathroom, so Elena went off to take a break herself, informing them that she would return in twenty minutes. After five minutes, and with still no sign of Louise, Carrie announced that she needed to pop to the loo herself so she would try to find her, to hurry her along.

Carrie entered the rustic outdoor toilets that were more like a glorified shed than a proper structure and painted shabbily in aqua blue all over the old floorboards, crudely constructed walls and toilet doors made of old planks of wood. It was quaint though, resembling an old beach hut. Beside the handbasins, strong lemon-smelling citronella candles burn to protect the bare bottoms of its visitors from the pesky local mosquitoes.

She quickly nipped into the first of the four cubicles, desperate for a pee herself. The toilet door was one of those that you often found abroad that she hated with a passion. It was so short that anyone waiting outside could either look at your legs up to shin level or look through the gaping gap at the sides. *Don't these people care about their privacy whilst doing such an intimate act?* she contemplated, but as she sat there, she listened carefully to establish if Louise was in there too, but apart from a dripping tap, it was totally silent.

As she washed her hands, water from the wobbly old sink splashed everywhere and all down her glamourous Elizabeth Hurley kaftan. She dried off her hands with a paper towel and popped the used napkin into the bin provided. She could also clearly see from underneath the annoying saloon type doors that all the cubicles were completely empty. Exiting the shack, she checked the pool bar and the patio restaurant, but she wasn't there either. Failing to locate her, the perplexed girl returned to the loungers to check if Louise had returned. She hadn't.

"No luck?" asked Belinda.

"Obviously *not*!" slurred Tracey, tipsy after she had hit the pool bar and consumed several glasses of Aperol that she had attempted to pass off as Tizer fizzy pop. The others knew full well that there was zero chance of her beverage being alcohol-free, but they didn't bother to call her out on it, knowing that they would simply be wasting their breath.

"Maybe she has nipped to the room and fallen asleep?" suggested Janet.

"I'll go and check," offered Carrie again, seeing that she was the one who was sharing with her. So, extracting her room card out of her stripey nautical beach bag, off she trotted again.

Carrie was relieved to see that her bedroom door was ajar as she approached. *Thank goodness*, she thought, but her elation was short-lived. It was only the cleaner. She entered anyway, thinking that maybe Louise might be in the bathroom or sitting on the balcony. She wasn't.

The Spanish maid spoke no English but attempted to explain that she would only be another ten minutes. In return, Carrie used a form of sign language to satisfy the confused woman that she was leaving first.

She checked the foyer next, followed by the lounge bar and then the gift shop. There was absolutely no sign of Louise anywhere. Giving in, she prepared to go back and give the others the bad news. She had been away from them for quite a while now, so she walked more quickly. Out of the hotel, she took a shortcut through the gardens to make her way to the pool area. As she passed the wooden gazebos that housed the indoor massage tables, she heard a noise that sounded like laughter, Louise's laughter. She stopped in her tracks to listen more carefully.

It was most *definitely* Louise!

She must have gone to the indoor massage area to get her treatment, Carrie thought as she barged in, about to tell her off for worrying them all so much. She was right. Louise was here. She had finally found her.

Louise was on the massage table, but to Carrie's horror, her friend was stark bollock-naked, and unfortunately for Carrie, she was not alone. She had caught her friend sitting astride the young golfer in his thirties who had been opposite them at the pool and who she had been admiring the defined abs of that afternoon. She was brazenly riding him like she was on a bucking bronco at the fair. From between the two bodies, loud slapping-slopping noises emerged, with splashes of liquid going everywhere, dripping off the edge of the table and onto the floor below.

"Yes. Yes. Yeeeeeeees. I'm squirting, I'm squirting," screamed out an ecstatic Louise.

"Oooh you are *sooooo* wet," came back his excitable reply.

Carrie gasped in horror. Louise looked up, mortified at being caught out, but before she, or the young man who Louise had firmly pinned to the table by the weight of her hefty thighs and ample bottom, could react, a nauseated Carrie panicked and fled.

Back at the pool, the others saw Carrie returning. She was alone, looked flushed and ruffled, and she was marching very rapidly towards them.

"Oh no, what's happened?" exclaimed Belinda, fearing that Louise had suffered an accident.

On reaching her sunbed, she flopped herself down, reached over to where Tracey's glass of Aperol sat, picked it up and necked the lot in one go.

"Hey! I was about to drink that," Tracey moaned, not grasping the seriousness of the situation.

"Well go and get another and bloody well get me one while you're at it!" gasped Carrie breathlessly.

Tracey was visibly shocked but leapt up to obey, scuttering off to the pool bar.

"What on earth has happened?" asked Janet.

Carrie regained her composure and her breath. "Please don't ask me. I can't say."

"Is she OK?" Belinda worried.

"Oh yes, she certainly is," replied a vexed and sweating Carrie, who then pulled off her kaftan, lay back and used the garment to cover the whole of her upper body and head in an attempt to block out any further questions. She didn't want to tell tales on her friend, and she was still traumatised from the sight that she desperately wished she could unsee.

The others all looked at each other, knowing that it must be bad. Tracey returned from the bar and placed a large glass of Aperol by the side of her.

"Your drink is here, Carrie," she said anxiously.

Carrie didn't reply, nor did she emerge from her cloth cave.

The atmosphere was still tense when a sheepish Louise returned. She approached defiantly and stood above them all, hands on her hips, expecting to be told off. "I suppose she has told you all?"

The kaftan was finally lowered. "No, I have not," objected a defensive Carrie.

"Oh," Louise felt bad for accusing her and was relieved that the others didn't know.

"Tell us what? Oooh, this must be gooooood," scoffed Tracey, loving the drama.

Louise didn't answer; ignoring everyone, she sat down, sighed heavily, then picked up Carrie's untouched drink and necked the lot.

TWENTY-FOUR

THE OLD TOWN

Palma, overlooking the Bay of Palma, was the capital of Majorca. City of dreams.

The widows had taken an excursion to spend the evening exploring the atmospheric Old Town. As they wandered aimlessly around the cobbled streets, they were blown away by the beauty of this majestic city, its rich cultural history exhibited by the castles and ruins, cathedrals and monasteries standing proud as they had done for hundreds of years. The tiny streets were kept cool by the shadows of the thick, stone walls of impressive old buildings that housed art galleries and museums.

They could have done with a couple of days here to fully appreciate all that it had to offer, but tonight, it was to be an evening stroll followed by supper at a wine bar that Amanda had booked for them. Having read so many travel magazines over the years, she knew all the best places, whether it was for the reputation of their food or to hang out with the in-crowd. This evening, she had selected the venue based on its reputation of excellent wine combined with an unusual experience.

They gasped in awe at the splendour of the Basilica Cathedral of Santa Maria, its Catalan Gothic architecture glowing in the early evening sun. They passed pretty courtyards with hanging baskets of colourful blooms and random clusters of terracotta pots containing lavender and mini olive trees. The scent of fresh herbs floated around the air, with hints of rosemary, mint and basil hitting their palates and making them peckish.

Spotting a free table at a little bistro in the Mayor Plaza, they took the opportunity to rest over glasses of pre-dinner gin and tonics. In the middle of the table was a tiny rustic vase of wild chicory. A harassed waiter briskly put down six menus and six paper bandages, each containing a knife and a fork, but he was disappointed to hear that they were not staying to dine too, so he abruptly swiped them back up again and walked off, huffing and puffing to himself. The historic city was a vibrant hub for foodies, so they hoped that the food where they were going tasted as good as the food here smelt.

Feeling replenished, they continued their walk, stopping to gaze into rustic shop windows at local produce such as exquisite lace and handmade pottery bowls in all shades of orange, green and yellow. Belinda wanted to buy the lot but acknowledged that she had more than enough at home, so she restricted herself to a matching set of three small dishes that she intended to use for dips. A shoe shop selling sandals and mules made from the softest leather she had ever felt got Janet reaching for her credit card.

Carrie bought herself a little summery dress. It cost her 80 euros, but she justified it to herself that she would never find anything like it back home; plus, this trip had cost her nothing, only her spending money. *I really ought to buy thank-you gifts for the others*, she thought, *seeing as they technically paid for it.* She knew they could afford it, being older than her, and having had husbands with good jobs, but even so, they had been very good to her, considering. Carrie stopped to look down a side street when an African street vendor caught her eye and called her over to look at his selection of *designer* handbags. She went to check them out but was dragged back by Tracey. "Noooo… buy the real thing, darling," she expressed in her best Patsy voice. Belinda stifled a giggle because Roger's nickname for Tracey had been Patsy. He had always said that she reminded him of Joanna Lumley's character in *Absolutely Fabulous*.

They passed rustic flower shops with displays, the likes of which they never saw at home. "Why do the Europeans dress their shop windows so much more stylishly than we do?" questioned Amanda. Belinda wholly agreed as they stood outside an artisan bread shop that was a work of art. Louise admired an oil painting in the foyer of a very expensive-looking studio that she dared not fully enter, fearful that her impulsive nature would allow her credit card to get severely caned.

The highlight for Belinda was a quaint little shop called *Forn des Teatre*. The most famous pastry shop in Palma. She bought a selection of small pastries, just so that she could dissect them (OK, taste as well then!) later to get ideas for her baking. What she didn't buy, she took photos of on her smart phone.

There were shops selling sunglasses, souvenirs and books both new and old. They admired the adorable children's clothing boutiques with outfits that looked like they were straight from the catwalks in Paris and far classier than the average British kid would ever wear. You didn't get outfits like that in Mothercare; mind you, at those prices, they were not surprised.

As the sun began to set, the Old Town turned even more magical. The lights from the shops lit up the narrow passageways like torchlight. The square had an abundance of fairy lights strung all around its buildings and hanging from the large brollies that covered the tables. It was an enchanting setting, one where quirky bars that hipsters frequented blended with traditional bars where old local men sat on benches playing dominoes and watching the world go by with an aperitif or two.

Amanda had a walking map app open on her iPhone which she relied on to guide them to the restaurant. She glanced down, letting the others know that it was only five more minutes away. When they were almost there, they suddenly stopped. Bewitching music bellowed out from an old wooden doorway and, being the curious creatures that they were, they couldn't resist taking a quick peek inside.

They were certainly not disappointed at what they came across. The widows stood captivated by a dramatic display of proper traditional flamenco dancing. A haggard, ex-rock-star-looking man in his late fifties played his guitar like the clappers, with such ease and expertise, only years of practice could result in such a performance. His long, grey-streaked hair was loosely swept back and tucked behind his ears, where a hand-rolled cigarette sat waiting for his post-performance treat. Amanda felt herself blush just looking at him.

Dancing to his beat was an athletic, lean man of about thirty, dressed head-to-toe in black. His trousers were circulation-cutting tight, his shirt unbuttoned over halfway down his chest. He had sharp, chiselled features and dark, wavy hair to his shoulders. He looked moody, angry even, adding to his allure. His nifty feet banged surprisingly heavily and aggressively onto the old wooden floor as he gyrated his slim snake hips around a couple of females who, to the surprise of the widows, were around their age.

"There's hope for us yet," joked Amanda.

"I've died and gone to heaven," Louise muttered, admiring both but mainly the younger of the two men. Carrie was standing next to her and, having been kind enough to not mention the incident from earlier, sarcastically chided her, "I think you've had more than enough for one day." Louise stared back at her, miffed. Carrie stared back defiantly. Then, they both burst into laughter, and they laughed, and they laughed, ending in a friendly bear hug from Carrie to let Louise know that all was forgiven.

"What's got into those two?" asked Janet to the others.

"I'll find out later," said Tracey, gagging to know what had gone on and suspecting it must be something extremely scandalous. She couldn't wait to find out!

They finally arrived at their pre-booked venue, and it did not disappoint. Belinda entered first, gasping in delight, followed by Janet who did the same, then the others, and finally Amanda. She had read about the place in one of her travel guides, then had googled it online, so she knew exactly what to expect, but the others hadn't, so the setting both amazed and astounded them. Carrie immediately got her phone out and started to take photos to upload to her Instagram. The enormous Gothic fireplaces, and all around the floor, had the most exceptional display of fruit and vegetables all bundled into old, vintage wicker baskets. The colourful masterpiece resembled a rainbow waterfall. It was like nothing they had ever seen before.

A practical Belinda wondered in awe how often they needed to change the produce and how long it must take to recreate. *Maybe they actually eat it*, she pondered. Giant iron candlesticks were everywhere, lighting up the magnificent display with their arms of wax burning away, adding to the ambience. Huge and extravagant floral displays were everywhere, their scents giving off an air of sophistication.

Abaco Bar was technically a cocktail bar, but Amanda had arranged a private table in the courtyard with a selection of Spanish tapas for them all. The old building, with its church-like interior and its extravagant, theatrical decor, made them feel they had been transported back to an era of opulence and grandeur. Classical music drifted out from the louder, busier bar area, mostly frequented by tourists.

The courtyard was heavenly. Tropical birds in cages sung out loud to them as they ate their stuffed peppers, garlic mushrooms and mini lamb kebabs infused with rosemary. They shared delicious plates of patatas bravas with aioli and anchovies.

"Well done for finding this place, Amanda," Janet praised her. "I have had the most wondrous evening."

"Me too," exclaimed Carrie. "It has been amaaazing."

"A surreal experience," added Belinda.

"We must do this more often," Louise insisted, thinking about the availability of men in Spain as much as the present company, although she had genuinely enjoyed coming away with them all. They had been having a calm and civilised night out until Tracey attempted to lower the tone. "I'm still waiting to hear what she got up to earlier."

Carrie made her shush, whispering, "It's not the time or place."

Louise was very grateful.

Amanda still had one surprise in store for them. She had ordered two local taxis to take them to a different location. "Just for coffee and desserts," she told them mysteriously as she bundled them all into two waiting cars. Three curious ladies climbed into the first one, and two more jumped into the second cab with Amanda.

A short journey ensued, after which they pulled up at a swanky, modern hotel in the marina. "Are we staying the night?" asked Carrie, confused, with them not having brought overnight bags.

"No, don't worry; our minibus is collecting us from here at midnight," Amanda reassured her, leading them over to the lift and squeezing them all inside. The all-glass lift whooshed up rapidly after Amanda had pressed the penthouse button. In the one mirrored wall of the lift, Louise checked out her appearance. *I'm looking well*, she thought, wondering if she was as tanned as she looked or if it was the tinted glass. Maybe it was the glow in her cheeks after her sexual awakenings. She was brought out of her vain thoughts by the pinging sound of the lift alerting them that they had arrived at their destination.

As the doors opened, they gasped. This was not at all what they expected. Carrie was immediately impressed, as was Louise. Belinda and Janet worried they were in some fancy nightclub. Tracey just wanted another drink.

The venue was the Blue Jazz roof bar, a swanky, sophisticated wine bar that turned into a nightclub after hours, and as its name suggested, funky jazz tunes echoed around the bar. Janet and Belinda looked at each other, both concerned that it seemed a tad too cool and trendy for them, so they were relieved when they were taken over to a quiet spot where three double sofas wrapped around a low coffee table awaited them. Amanda had somehow managed to secure them the best seats in the house, with phenomenal views.

To the widows' delight, and as the cool jazz played softly in the background, they were now sat overlooking Palma's marina, with only a glass screen between themselves and the open sea. Luxury yachts, gin-palace catamarans and smaller speed boats all bobbed about together under the bright night sky, some lit up, having lucky residents on board. The stars in the sky were as clear as they'd ever be. It was a truly heavenly night.

A stunning and glamourous hostess came over to serve them, a heavy Lithuanian accent asking, "Cocktails?" and handing out drink menus.

"Just coffees please," replied Amanda.

"And cakes," piped up Janet, to the relief of Belinda, hoping she wasn't going to be the only one who still wanted cake at this time of night.

Before the waitress went off to fetch different menus, Tracey quickly shouted out, "I'll have an espresso martini, please."

"Anyone else?" offered the hostess.

"Go on then," agreed both Louise and Carrie, deciding they would have the same as Tracey considering the setting. With three coffee cocktails, three normal coffees and three cakes now on the table, the ladies enjoyed the relaxing ambience of their luxurious surroundings. The music was mesmerising, the women as chilled as the jazz. They could happily sit there all night in their penthouse heaven.

After a while Carrie excused herself as she got up to go and find the bathroom, with Tracey jumping up and offering to accompany her but not really needing to go. They found that the venue had really filled up since they arrived, with them now having to squeeze through the trendy crowd to get to the toilets. Frustratingly, the queue was out of the door as Carrie took her place in line and waited patiently.

"I can't be bothered to wait," Tracey called to her over the noise of the music and the chattering of the revellers, then she disappeared, and not in the direction of their table. Carrie watched her in amusement, knowing that she would head straight to the bar.

As she waited in line, a muscly, tall, dark and handsome man walked past her on his way to the gents' loos. He smiled at her as he passed, and she smiled back politely. She was still in the same spot when he came out, so he took his chance and tried to chat her up. "Don't I know you from somewhere?" he asked her. She thought he looked familiar but was not sure, but after chatting for a while, they established that they both worked in Guildford.

"We must have passed each other in town," he told her.

She excused herself when she finally got her turn to go into the loo, bidding him goodbye, but to her surprise, when she came out, he was still there. In his hand was now a sparkling chilled glass of champagne that he had bought for her, handing it over and assuring her, "No pressure. I just wanted to get you a drink."

She thought he was a bit full of himself and presumptuous, and she was most definitely not interested in him, so she explained she was with friends and must go, thanking him for the drink and quickly escaping to rejoin the others.

Tracey had beaten her back to their sofas and spotted straight away that she was holding a glass of champers. "Where did you get that?" she asked jealously.

"Oh, some cocky bloke gave it to me, but I'm not drinking it," replied Carrie, "you can't be too careful these days with all the drink-spiking that goes on" putting it down on the table with a grimace, as though it were a glass of poison.

Tracey smiled as she picked it up. "Result!" she said.

Janet looked at her watch and alerted everyone that their minibus would be outside in five minutes, so they got up and prepared to leave, weaving their way through the revellers and towards the lifts. Carrie spotted the man again but pretended that she hadn't noticed him and kept on walking, staring straight ahead. He had been searching everywhere for her, so he followed her group to the lifts, not wanting to let her out of his sight again.

As the women waited for the lift to reach their floor, he dashed over to her, not caring that she was not alone, as he arrogantly handed her his business card. 'David Westwood. Director of Sales' it read. It advertised that he worked at the biggest double-glazing company in town. The others watched on unimpressed as he demanded arrogantly, rather than asking politely, that she call him as soon as she got back home to England. Carrie held the card in her hand but failed to put it away into her handbag for safekeeping, having absolutely no intention whatsoever of calling him. It would be going straight into the first bin that she passed.

Louise, who had stayed behind to sort out the bill, finally caught up with them. On spotting the man, and to everyone's surprise, she ran over to hug him. "Ahh, so lovely to see you again." His horrified face was a picture as he squirmed, clearly not as pleased to see her as she was to see him. As soon as Carrie saw them together, she gasped in horror as she realised where she knew him from. He was the man who she had caught Louise having sex with earlier that day!

The mood in the minibus was strained. The others baffled as to what was going on. Louise sat silently, sulking, as well as looking embarrassed.

"I didn't know it was your man," said Carrie. "I don't even like him."

"It didn't look like it," she accused Carrie.

"What do you mean your man?" Tracey interjected. "Is he actually your man?"

"He was," sulked Louise.

"Was he?" chorused the others.

"How was he?" asked Amanda, now curious.

They all went quiet, with everyone waiting for Carrie or Louise to elaborate. Belinda cleverly put two and two together. "Is that where you were today then?"

"What, when she disappeared?" added Janet disapprovingly.

"You're such a bloody dark horse," bellowed Tracey, clapping her hands in delight and loving the scandal.

"Yes, OK, I saw him today. *So what?!*" Louise snapped.

"I didn't recognise him," explained a worried Carrie. "He bought me a drink and tried to chat me up, but I wasn't interested."

"That's true," added Tracey. "I drank the drink he bought her."

"Whatever," muttered Louise.

The rest of the journey was silent.

Relieved to be back at the hotel, the widows headed straight for the lift. It had been a good night, but they were all exhausted. No one mentioned again what had just happened and they all bade each other goodnight, arranging to meet at breakfast the next day, prepared to head out to the beach. It would make a nice change from the pool, and they most certainly did not want to be around the hotel the next day, seeing as the dreaded David Westwood might still be there.

As the other four closed their bedroom doors, Carrie and Louise walked awkwardly into theirs. "I wouldn't like to be in their room right now," Amanda told Tracey.

"Oooh I would. I'd love to be a little fly on that wall," laughed Tracey.

TWENTY-FIVE

BEACH DAYS

By the next morning, all was well again between Carrie and Louise, but they decided to give the breakfast dining room a wide berth that day as neither of them fancied bumping into David, nor the bunch of prats that he was with. They guessed he would have most likely bragged to his chums by now, so they did not want to be the subject of crude jokes from their male pack mentality.

As they left their room to set off, they knocked on Belinda's door to inform her that they were going to have their breakfast at the harbour instead and would meet the others down at the beach. "We'll get there first and organise the sunbeds," offered Louise, clearly in a better mood having slept on it and having realised that she had overreacted. As soon as she had woken, she had apologised profusely to Carrie who had immediately forgiven her. Although Belinda was still Carrie's favourite, she was closest to Louise, their ages being nearer and them having an easy rapport and a great fondness for each other.

Belinda shared the news with Janet, who was pleased that all was harmonious again. The holiday was meant to be a bonding experience after all that they had been through lately. She didn't want anyone falling out. When they exited their room to go down to breakfast, they did so at the same time as Amanda and Tracey, bumping into them in the hallway and then walking down with them. They shared the good news that all was now well with Carrie and Louise. The foursome occupied their usual table in the dining room, with Amanda observing that all the guests did the same. *Why do people sit in the same place every morning?* she wondered.

Belinda, wanting a full English again, found herself in the queue right next to David Westwood, who didn't recognise her from the night before but smiled at her regardless. She just glared back at him, quitting the queue and storming off to get an omelette instead. She had no intention of being friendly with anyone who had upset her girls. As she looked down at the bland, eggy offering on her plate, she fumed thinking of him. Those sausages had looked delicious.

Meanwhile in the harbour, Carrie and Louise were seated at the Cappuccino Café, a renowned trendy café, popular with affluent locals, yacht owners and tourists. The location was superb, right on the water's edge, so its diners could either admire the myriad of high-quality floating vessels nearby or just keep an eye on their own boat instead. Even though it was still early, the famous café was jam-packed, and they had been lucky to even get a table. Its fashionable reputation meant that it also got its share of Instagrammers, dolled up unnecessarily for breakfast, posing for photos, and snapping away at their food and drinks.

They sat in wicker armchairs with nautical cushions that suited its location, but they had red-and-white stripes, a refreshing change from the popular blue-and-white vertical lines. The girls ordered cappuccinos, believing that their namesake beverage must be particularly good in this establishment. The Wi-Fi was strong and the coffee even more so, which had impressed Louise, who needed to check in on her office. She had two clients due to exchange on their house purchases that day, so she needed to chase the solicitors to give them a kick up their backsides, otherwise the paperwork would remain untouched on their desks. She was never impressed with the service they provided. They were overpriced and far too slow. She disliked solicitors immensely, telling Carrie they were 'too much up their own arses'.

They both devoured two pastries each, with Carrie dunking hers in the frothy coffee, both glad that they'd ventured out somewhere new for breakfast. It made a nice change from the boring breakfast room of their hotel, not to mention that the atmosphere here was vibrant, with them both starting to thoroughly enjoy socialising again after their previous mourning period. The discovery of the fake competition wins meant that none of the widows felt guilty for enjoying themselves anymore. The men's deviousness and misbehaviour had certainly done them all a huge favour.

After breakfast, they wandered through the town and headed towards Oratori beach which, to their delight, was in a sheltered bay, ensuring a flat and serene sea, perfect for bathing. Hopefully, it would be warm and welcoming later when the sun had been given time to heat it. The sunloungers were just being laid out when they arrived, so they were successful in nabbing six together, and right on the front row too. With their own towels placed on their beds, they scattered an array of books, suntan lotion and flip-flops across the other four loungers. This was a warning to any newcomers to the beach. It meant 'bog off, they are ours'!

They had been spotted by an eagle-eyed man who was the owner of the beds, and before they even got a chance to sit down, he was there in a flash to collect his rent. "Sixty euros," he told them bluntly.

"*Each?*" shrieked Carrie, alarmed that he meant €60 per bed and about to stuff her belongings back into her bag.

"No, señorita, ten euros for one bed. For six beds, sixty euros," he informed her.

Louise laughed and handed over three €20 notes. "My treat," she insisted. "For being such a bitch last night."

He stuffed the notes greedily into the large leather bumbag that sat over his sweaty crotch.

Before the others arrived, Carrie got Mr Bumbag to set up an umbrella for Janet and Belinda, and whilst he erected it, she dragged over three little plastic tables so that they all had somewhere to put their drinks. She also spotted an unattended plastic ice bucket, which she swiftly took ownership of, knowing that Tracey would appreciate it.

"Don't encourage her," laughed Louise.

Mr Bumbag asked Carrie for another ten euros, pointing up at the brolly. Carrie tutted, outraged at the additional price for an umbrella, so Louise went to get her purse, but Carrie beat her to it, telling her friend, "It's OK, I'll get it."

With his greedy bumbag having been fed again, the man marched off to find his next victims. An hour later, they were joined by the others. A very slight sea breeze blew, making the beach far more comfortable than the baking heat of the pool area, which was greatly appreciated by Belinda. "Oh, this is much better," she exclaimed. "I think I'll have a dip later."

The others had noticed that her inhibitions were disappearing the longer they were there. She had stopped hiding behind her baggy kaftan and was embracing the summer sun. She looked well too, her suntan really suiting her. She looked younger, invigorated and, more importantly, happier.

They were all in such upbeat moods, they weren't even ruffled when every half hour they were pestered by someone trying to flog something. So far, they had turned down aloe vera gel, fake sunglasses that looked like they would snap after one wear, wooden painted toys and enormous tablecloths that fluttered gracefully in the wind as they were being displayed.

Belinda had made a purchase of a small plastic fan for her hot flushes. She delighted in cooling herself, wishing she had owned this gadget from the start of the holiday. "Best five euros I've ever spent," she told her friends.

The hardest sell was from the hawker whose dresses, she claimed, were 'one size fits all', but they all knew they wouldn't even fit one leg into them.

Carrie almost succumbed when she spotted the tall, slim African vendor again, this time with the latest collection of

Mulberry-inspired, or fraudulently copied rather, handbags. She went to call him over.

"*Noooo!*" the others screamed in unison.

"Just don't do it," yelled Tracey, shooing the man away.

Carrie had got his hopes up of a sale, so now he walked off, disappointed. He looked seven feet tall thanks to the high stack of 'Armani' baseball caps piled up on his head. All the real thing, of course! Carrie sat back, laughing. "It's alright for you lot, I can only afford the fake ones."

Belinda had joked that she was really missing her daily massage, and they all agreed that they were too, so when Carrie went to the bathroom and noticed a small Asian lady offering them, she signed them all up, promising to pay the lady in cash back at the sunbed. She had spotted her walking around holding up a 'massage menu' and shouting out loud. "Massaaaaaaaaaage. Twenty euro. Massaaaaaaaaaage."

It turned out that she would come to your sunbed, then do you whilst you lay on your lounger. Carrie had wanted to buy a gift for the others as a thank you gesture, so when she returned from the loo, she was now accompanied by the little lady, who proceeded to give them all a damn good pummelling. Although barely five foot two, she put Fernando and Elena to shame. By the time she had finished with them, they didn't have one knotty shoulder between them, and for far less money than the hotel had charged, she had given them a full body, which had included head and feet. Although they were now left with oily hair, they wished they had spent more time at the beach rather than around the hotel pool.

The last day of their trip was going so swimmingly, and not one of them wanted to go home just yet, all of them craving a couple more days before flying home. The Majorcan sun, good friends, good food and being away from home had been a real tonic.

By lunchtime, they were enjoying the beach so much, they didn't want to leave it to go and sit inside a café, so Tracey offered to go and fetch food instead, which they all appreciated, especially when she returned carrying two large carrier bags that smelt exceedingly appetising. From the first steaming plastic carrier bag, she took out six white polystyrene food cartons, the mouth-watering smell letting them know they were going to like her wares. Inside were chicken kebabs with salad and garlic sauce, which tasted as good as anything they could have got from any restaurant. It was Janet's first-ever takeaway, and she wasn't sure that she liked the idea of eating from her lap like a common savage. She had to watch the others to see how she was meant to manage it, but once she'd started, her senses went into overdrive, and she tucked right in and devoured the lot.

From the other bag, Tracey produced six bottles of Evian water for them to wash it down with. They saw that she had also purchased a bottle of cava, which she cheerily plonked inside the waiting, but still empty, bucket. After licking her fingers to remove the last of the garlicky sauce, she wiped them on her paper napkin, before beckoning Mr Bumbag. He took their order of ice for the bucket and more drinks for the others, who all ordered a Coke, except for Amanda who fancied a beer. As they sipped the refreshing, brown, fizzy liquid, Louise posed a question: "Why does Coke always taste better from a proper glass bottle?"

No one knew the answer, but they all agreed that it was true.

After their delicious lunch, Belinda nipped to the ladies and brought back ice creams for everyone. She hadn't known what they would prefer so she had bought two strawberry Cornettos, two Magnums and two Mars ice creams which they all leapt on like little kids. No one had given a toss about their waistline this week. It had been a time for treating themselves.

Mid-afternoon, and with bellies full, they lazed on the loungers, knowing that by this time tomorrow they would be back home in the gloomy British weather and back to their normal lives, whatever normal was these days. They still didn't know.

Amanda decided that she simply could not go home without having a swim in the ocean, so she asked the others to come in too, with Janet and Belinda being the only ones willing to join her. Carrie protested that she didn't like going in the sea. Too many slimy things touching her legs, she explained. Louise was busy on her phone, pretended to be replying to work emails, but she was really researching the best dating apps, and wondering if anyone would judge her if she joined one so soon after Chris's death, and Tracey declared that she was, "Too drunk. Sorry," the bottle by her side having been turned upside down in the bucket.

Amanda, Belinda and Janet frolicked chest deep in the warm afternoon sea, treading water as they casually chatted about the night ahead. "We're being picked up for the airport at eight-thirty in the morning, so shall we eat in the hotel tonight?" suggested Janet. "I don't think we should have another late one."

"Good idea," agreed Belinda. "We could do the patio restaurant again?"

"Perfect. Their paella was delicious. I could certainly eat that again," concurred Amanda, then added in jest, "And at least we can keep a closer eye on Louise and Tracey."

"I'm rather concerned about Louise going off with all these men. You just don't know what they've got, do you?" Belinda said with genuine motherly concern.

"What have they got?" Janet asked, confused.

"Diseases," laughed Amanda. "Sexual ones. Well, hopefully they *don't* have any."

"I read that the biggest age group catching STDs now are people in their fifties," Belinda stated, glad that she had absolutely no intention of having sex with anyone.

Janet was deep in thought about the events and conversations they had had that week. She curiously asked them, "I didn't like to say this in front of the others, but when you both used to have intercourse—"

Amanda interrupted, laughing out loud. "Please Janet, just call it *sex*, or I can't take you seriously."

She continued, "When you two used to have… sex," she whispered it, "with your husbands, did you always have orgasms?" she asked, thinking that she was cool now that she knew what one was. "Because I can't believe that I went sixty-one years without it happening to me, yet it appears to be normal for everyone else."

Belinda tried to help her out. "Sometimes, but not always. Maybe more in the early days. Most women do, but not every time."

Amanda attempted to expand and explain it better. "If it's

just a quickie, and the man is selfish and makes no effort to arouse the woman, then it probably won't happen. Maybe the major was like that?"

Janet still appeared confused but admitted, "Yes, I suppose he was. I can't really remember. We only did that sort of thing in the early days when we were newly-weds. Then we had separate bedrooms so that part of our marriage stopped altogether."

Belinda took her turn again. "Sometimes if the man has a very small penis, that might not help either if it doesn't reach where you need it to, unless he makes up for it in other ways." She held up her fingers to indicate a small willy.

"Oh my God" shrieked Amanda in joy. "Are you saying Roger the stud only had a tiny todger?"

Belinda giggled and put her finger up to her mouth. "I'm saying no more… but shush, don't let Carrie hear us."

"Hahahaha. Oh, that has made my day," laughed Amanda again, until Belinda frowned at her to shut up, which she obediently did.

"Stop it, you'll have Carrie pining for him again," chided Belinda.

Janet lay back to float on top of the water. She looked up at the sun and smiled contentedly, letting out a huge, blissful sigh. "I've learnt so much this week thanks to you all. The women at the WI would never talk like this."

"I'm not surprised," laughed Belinda.

"Mind you, they did start getting a tad fruity when those rude calendars came out. Charles was so outraged he wouldn't allow me to go for a month until all the fuss had died down," she giggled.

Amanda was annoyed at how much Charles had controlled Janet. "Shame you didn't rebel and do one too. I can see you now... Miss January Janet."

"Or the centrefold!" quipped Belinda.

Amanda confessed mischievously, "When I had sex with Christopher, I used to have to finish myself off afterwards when he went to the loo... and if he didn't need the loo, I would pretend I had left the back door open. He was soooo neurotic about security that by the time he had come back upstairs I would have sorted myself out!"

They all laughed, accepting of the fact that none of them had a perfect relationship or sex life.

"I did think that Charles was very small until I met Bertie, but now I realise he was normal after all," Janet said innocently.

Amanda snorted and choked in the salty water. She was laughing so hard, she couldn't breathe. "*Belinda!* She thinks the *bullet* is the size of a *normal penis!*"

Janet didn't get why Belinda and Amanda were cracking up. She looked baffled, but their laughter was so infectious that she joined in, and the three friends could be heard from the beach guffawing like buffaloes.

"Crikey, what's tickled them?" said Carrie to Louise and Tracey, who had also heard the commotion. The three on the beach were now laughing with them, despite not even knowing what they were laughing at.

"Help, I'm going to drown," gurgled Amanda, who couldn't stop laughing.

Belinda kindly educated Janet. "The bullet is only a little finger-sized one to masturbate with, Janet. At least I think so.

233

I've heard it can be used for other things, so I am not entirely sure myself."

"Since the menopause, I haven't even wanted to do that," admitted Amanda. "But with what happened with Fernando and my toes, it's given me hope that I might come back to life after all."

Belinda suddenly started to sing a song, meaning it comically, but she had a fine voice and sung it extremely well. "Can you hear the drums, *Fernando*?"

Amanda and Janet joined in spontaneously, singing at the top of their voices in the calm sea, without a care in the world.

Louise jumped up and looked around frantically and hopefully. "Fernando? Is he here?"

Tracey pulled her back down. "Don't be daft; they are just having a laugh."

"It's great to see them having fun," Carrie said, chuffed to see that Belinda was finally letting her hair down.

"I think the three of them could do with a good session with Fernando themselves," laughed Tracey.

"Actually, I think I could too!" said Carrie, laughing merrily.

"*Hallelujah!* She is getting over Roger," declared Tracey.

Louise glared at them both. "Fernando is *mine*, thank you very much."

To tease Louise, and in an attempt to make her stop being so silly, Tracey started to contribute to the singing. Carrie immediately got in on the act too.

Luckily, Louise saw the funny side of it, so she then joined in too. The two choirs sung out to each other, the belles on the beach and the sirens in the sea. A perfect end to a perfect last day...

"Yes, if I had to do the same again, I would, my friend, Fernando."

"Yes, if I had to do the same again, I would, my friend, Fernando."

TWENTY-SIX

THE LAST SUPPER

The walk home from the beach was such fun. All the way from their sunbeds, along the harbour and back up the hill to the hotel, they sauntered along in high spirits, singing ABBA songs. It turned out that Carrie and Belinda were huge fans of musical theatre and they'd both been to see *Mamma Mia* in the West End, so they knew every single word of every song, as did Amanda from watching the movie so many times with her daughter. By the time they reached the hotel, Carrie had talked everyone into going to see it.

Tracey wanted to go the supermarket again to fetch a bottle of cava for her evening nightcap, so she persuaded Amanda to accompany her there once more, so the other four continued back to their hotel. As they entered the lobby, Belinda remembered that she must take a gift home for her neighbour Barbara, who had been dog-sitting Hugo while she'd been away, so Janet suggested that they go and check out the hotel gift shop. Carrie and Louise declined to join them, excusing themselves to go and get ready for their last night out, both super keen to wash their hair to remove the oil from their earlier massage. As good as it had been, their locks now hung lanky and greasy. Eyeing that the lift door had just opened, they raced towards it before the doors closed as magically as they had opened.

As Amanda and Tracey headed back from the supermarket, they passed the same shop from which they had purchased Bertie a couple of nights earlier. Amanda filled Tracey in on what had made her laugh so much when she had been in the sea with Janet.

"I told you we should have got the bigger one," chuckled Tracey.

Amanda didn't reply, instead pulling Tracey into the shop. "Let's do it then. She really hasn't got a clue. We need to educate her." They settled on an average, realistic-sized dildo, in pale pink. "If she does get a new man, she'll need to know what to expect," Amanda said as she paid.

"That's true, and fancy the major only having a little maggot," Tracey sniggered.

With the gift wrapped discreetly in a plain brown bag, they scurried out, also keen to get back as soon as possible, seeing as their reservation at the patio restaurant was booked for 8pm.

Back at the hotel, Amanda and Tracey found themselves at the bottom of the lifts at the same time as Janet and Belinda, who had just exited the gift shop. Belinda was excited to show them the funky door stopper that she has just purchased for her neighbour. It was wooden and painted with a dog's head on the end. "He looks just like my Hugo," she enthused.

The lift door pinged as it opened at floor number five, with everyone spilling out into the corridor. While Belinda fumbled for her room card, Amanda took the opportunity to sneakily drop the brown paper bag into Janet's beach bag. "This is what a normal size is," she whispered.

Belinda managed to locate her card, open her door and go inside, as did Tracey, but before Janet did too, Amanda cheekily shouted along the corridor to her, "By the way, his name is Percy!"

"Who is Percy?" asked Belinda comically, totally unaware of what had gone on.

Two hours later, Carrie and Louise, despite going up to get ready first, were the last to make it down to dinner. "Ahh, here you are," Janet said. "I was about to send out a search party."

"Sorry, everyone," Carrie groaned. "My fault. My hair takes sooooo long to do."

"It is beautiful though. You look gorgeous," smiled Belinda genuinely, as she handed the latecomers a glass of champagne from the magnum that she had generously pre-ordered and paid for. "A toast for our last supper," she explained.

"Thank you, and you look lovely too," Carrie returned a compliment to Belinda, too modest to have the attention all on herself, then added, "And I love your necklace, Janet," careful not to leave her out. The older two ladies felt like mother figures to her now, even more than her own mum did.

"Oh this, I've had it for donkey's years," Janet replied. "Charles bought it." Then she changed the subject, keen to get everyone's attention… "Now that you are all here," she raised her glass, "here's to a very successful holiday."

"The first of many, I hope," Belinda added cheerily.

"We must make this a regular thing. We have so much catching up to do," said a determined Amanda.

"I'm definitely up for that," confirmed Louise.

"Me too… if you boring lot will start having a proper drink," joked Tracey.

It was a chillier night than usual in Puerto Portals. They had been fortunate to have enjoyed wall-to-wall sunshine every day since they had arrived, but the weather was about to change. It was forecast to soon turn cloudy and windy, with a high chance of rain. Their waiter Pablo informed them that a storm was brewing as he closed all the umbrellas in the patio restaurant, tying them securely, while the other staff rushed around taking indoors the fabric padded cushions from empty chairs. The widows were grateful that he had kindly provided them all with soft, woollen blankets, which were now under the table cuddling their knees, their own pashminas hugging their shoulders. They had managed to enjoy their last supper before the sun went down and before the temperature had dropped, but now it was too cold to remain al fresco, so they moved inside to the warmth of the lounge bar.

"Our last nightcap," said Belinda sadly.

"I really don't want to go back," groaned Amanda.

"Me neither," added Carrie. "I'm going to miss you all so much, and thank you for inviting me." Belinda put a protective arm around the young girl's shoulder. "I really appreciate how kind you have all been to me," Carrie added, tears welling up in her eyes.

"Seeing as it's our last night, who's up for clubbing?" Tracey wanted to make the most of her last chance to let her hair down with friends. Tomorrow night she would be at home, drinking alone.

"Sorry. My clubbing days are over," Amanda pooh-poohed the idea.

"And mine never started," laughed Janet.

"My feet are killing me," Belinda used as her excuse, rotating her ankles as if to prove so.

"Well, what about you two? Someone join me, please?" pleaded Tracey.

"Oh, alright then," Louise agreed, already having secret plans to meet up with Fernando later anyway.

"Just one drink then," Carrie conceded.

"Don't forget our flight is in the morning. We've got an eight-thirty pick-up," Janet reminded them, concerned that they might have bad heads the next day. She didn't want anyone throwing up on the plane.

"Don't worry, Janet. One nightcap in the bar won't hurt," Tracey replied, glancing in amusement at Louise and Carrie.

Goodnight hugs were exchanged, and plans were made to meet at 7.30am for breakfast. With a noisy ping of the lift, half the group disappeared into its sliding metal doors. No sooner had they gone, Tracey pulled the other two up onto their feet. "Come on, let's get out of here," she squealed giddily. They followed obediently, knowing there was no point trying to argue with her. Like naughty schoolgirls, they shuffled around in the revolving door, giggling in conspiracy and excitement. "*Freedom!*" yelled Tracey.

Ten minutes later, the threesome strutted along the harbour with an extra bounce in their step, all in high spirits at the thought of a proper night out, the fact it was their last meant they were determined to make it a good one. The cold wind caused them to walk faster, eager to find somewhere they could go inside. Louise dragged them into the first bar they passed. She'd heard a commotion going on inside, and from what she could see, it was full of men. As they pushed their way through the noisy bar, they saw that an international football game was playing on a big screen. Louise was miffed that the rowdy men appeared more interested in the game than chatting her up, so she knocked back her drink. "Come on, drink up. Next bar," she ordered bossily, Carrie and Tracey having to neck the lot to keep up with her.

The next watering hole was a more civilised wine bar, so they sat leisurely, chewing the fat over a bottle of Torres Vina Sol and making plans that they would meet up in town the following week to return to Baileys Wine Bar. Louise was chuffed that she now had two groups of girlfriends to socialise with. She sheepishly confessed to them that she was meeting Fernando in an hour.

"Dumping us for a man, are you?" ribbed Tracey but not really minding; after all, she still had Carrie to drink with. Louise informed her pals that they must help her find the Sailors Bar, where she had promised to meet him.

***

In Amanda's room, she checked her phone again for the umpteenth time. It was after midnight and she couldn't stay awake any longer. She prayed Tracey wasn't going to be too noisy when she got in, and she hadn't even started to pack!

***

It was a lively and cosmopolitan vibe at Sailors, where the girls sat jubilantly at the bar. They were in the minority, seeing as there were more golfers than holidaymakers, and the attention they were getting was unrelenting. Louise was in her element because she had never experienced this before, and it felt so exhilarating, so good. Tracey was happy because the drinks were flowing, and even better, they were complimentary, thanks to the company expense accounts of the golfers, who had generously been sending them over, keen to impress.

Carrie had enjoyed a boogie and was having fun, but she was worried about getting up in the morning. She didn't even bother trying to persuade the others to go back because they were drunk and on a mission. Maybe she would sneak off soon, she decided.

Another hour passed and Louise was upset. Fernando had clearly stood her up. Feeling insecure and unwanted, she drowned her sorrows, matching Tracey drink for drink, to the dismay of Carrie, who couldn't handle the out-of-control pair. When a couple of extremely tall Germans came over to chat them up, Louise switched her affections. Maybe a gorgeous German would be better than a silly Spaniard anyway, she attempted to convince herself, and ten minutes later, she was snogging the face off Hans from Heidelberg.

Carrie had had enough, so she excused herself for the loo, then she snuck off, legging it out of the bar and into the street outside. She felt bad for abandoning her friends, but she knew that they would never have allowed her to leave. It was blowing a gale when she got outside into the cold night air, and to her dismay, there were no taxis in sight, so she reluctantly started to trek back to the hotel, just as it started to rain. *Bugger!* she thought. She hated being out so late at night, and especially all alone, but having no choice, she removed her high heels and started to power-walk as fast as she could.

Suddenly, a van full of men screeched up beside her, scaring the life out of her until she heard, "Hey, Carrie. Need a lift?" To her relief, it was David Westwood and the other golfers from her hotel. A relieved Carrie hopped in, thanking them, not caring who he had shagged.

Back at the Sailors Bar, and with Hans preoccupied by having Louise's tongue rammed down the back of his throat, his sidekick Franz tried his luck with Tracey. Unfortunately, he was not as good-looking as his friend, and even though she was extremely drunk, she could still see that he had terrible teeth, a whopper for a snout and a horrendous mullet haircut. His double denim look, with too-short jeans, did nothing to help his allure. She might have been pissed, but she was not that pissed. She decided to take herself off to the loo to find Carrie. She needed her friend to save her from this dreadful German sausage-nosher.

To her bewilderment, Carrie was nowhere to be seen, so she went back into the bar to tell Louise that their friend had gone AWOL. Tracey was unimpressed and hoped that Carrie hadn't snuck back to the hotel and left them there. *What a flippin' goody two shoes*, she thought. But back in the bar, she discovered that Louise had also disappeared. In her place, Franz was now sat on Louise's barstool. Stumped, she looked around for Hans and Louise. "Have they gone for a dance?" Tracey asked him.

"No. They leave. Back to boat. For Sex," he told her very directly in harsh German tones. That had flummoxed her, and she was too stunned to comment. Instead, she knocked back her drink, bid him goodnight and turned to leave. "*Vait!*" he called out loudly. She turned round to see what he wanted. "You vant to come to boat too? We fuck?"

A horrified Tracey retorted, "No, thank you." Then, thinking what a cheeky sod he was, she snapped at him, "And I don't care how big your bloody boat is!" before storming off.

Later that night, Louise tried to sneak into her room without waking Carrie. She failed. "You can stop trying to be quiet; I can hear you," Carrie mumbled, still half asleep.

"I've had sex on a *boat!*" she said excitedly to the drowsy girl, who was far too tired to care.

"Tell me in the morning," she replied grumpily, pulling the pillow over her head to block out the racket from her annoying room-mate.

TWENTY-SEVEN

MISSING IN ACTION

As arranged, at 7.30am sharp, a punctual Janet and Belinda were downstairs in the dining room for their last breakfast before they left. Their suitcases were parked near to their table, and they would be ready to depart as soon as they'd eaten. They still had an hour until the airport shuttle picked them up, so Janet told Belinda she would join her for a full English, seeing that they had a day of travelling ahead. Belinda was pleased that their early start meant she was finally able to get served immediately, without having to queue up behind a gaggle of golfers.

Carrie came up behind them and grabbed a plate to join them, opting to have whatever they were having.

"Where is Louise?" Belinda asked her.

"Don't ask!" Carrie huffed. "She didn't get in until four, then she woke me up."

"Well, I do hope she isn't late; the transportation will be here in an hour," Janet reminded her.

"I know," said Carrie sensibly. "I'm going to go back upstairs at eight to clean my teeth and grab my case, so I'll make sure she gets up."

The trio were seated and about to tuck into their fry-ups. As Carrie put her first bite of bacon into her mouth, they were alarmed to see Amanda come running in, bright red and panting. "We've lost Tracey," she gasped.

"What?" Belinda shrieked. "Where is she?"

"If I knew that I wouldn't be standing here," flapped Amanda. "She hasn't come home from last night."

They all turned to Carrie for the answer. "You were with them last night." said Janet "Where did you go?"

Carrie now felt concerned and guilty that she left them. "They were with two German men, so I left them and came home," she panicked.

"Is Louise back then?" queried Amanda.

"Yes, she's in bed with a hangover. She said she felt too ill to eat breakfast."

Amanda grabbed Carrie's untouched orange juice and glugged the lot thirstily. "I woke up at six and she wasn't back, so I have been out looking for her. I've checked the grounds, the bushes, the pool area and all the lounges." She stopped to catch her breath. "So, I asked reception to check the CCTV and only one person arrived back at the hotel after two o'clock, and they showed me the footage, but that was Louise staggering in at four," she gasped again. "Tracey isn't anywhere. She didn't come back to the hotel at all last night."

Janet was not impressed. "I knew this would happen if you all went out," she said accusingly, Carrie feeling like a child being told off by the headmistress.

Amanda pushed Carrie's plate away from her. "Come on, we need to speak to Louise."

Amanda and Carrie got up, but Belinda did so too, taking charge for once. "Are both your cases packed?" she asked them, with them both confirming that they were. "Right then. Janet, you stay and finish your breakfast, then you bring our two cases and wait in the lounge for the minibus. You two come with me. You pair can get Louise up and go out to find Tracey, and I'll get all the suitcases down to Janet, then I'll check us out." With that, the three women legged it to the lift as Janet stared after them, astounded.

Louise was abruptly awoken from her drunken slumber by Amanda tugging the sheet off her still-clothed body. "*Quickly! Get up!*" she screamed.

"What's happened?" Louise asked groggily. Her head was throbbing, her brain fuzzy, but she could tell this was serious, seeing as she was faced with three angry women staring at her. She quickly sidled out of bed, grabbing the velour tracksuit that she had left out in preparation for the journey, then pulling off last night's dress that she had slept in and shoving it into the side pocket of her suitcase, getting redressed as quickly as she could.

"Louise. Where is Tracey?" Belinda shouted, a new strong, powerful side emerging from her.

"I don't know. I left with Hans, the German, to see his boat." She had to think hard, her memories blurry. "She was with his mate Frank."

"It was Franz! And I didn't like the look of him," Carrie butted in.

Belinda held out her hand to Amanda. "Give me your key," she ordered, then she told them all, "You lot get down to the harbour and find her. I'll get all the suitcases downstairs, then I'll meet you back in the foyer with Janet."

Amanda passed her key to Belinda. "Oh, I forgot. Tracey hasn't even packed yet." Then, they all scarpered from the room before Belinda could react.

Three women ran as fast as they could down to the harbour. Louise was struggling. She wanted to vomit.

"Come on. Hurry up," urged Amanda.

"I'm trying my best," she puffed back.

"This way," Carrie shouted to Amanda, suddenly having a flashback and remembering the route they took and where the Sailors Bar was. In the cold light of day, the venue that had seemed sparkly and glamourous now looked dull, damp and seedy. It was all locked up. "What if she's asleep in the toilets?" Carrie suggested.

"Or dead," Louise said, immediately regretting her words.

"She might be," worried Carrie. "Those Germans might have murdered her."

"Carrie, they are tourists not terrorists!" Amanda sighed at her. "But she could have choked on her own vomit."

"Or fallen into the sea," deadpanned Louise.

They looked at each other in sheer panic, all now convinced that it was the most likely outcome. They ran to the harbour's edge to look over the edge into the deep water, which no longer looked inviting. Continuing towards the boat moorings, they scanned the rippled surface, expecting to see a face-down bloated body floating past. On reaching the boats, they started to shout out her name loudly. "She is probably still fast asleep in one of those," Amanda accused.

"Which one belongs to your German men?" asked detective Carrie.

"Oh err, I don't remember, except it was big and white."

"Great. That rules out about two boats out of hundreds then," Amanda snapped.

They jogged along the harbour, continuing to call out, "Traaaaacey, Traaaaacey," but to no avail. A few owners tutted at them for ruining their early morning meditations. At the end of the harbour, there was an additional owner's jetty, but it was closed to the public, and you needed to swipe a member's card to enter. *Most probably a platinum one*, Amanda thought as she rebelliously clambered over the metal barrier and ran down the private wooden gangway calling out her friend's name. Unfortunately, in less than a minute, she was noticed and escorted off unceremoniously by a smartly dressed, but foul-mouthed, security guard.

"Get out of here," he snarled in a heavy Russian accent. "*Ty che B'lyad!*"

They were utterly frustrated, not to mention worried sick. They simply couldn't find her anywhere. "Janet and Belinda are going to be so mad," Carrie said. "I'm scared to go back empty-handed."

At that comment, Amanda checked her watch. It was 8.10am. "Shit, we have to get back; we've only got twenty minutes before our minibus arrives."

They started to run back to the hotel. Unfortunately for Louise, it was all uphill on the way back, and she was starting to feel even worse. "This is not what I want to be doing with a raging hangover," she groaned.

"It's your own fault. You were the one out boozing with her. You should have kept an eye on her," Amanda panted.

"I don't think Janet and Belinda will be impressed. They're far too old for all this. I feel bad for them," Carrie commented.

"I agree," Amanda panted as they strode purposefully up the hill. "This is going to ruin what has been a lovely break, especially after she has booked the plane for us."

"Oh, bugger off, you two," Louise snapped. "Stop blaming me for what Tracey has done. At least she is having fun, wherever she is," she gasped, attempting to keep up with them. "You lot just need to lighten up!"

Carrie looked upset. "Take no notice," Amanda told her. "She doesn't mean it; she's probably still drunk."

The sombre trio came back inside the hotel. As they were spewed out of the revolving doors and appeared back in the foyer, Janet and Belinda were alarmed to see that they were only three and not four. Amanda held her hands up in despair. "No joy. We couldn't find her anywhere."

Janet was furious. "I'm sorry, ladies, but I am not wasting the private jet. It cost a small fortune and I am *not* travelling back cattle class because of her *debauchery.*"

The others went quiet and glanced at each other nervously as Janet continued, "She's a big girl, so I'm sure she'll be able to look after herself. She will just have to book herself a scheduled flight if she misses this one."

Belinda shook her head at Tracey's behaviour. "I'm with Janet on this one. Tracey is fully aware of what time our flight is."

"And I have to go back today. I've got work tomorrow," Carrie added. "I've had so much time off, what with the funeral and grieving. I've got no more leave left."

The six suitcases stood beside Belinda's leg. "Should we take her suitcase? And passport?" she asked.

"We could take them with us to the airport, and if she isn't waiting there, we'll send them back here with the driver," Janet stated formally. She had suddenly reverted to her strict Margaret Thatcher demeanour. Her holiday clothes were now packed away, and she looked very smart and classy again but cold and detached, in formal mode again. They had pushed her too far with their bad behaviour. She was not impressed.

Amanda looked nervously at her watch again. "The driver must be waiting outside by now," she told the group. "Shall we take the cases out?"

They all went to pick the bags up, except Janet, who stood still, not moving. She was still very angry. Suddenly, a Spanish policeman came rushing in and headed over towards them. Janet quickly took charge of the situation and went to speak to him to, fearing that Tracey had suffered a terrible accident. To the astonishment and bewilderment of the others, the *Guardia Civil* roughly grabbed hold of Janet's arm and swiftly frogmarched her away, behind the reception desk and into the hotel office. The others stood frozen in shock.

Ten minutes later, Janet was still being held in the office, with the hotel manager, the policeman and another member of staff. Through the gaps in the blinds, they saw that their friend was crying. The women huddled together in the lounge, concerned at what on earth could be happening to their friend.

Amanda had organised their suitcases onto the minibus and instructed their driver to give them another fifteen minutes. Belinda was stood at the reception desk, attempting to establish what was wrong. After another five minutes, Belinda returned to the others to break the bad news that Janet was being accused of stealing a necklace from the hotel gift shop. It had happened the day before apparently, whilst Belinda was buying the gift for her neighbour.

"Oh my God," exclaimed Carrie. "It's the one she had on last night. The one I complimented, and she said Charles had bought it for her."

Belinda looked equally worried. "I did see her handling the jewellery when I was buying my doggie doorstopper."

Suddenly, Carrie bolted over to the desk, and the others watched in amazement as she was taken into the office too. They craned their necks to see why Carrie was being so animated. After a few minutes, she rushed back out and requested that Louise would pass her handbag to her, from which she then removed her purse. As she handed her bag back to Louise to hold, she whispered to them all, "Just pretend Janet has got dementia, OK?"

They were all shocked but nodded in agreement. After another few minutes, Carrie had paid for the necklace and she walked out with Janet on her arm, who couldn't look anyone in the eye. She suddenly looked very small and frail. The others were shocked again when Carrie shouted out loudly to them, "I'm just going to get Mother into the minibus. Come along, girls."

Without any hesitation, they all exited the hotel as quickly as they could, scrambling into the waiting vehicle so they could be on their way and far away from the hotel and scary policeman. In the safety of the vehicle, and on their way to the airport, Janet had again chosen to sit in the front with the driver, but this time she had put on a headscarf and her sunglasses, sinking herself down into her seat to go to sleep, or so she pretended. The others were all subdued but mightily relieved that Carrie's clever trick had got Janet off the hook.

The tense journey to the airport was over in no time, and they all clambered out. They were worried about Janet but were also keen to see if Tracey had turned up. She hadn't. Janet remained silent, so they allowed her some space. She was clearly mortified and ashamed.

With everyone settled on board the jet, and the engines warming up, the pilot came out to inform everyone that he was only able to wait for another ten minutes, or they would miss their take-off slot altogether. Tracey's suitcase remained at the bottom of the steps. It was stood waiting by the feet of their minibus driver, who now leant back against his vehicle, hands in pockets, waiting patiently to see if he was going to be returning the suitcase and passport to the hotel. After what had just happened with Janet, they all sincerely hoped that wouldn't be the case.

"Can you really not think where she might have got to?" an exasperated Belinda asked Louise. "Just talk us through your night again, please?"

"Well, I was with a lovely man called Hans who asked me to go for a nightcap on his yacht. I was feeling a bit put out because I was meant to meet Fernando, and he hadn't shown up. I was a bit upset, so I thought, sod him, I may as well go and see what it's like to have sex on a boat." Amanda rolled her eyes, not sure which was worse, her insecurity or her promiscuity. Louise continued, "I wonder if there's a name for that? Y'know, like the mile high club when you do it on a plane."

"Just get on with it," snapped Amanda, seeing the irritation on Belinda's face.

"Well, anyway, I had a session with him." She then laughed, attempting to make a joke, "Just to keep up the EU relationships after Brexit, of course," but she realised that no one was amused so attempted to justify herself, "I really did mean to go straight back to her, but I must have fallen asleep for a while, then by the time I woke up and went back to the bar, it was closed, so I came back to the hotel." She looked round to try to gain forgiveness. "I assumed she had come back to the hotel and was already tucked up in bed."

Belinda sighed. "She is a silly girl, but I hope she learns her lesson after this."

By now, Louise was feeling worse. With all the running round that day, she hadn't had anything to eat or drink all day, so she felt terribly sick. Having missed breakfast, they were all starving, so whilst they waited for take-off and their food to be served, they had to make do with the complimentary mini packets of pretzels and nuts. Marcus, the same male steward that flew them out, now handed out the obligatory champagne, but no one much felt like celebrating. After eating her weight in snacks, Louise had another drink or two. *Hair of the dog*, she thought, and she certainly felt better but had simply topped herself right back up again.

Amanda muttered her disbelief, "Well, that's it then. She has actually gone and missed the bloody flight."

Tracey was obviously a no-show, so the group reluctantly resigned themselves to leaving without her. As the pilot came out to do his final checks, and was about to lock the door, they heard an almighty noise. A local taxi came roaring up to the plane beeping its horn incessantly, then screeching to a halt right at the bottom of the plane's steps.

"It's *Tracey*!" squealed Carrie, her face pressed excitedly up against the tiny oval window. Everyone, even Janet, leapt up to dart over to the nearest window on the port side of the plane to take a look for themselves. They watched as Tracey exuberantly jumped out of the taxi, then spoke to the waiting minibus driver, who had rushed over to her, given her the suitcase and her passport, then pointed at the plane steps and then to his watch, indicating that she only had minutes to get herself onto the plane. He had then climbed back into his own vehicle and driven away.

They expected her to quickly grab her suitcase and leg it on board full of apologies, so they were surprised when she calmly turned around and walked back towards the taxi, where a male companion climbed out. They embraced, kissing passionately. An animalistic guttural scream echoed around the plane as Louise exploded with fury. "It's *my Fernando!*"

TWENTY-EIGHT

JOURNEY FROM HELL

Tracey finally decided to grace them with her presence as she began to make her way up the steps of the jet. She still didn't rush, wobbly and unsteady on her feet, stopping and turning three times to wave goodbye to Fernando who, from the foot of the steps, stood gazing up adoringly at her, blowing kisses in return, until he spotted an irate Louise, glaring intently out of the window at him, mouthing something clearly abusive, her middle finger held up high in furious gesture. He swiftly got back in the cab, and it screeched off again. When she finally staggered inside the jet, she did so grinning like a Cheshire cat, giddy like a teenager. Drunk on love but also still drunk on cava.

As soon as Tracey entered, Louise flipped, flying across the cabin towards her like a savage dog after the postman. Marcus instinctively jumped in front of Tracey to protect her from the crazy lady. "You bitch. How could you?" Louise screamed at her, totally ignoring the poor man stuck in the middle of them. Louise was drunk, the few drinks she'd just consumed on the plane topping her up from the previous night.

Unfortunately for her, Tracey was far worse and still half cut herself. "Why shouldn't I?" she slurred back at Louise, amused as usual by any drama but also too drunk to have any empathy with her friend or to realise she had broken the girl code and gone off with her friend's man.

The commotion even caused Janet to come out of hiding, who now sat up, shocked and concerned that they might be delayed or even thrown off altogether. Her fears were confirmed by the entrance of the concerned pilot. "Do we have a problem here, ladies?"

The two women stopped arguing when they were firmly told by the authoritarian male that they had literally two minutes to sit down, or they would be escorted from the plane. To the relief of the others, they obeyed the captain who, in his smart navy uniform, now looked even sexier when angry, so they swiftly took their places and buckled up like a pair of sulking naughty schoolgirls. The unamused captain abruptly left them, and his cockpit door slammed behind him. Just moments later, the plane's engines roared as it began to slowly manoeuvre along the airfield, seeking its designated take-off lane.

"You're just a drunken slut," Louise whispered not too quietly, so everyone else could hear.

"Yes, that's me! And who's the drunk now?" Tracey retorted defiantly.

A frustrated Louise slung a cushion across the cabin in Tracey's direction, but it bounced off Amanda instead, who pleaded, "Louise, please stop, we'll get thrown off."

Marcus, sitting nearby on the staff pull-down seat, with his hands positioned underneath his thighs in the crew take off position, looked up in alarm. "She's right, madam, the captain will stop the plane if you two don't calm down," he said unconvincingly to the pair of them.

"I only spoke. No laws against that, are there?" Tracey answered him back. Receiving no reply, she realised that her tongue could still be used as a weapon. She turned back to Louise and sniped, "Oh, and by the way, he does know that you pissed yourself!"

The others now gasped in outrage that Tracey, after her already ruining everyone's morning, was now blatantly goading Louise, especially on what was a very sensitive subject.

"You actually told him? How could you?" Louise looked at the others for support. "Can you fucking believe she would do that?" Then she turned back to Tracey. "You absolute spiteful bitch."

Tracey realised that she had overstepped the mark, so she suddenly stopped arguing and pulled the complimentary eye mask over her face to hide behind, muttering, "Sorry. I didn't mean to. I was just drunk."

"You are always drunk, you old soak," an upset Louise snapped, not accepting Tracey's feeble apology.

Unfortunately, her remark had goaded Tracey into reigniting the argument. "How dare you judge me. You're the one who has been misbehaving all week. You've shagged for England. At least I only slept with one man."

"But he was my man. You know how much I liked him," bleated Louise.

"Well, you shouldn't have stood him up then, should you?" retorted Tracey. "And he isn't *your* man. He turned up to meet you, but you had gone off with that lanky sausage-nosher." Louise looked absolutely gutted to hear that Fernando had indeed turned up in the end and that she had missed him, so she huffed in irritation. Tracey continued to rub it in. "I bumped into him when I was about to leave. So, we had a drink together, then one thing led to another…"

"Oh, I bet you loved that, didn't you?" exclaimed Louise.

"Actually, I did. And you were right. He was amazing," Tracey smugly responded.

The others were concerned that the dispute was escalating again, and Carrie, with the very best of intentions, attempted to defuse the situation. "She is just upset, Tracey, that's all. And you did nab her man. You knew she really liked Fernando."

A furious Tracey swung round to face the girl who had dared to criticise her. "That's a bit rich. You nicked my friend's fucking husband. You home-wrecking little slut."

Her harsh remarks immediately shut up an alarmed Carrie, who quicky backed down and then stayed out of it, aware that Tracey had a point. She glanced up at Belinda sheepishly, now ashamed of her past, but Belinda, always beyond kind, charitably shook her head and mouthed to Carrie, "It's fine. Ignore her," and gave her a supportive smile.

Janet had heard enough and now came out of her self-induced bubble to join in the conversation, determined to put a stop to this malarky. "Please stop, you two. I will never be able to use this company again." She tutted and sighed in disapproval at Louise and Tracey, adding, "I'm so glad that Charles isn't here to witness these shenanigans. I am so embarrassed."

An irritated Louise was in no mood to be lectured. "You are?" she shouted at Janet. "Not as much as we were when you robbed the gift shop."

Tracey had no idea what Louise meant by her statement. "She robbed what?" She suddenly cheered up and guffawed at the thought of more drama, especially as it took the emphasis off herself.

The others gasped in shock that Louise had brought this up, especially as Janet was already distraught enough, but it was too late, and she immediately retreated into her cocoon, pulling her eye mask on and her shawl over her head, traumatised, embarrassed again and keen to avoid everyone.

Belinda had heard enough. "That was totally unnecessary, Louise. You know how upset Janet is. Are you forgetting how kind she is and the fact she organised this plane for us?"

And Amanda scold Tracey. "And you too, you ungrateful mare. I was up at six looking for you, then we were trawling all the bars looking for you. We thought you had drowned." With no reply from Tracey, she continued, "We did *everything* we could to find you, *and* we brought your suitcase here."

Tracey now looked ashamed, but she still couldn't let it go. "She started it."

"Yeah, that's right, blame me for everything," butted in Louise.

"Will you children calm down and *behave* yourselves?" snarled an irate Belinda. She was keen to defend and protect a clearly fragile Janet. Her outburst managed to save the day, the group astounded by her demanding and extremely strict voice. No one had ever seen this side of Belinda, but with her being the mother hen of the group, they both obeyed, and the plane finally fell silent. The argument ended.

The steward observed the spectacle from these women, most of whom were the same age as his mother. This was the best entertainment he had had all month. He thought this lot were boring on the way over, but *crikey*, he thought, *they have certainly put the rock stars and boy bands to shame!*

An hour later, they were now up in the sky and halfway home to England. Their sleek jet soared silently above the craggy, bare mountain ranges below that glowed a deep burnt-orange colour beneath the searing midday sun. Janet, still hiding behind her eye mask, remained huddled beneath her blanket and lay with her back to everyone in her reclined seat. They wouldn't hear from her again for the remainder of the flight. Even when Belinda went over later with a cup of tea and tried to gently give her comfort, Janet just took it and whispered to thank her gratefully, but she left it on her side table, then closed her eyes again.

Belinda hated seeing her friend like this. She had discovered that Janet was no Iron Lady after all and more a fragile little bird. It had been a pleasure to see her come out of her shell these last few days, so it was such a shame that their trip had ended like this. This holiday had been such an uplifting experience, one that she had thoroughly enjoyed, and which had given her faith that her future was going to be more fun than her previous few years had been. Now she wasn't so sure. How could the group recover from this? She doubted they would ever go away again. Suddenly, she dreaded getting back to her house. She would be all alone again. Firstly, she had lost her husband, and now it looked like she'd lost her friendship group too.

Carrie peeked over at Belinda. She had watched her take a drink over to Janet. She was such a caring woman. She wished her own mother was as nurturing. She decided to stay quiet for the rest of the flight. What Tracey had said was right. She was a home-wrecking little slut. She couldn't face speaking to Belinda. She felt so guilty. Maybe when she got home, she should start seeing her old friends instead. She didn't belong in this group. She was an intruder.

Amanda looked around the plane at everyone. Just when they had really got to know each other properly, and she had found herself some travel buddies, look what had happened. It was disastrous. *Maybe Belinda, Janet and I should go by ourselves next time*, she thought but doubted that Janet would ever want to do it again, or maybe she should get herself a man to travel with instead. She didn't particularly want one, but she desperately did not want this to be the last adventure that she had.

Louise felt desperately sad. The alcohol was wearing off and her hungry belly rumbled, making her feel nauseous. Why did she go out last night? She would be feeling refreshed and rested by now if she had only behaved and gone to bed early. She would have managed to have a cooked breakfast, and everyone would still be friends, instead of this awful atmosphere. Damn, it was all her own fault. To make matters worse, she only went out in the first place to meet up with Fernando. He must have obviously turned up late. If only she hadn't gone off with that bloody German, then she could have had the pleasure of him again. She secretly kicked herself. Then she thought of him with Tracey, and she was gutted. She really liked him. A lot.

Tracey's eyes were closed behind her mask. She was totally oblivious to anybody else. A satisfied smile spread across her face. She was having flashbacks from the night before. And didn't she well and truly FUCK FERNANDO!

TWENTY-NINE

KISS AND MAKE UP

Back at home, six women were going about their normal lives. They all appeared OK from the outside, but inside, they were not. Each one was equally distraught.

The journey home from Majorca had been awkward. No one had spoken again for the remainder of the flight, each of them worried that any conversation might start another argument. It had been the same in the minibus from the airport to their individual homes. As the driver pulled up outside each house, they would each mutter a polite goodbye, but that was it.

Belinda had wanted to talk to Janet, but seeing as she had chosen to sit up the front with the driver again, it had been impossible. As Janet had departed from the vehicle, Belinda had called out that she would telephone her the next day, and even though she had tried every single day since, her calls were never picked up.

Tracey was dropped off next, getting out as though nothing had happened, but very sleepily, and only muttering a quick goodbye to everyone. They watched as she staggered up her path, the minibus only driving off after the driver had seen that she was safely inside her house. As she watched them drive off, she muttered to herself under her breath as she closed the door, "Boring bastards."

No sooner had she gone, Louise attempted to ask the group, "Do you all agree that was her doing? It wasn't my fault, was it?" But no one was in the mood to hear it.

"Just leave it for now, please. We've all had enough for one day," Amanda had requested, so she returned to silently sulking.

Carrie had been dropped off next, followed by Louise, then Amanda and finally Belinda. Carrie had been polite and had thanked everyone for the trip. Belinda and Amanda nodded in response. "We'll speak soon," Belinda reassured her, but she clambered out feeling both awkward and upset and thinking to herself that was the last time she would ever see them again.

Louise had said goodbye politely when she exited the vehicle but was clearly still sulking that they had not taken her side against Tracey. Unbeknown to the others, she was genuinely upset about Fernando. He was the first man in her entire life that she had felt a deep connection with, failing to realise that it had simply been a case of sheer lust. Now she just wanted to get back into her own house and return to the safe routine of work.

When just Belinda and Amanda remained, they discussed Janet. The Tracey/Louise situation had been awful, but right then, their only concern was that the elder member of the group would be OK. They made a plan that they would give Janet a few days to get over her ordeal, but that Belinda would call her every day to keep an eye on her. They both agreed that maybe the group was just too many women, of differing ages, that were too different, and maybe their late husbands had been the only thing that they had in common after all. Amanda suggested that she and Belinda should meet up in a week when everything had calmed down, but even as they planned it, neither of them felt sure that it would happen. Amanda just wanted to get home and have a relaxing bubble bath in peace and quiet. Belinda just wanted to pick up her dog Hugo and get back into the sanctuary that was her own kitchen.

Over a week had passed and still no one had spoken to each other. Amanda had kept herself busy by organising her house. She felt incredibly guilty for doing so, but she had removed every single item of Christopher's and had sent all his belongings to the local hospice charity shop. It wasn't done with any malice towards him but because she had called an estate agent to come and value her house; therefore, she was ruthlessly decluttering to ensure that her home was at its most attractive for viewings. She also donated an assortment of ornaments, books, old toys of Sophies and some of her own clothing too. She found the process very therapeutic. Clearing out the old and making way for a new chapter. Whatever that would be. She still didn't know what she would do, or even where she wanted to live, and she realised that she had no one close to discuss it with. The only people she wanted to share her news with were all not speaking to each other. She kept going to pick up the phone, but she was unsure that her call would be what any of them wanted and she was wholly convinced that Janet was totally done with them all. She also assumed that there was no way that Tracey and Louise would ever speak to each other again.

She knew that she should've called Louise's estate agency to value her property, rather than her rival's Berrymans, but she hadn't wanted it to seem as though she expected any favours or mates' rates. Amanda had pondered on whether Louise might have thought her call was just an excuse to speak to her, but then she worried that using her competition might upset her even more so. She certainly didn't want to offend her, so maybe she should call her after all.

Carrie kept herself extra busy at work and had even been for a night out with Charlotte, but although her friend had cheered her up slightly, the wine bar and clubbing scene was not her thing. She was an old soul at heart. She wanted a quiet family life and babies. She really missed the widows.

Louise had also thrown herself into work. She had begun to redesign the office with the help of Samantha, finally putting plans into place to update it the way she had always wanted to. Despite being excited by what was now solely her estate agency, she still felt flat. Something was still missing from her life, and it was not her husband.

Tracey had initially been oblivious to her actions, and the devastation that they had caused, but over the next few days, she kept having flashbacks, and she was starting to finally see that she had been out of order. For the first time in her life, she felt remorseful. The women had been good to her, she now realised. She really did care whether she saw them again, but she was sure that she had pushed them too far. She knew that they would never forgive her, and there was nothing that she could do about it. She knew that she just had to accept it, so she sighed sadly and cracked open a bottle.

Janet had never felt so low. She had been on top of the world on holiday, finally letting go of the shackles of her prudish upbringing and her controlling husband. Her inhibitions had been discarded, and she had thoroughly enjoyed herself. Her new confidence had given her the boost to make many exciting plans for her future, but now she had crashed dramatically back down to earth. She was trapped again. How could she go out and face anyone now that everyone knew that she was nothing but a common thief? They must think so badly of her. She was so ashamed of herself. She prayed that people from the golf club wouldn't find out. How could she ever show her face in public again?

Belinda was stood at her kitchen island, baking. She daydreamed about the fact that it was going to be autumn soon, then Christmas. This year would be her first Christmas as a widow. She'd hoped to be spending it with the golf widows, but that wouldn't be happening now. If Janet had cut them all off and no longer wanted to be their friend, and the others had fallen out with each other, how could they possibly return from this?

She was making a banoffee pie, Janet's favourite. She thought of her friend and worried that she might have returned to eating like a sparrow. She couldn't have that. Tipping double the mixture into her mixing bowl, she decided to make two pies, one for herself and one for her friend in need of fattening up. She decided to take it round the next day, seeing as Janet wouldn't pick up the phone, so she'd just have to turn up on her doorstep and give her no choice. After all, that's what Janet had done to her when she was avoiding everyone after Roger had left. That's what friends did, and she had absolutely no intention of losing her posse, not one of them.

The following day, she turned up at Janet's house laden with both a quiche Lorraine and the delicious dessert. She knocked on the door, but there was no answer. Janet's car was parked outside though, so she must be home. Walking around the back of the house, Belinda found her friend sitting dejectedly on a garden bench, throwing crumbs of stale bread to the birds.

Janet looked up, mortified at being caught out. She looked a mess. Not by most people's standards but by her own. She obviously hadn't been to the hairdressers for her regular blow-dry, and Belinda had been right in her suspicions, as a frail-looking Janet looked up at her, pale and drawn, like she hadn't been eating properly.

Belinda was in no mood for any excuses. "Come on, Janet. Snap out of it and put the kettle on."

Not knowing how to respond to the new, determined Belinda, Janet obediently got up and walked towards her kitchen, followed by Belinda. As they walked through the back door and into her kitchen, a silent Janet filled the kettle with water as Belinda put the quiche into her friend's oven. "We are having quiche for lunch, no arguments."

Janet nodded, gratefully. They looked at one another and Belinda enveloped her frail friend into a big bear hug, holding her tight. She was safe. The older lady cried, making Belinda cry too. "It's OK, I've got you," Belinda told her kindly.

An hour later, they sat at Janet's table, having eaten the quiche and drunk the tea. Belinda now served up two enormous portions of banoffee pie. "Thank you so much. I wanted to call you, but I didn't know what to say," Janet offered, trying to explain why she hadn't been in touch.

"I don't care if you nicked the Crown Jewels, you daft bat. You're my best friend." They both started to laugh.

Janet went on to explain why she started her little habit. It was born out of rebellion at Charles and his highly controlling rules. She also promised that the shock of getting caught meant that she had never done it since, nor planned to ever again. They both agreed that what they had was too special to throw away over being embarrassed. None of the women were perfect, but they were perfect for each other. They were a team.

Janet was back in the game. After speaking to Belinda, she felt reassured that only their group knew about what she did and she trusted that none of them would have talked about her or judged her, acknowledging that they would all have her back, and they praised Carrie's quick thinking that saved the day.

Feeling much better, she announced to Belinda that she was going to book herself into the hairdressers on Saturday and that she wanted them all to come to her for lunch that Sunday. It would give her something to do, and it felt good to be needed again. The Sunday Lunch Club was back in business.

Belinda drove off elated, keen to get home as soon as possible to set about the task that Janet had given her: to inform all the others that Sunday lunch was at Janet's, and she expected them all to turn up. No excuses. Her second task, one that she would enjoy even more, was to make desserts for the occasion.

Amanda received the call first and gladly accepted, informing Belinda that she had been on the verge of calling Louise about her house sale, so she was rather glad that she would now have the opportunity to do so in person instead. They both agreed that it would give them something to talk about over lunch if it got awkward, or it could be a distraction if Louise and Tracey started arguing again. She admitted that she was so relieved to hear from her, and she signed off telling her friend that she couldn't wait to see her at the weekend.

Louise acted cooler, still childishly sulking. She informed Belinda that she had been planning to go to the cinema on Sunday but was willing to rearrange, so she would attend. She failed to mention that she had been going alone, and as soon as she put the phone down, she did a little dance in her hallway. She had missed them all so much, but she still dreaded seeing Tracey.

Carrie squealed in delight upon hearing the news that Janet was OK. She had been so worried about her, and once again, she thanked Belinda for being so kind to her.

Tracey answered cheerfully and immediately expressed her pleasure at hearing the invite. Belinda expected her to be the one who might act shirty, but she told an astounded Belinda that she was very keen to apologise to them all, but Louise in particular. Belinda hung up surprised and very impressed. She didn't even sound drunk!

THIRTY

SUNDAY SUNDAE

On Sunday morning, Janet was up, showered and dressed by 7.30am sharp. Major Charles would have been impressed. She didn't have to do it anymore, and she'd certainly not done so in memory of him. In fact, it was the first time for a while that she had actually done so, but today, she was up bright and breezy because she was so excited. She simply could not wait until her house was full again. Full of friends.

She had gotten over her faux pas in Majorca and had finally stopped beating herself up about it.

Her period of self-imposed isolation had seen her googling and studying everything she could on the topic of shoplifting, and she had thoroughly analysed herself to understand what had driven her to behave in such a manner. Now that all the family finances belonged to her, she finally felt in control of her life, and therefore, she had no reason to rebel. She was satisfied that she would never do it again and, reassuringly, she felt confident that she was not a raving kleptomaniac.

By midday, the beef was in the oven, the potatoes and vegetables prepared, and the table laid with fresh flowers picked from her own garden. The free time that she had finally been able to enjoy since Charles's death meant that her garden was now coming along nicely, thanks to the assistance of her new gardener who did the lawn, the trimming of trees and bushes and all the other boring jobs that she was not inclined to get involved with. He left the flowers, hanging baskets and the fun bits to Janet, on her orders.

Janet had rehearsed exactly how she planned to address the group that day, to explain why she had done what she did, but mainly she wanted everyone to address any other elephants that would no doubt be lurking in the room so that they could all put it behind them and return to how they were before. Life was simply too short to hold grudges, and the dramatic departure of their husbands should be a warning of exactly how much.

By 2pm, the women started to arrive, all slightly apprehensive but more excited. Time was a great healer and even Tracey and Louise were both looking forward to burying the hatchet. Luckily for everyone, they were the first two to arrive, both parking at the same time on Janet's smart private avenue and being forced to face one another in the road. Louise took the moral high ground by smiling and offering her open arms to Tracey, who in response leapt into them, thanking her profusely and begging for forgiveness.

"Hey, let's not mention it again," Louise suggested. "Friends before men, I say?" As a pact, they clanged together the bottles of wine that they had brought along, before they bounced into Janet's home, arm in arm, to the relief of the host who would no longer need to use her prepared speech to urge them to be pals again.

Belinda arrived next, followed by Carrie who spotted her struggling to lift the box of desserts from her car, so she rushed over to help, keen to have someone to walk in with, still so unsure of herself and back to being shy again. Janet's front door had been left propped open, so they entered laden with the goodies to find her pouring drinks for an extremely jovial Louise and Tracey, chatting and giggling, so obviously friends once more. It was as though nothing had ever happened.

Carrie put Belinda's box down, then enthusiastically greeted everyone with hugs, before suddenly exclaiming that she had forgotten the flowers that she had brought, so she disappeared again, dashing back out to her car to fetch them. Outside, and now carrying the giant bunch of lilies she had brought along for Janet, she bumped into Amanda. They too gave each other a friendly hug to demonstrate how much they had missed each other; then, before they went in, Carrie quickly informed the latest arrival that Louise and Tracey had made up and were friends again.

"Thank God for that," laughed Amanda. She had brought along a Diptyque Feu de Bois three-wick candle for Janet, one that she had been saving for herself, but now she wanted Janet to enjoy it. After her generous gesture of the private plane, then insisting that they all came for lunch, she certainly deserved a treat.

It turned out that Janet didn't need to make her speech, or address any issues, because they all just got on with it, slipping straight back into exactly as they were before. *There was no need to rake it all up again*, they had all individually thought. They were all just happy to be together and friends once more.

With Amanda, Carrie, Louise and Tracey outside enjoying a pre-lunch champagne in her garden, Janet made room in her fridge for Belinda's goodies. She gasped at the exquisite-looking Key lime pie as Belinda took out six fancy glasses from the other box. "Oooh, what are they?" asked Janet. She had missed being introduced to new flavours.

"Raspberry and white chocolate sundaes. For Sunday lunch," beamed Belinda proudly, knowing that they would be greatly appreciated by all, but especially by Janet.

With the roast beef dinner finished and the sundaes being devoured, Janet finally mentioned the trip, but only to offer that no wonder things had gotten a little crazy, seeing as they had tried to catch up on years of missing out in just a few days.

"Well, I certainly did," admitted Louise. "I'm sorry if I was too much."

"No apologies required," Janet reassured her. "I for one thoroughly enjoyed myself," she laughed, causing them all to burst into floods of laughter too.

"I guess we all needed to go crazy," said Belinda.

"You still haven't yet," joked Amanda. "Maybe next time?" She knew that she might have to wait a very long time to see the day that would happen.

"If anyone needs to apologise, then it's me," offered Tracey. "I do know that my drinking was getting out of hand." No one tried to deny this, so she continued, "I have actually been cutting down a lot, and although I have no plans to stop altogether, I am taking it a little easier."

"Well done, Tracey," Belinda stated in all seriousness. "I'm sure I can speak for everyone to say that we support you, and we are very proud of you."

"If anyone is interested, I've stopped stealing!" Janet astounded them all, but then they saw that she was teasing them, and guffaws of laughter echoed around the table as the day ended on a high.

THIRTY-ONE

FIRST CHRISTMAS

It would soon be Christmas, their first without their husbands, but thankfully, they would not be alone as they were all back to being the best of friends, so at least they still had each other.

Everyone had long forgotten about Majorca. Tracey and Louise had been able to laugh about it, vowing to never go after the same man again. In fact, Tracey had gone back to being uninterested in men altogether and had resumed her painting, finally enjoying her craft once more, which was a blessing seeing as she was actually a very talented artist.

Louise still very much liked men and had recently started to date Steve the window cleaner, much to the surprise of the town gossips, whose raised eyebrows indicated that they either didn't approve of the swift manner in which she had replaced her husband or the fact that he was ten years younger than her. She had no plans to do anything silly though, confessing to

277

Samantha that she did not see him as a long-term partner and was actually starting to get a little bit bored of him, his physical attributes being the only thing that still held her interest. "He is a bit thick, bless him," she confided.

Carrie was still resolutely single. She had been working exceptionally hard, putting in many hours of overtime at work, keen to get a promotion so that she could earn extra money to have more experiences like the holiday that she had just enjoyed with the others. Apart from that, nothing exciting had happened to her. Charlotte had tried unsuccessfully to fix her up a few times, sending her a stream of photos via WhatsApp, all of handsome, available men, but she was simply not interested. It would be a long time before she fell in love again.

Amanda had cancelled the other estate agent. Louise, who was now handling her property sale, for mates' rates of course, had already organised the photographs and the floorplans, and it was due to be marketed in January, immediately after the festive holidays. A new year and a new start beckoned for her. She figured whatever that might entail, it would surely be more fun than the last few years that she endured with Christopher.

Janet had finally begun her golf lessons, and she was rather good, if she said so herself. Even her coach had informed her that she had a natural talent. She had also started going out to the cinema every Saturday evening with Burt her loyal gardener. There was nothing romantic between them though, just pleasant companionship, with him preferring widowers to widows!

The baker was in her element. Standing at her kitchen island, Belinda cheerfully sung along to Christmas carols on the radio as she got to work on making the desserts for the big day. Six weeks ago, she made a traditional Christmas pudding, complete with hidden sixpences, which now sat slowly maturing in her larder, but right now, she was making profiteroles and a winter berry cheesecake. Both Carrie and Amanda had dropped hints that they didn't really like Christmas pudding or mince pies, so she would hate anyone to not have the choice of a couple of her offerings. Even though the women always took it in turns to cook, every single week now Belinda made the desserts, and she refused to have it any other way. After experiencing her delights, none of the others would even dare to try and compete.

They had all taken their turn to cook lunch over the previous Sundays, except for Louise who had insisted on walking them down to her local pub, but Christmas Day now fell when it was Janet's turn to host again. Fortunately, she was only too happy to oblige, much to the relief of the others. The fact that she had the biggest and grandest house also suited the occasion, so when she requested that Belinda escort her to midnight Mass on Christmas Eve, Belinda thought it was the least she could do for her generous, caring friend.

There was a chill in the air that evening when Belinda arrived to collect Janet for church. It wasn't really her thing, but Janet had specifically asked that she take her, so she was more than happy to accompany her friend. Besides, what else did she have to do that night? Much to her surprise, she found that she thoroughly enjoyed it, but whether it was the setting, the carols or simply the time of year, it was far more emotional than either of them anticipated.

Afterwards, Belinda dropped Janet back home, using the visit to deliver the puddings in readiness for their Christmas lunch. Having stored them all in the fridge, the two women now sat in Janet's kitchen nursing a late-night cocoa to warm themselves up from the cold dampness of the chapel.

"That was so emotional," Belinda said as she dabbed away a tear.

"Are you OK?" Janet asked, concerned.

"Oh, ignore me, I think I am getting sentimental because it's Christmas. I'm not missing Roger, but I do miss my Max. It's a shame he can't get back to England for Christmas, but he has a gig on Boxing Day." She sighs sadly. "No doubt Amanda will be feeling the same," she added. "Her Sophie is still away. She has to work over Christmas so she can save up for her next flight."

"Well, at least you have us," consoled Janet, as they bade each other goodnight.

On Christmas morning, they each got dressed up, all keen to make an extra effort with it being the sacred day. It was not just another Sunday lunch, and they were all aware of the significance of it, with it being their first Christmas as widows. Although they were very angry with the men for their deceit over the competitions, they had since calmed down. It was very difficult to remain resentful to a dead person.

All of them prepared to bring along Christmas presents, each feeling like Santa with five gifts to distribute. Amanda had bought everyone an Emma J Shipley candle, each in a different but exquisitely decorated china jar. She hoped that they realised how expensive they were. Her choice in candles was not what you could pick up in TK Maxx for a tenner.

Louise had gone for Liberty designer scarves, each with a different pattern to suit her friends' individual styles. She had taken great care to select colours that each woman tended to wear.

Belinda had bought them all books, and although they suited each woman's hobbies and lifestyles, she now doubted herself, thinking that it might be a boring choice of gift.

Carrie had bought them all tickets to see *Mamma Mia* in London in February. She thought it would be a good excuse for them to have a weekend away together, and more importantly, she knew that it would make Belinda happy.

Tracey had only thought about it at the very last minute. She had been out drinking with her cousin all afternoon, so she'd been rather tipsy and she'd done what men often did when they came out of the pub at 5pm on Christmas Eve. She'd dashed at the last minute into the nearest department store and grabbed perfume. Five bottles of perfume. "All the same to save any favouritism," she told the woman on the counter, but the truth was she was too drunk to deliberate on who would like what, and after all, what woman doesn't love Chanel No. 5?

Janet was ready. Her home was as welcoming as she was. A festive wreath of mistletoe and holly adorned the front door, which she personally opened to greet each one of her guests. She embraced them all warmly, then they gathered in her kitchen which smelt of the roast turkey, almost cooked to perfection in her new fancy La Cornue cooker, purchased with the proceeds of one of Charles's insurance policies.

With everyone present, they made a toast with the champagne that Janet had pre-chilled for their arrival. They had all had an eventful year, and the fact they shared this experience meant a lot, with them all having sincere empathy with one another. After saying a few kind words about their departed husbands, they declared their fondest wishes for each other to find fulfilment, love and happiness.

The prawn cocktail starter was already prepared, so Janet handed two each of the six crystal glass dishes to Carrie, Louise and Tracey to set down on the dining table. They gasped in awe at the effort that Janet had gone to, both in decorating the table and the room. Her taste was traditional, old-fashioned even, but the atmosphere was warm and there was nowhere any of them would rather be. Amanda carried in bottles of wine, one red and one white, with Belinda and Janet following behind her. As they took their seats, Janet wished her guests a very Merry Christmas but insisted that no gifts were to be opened until after lunch.

When the turkey was ready, Belinda and Janet returned to the kitchen so that Belinda could carve the big festive bird for her. Janet had never known how to, seeing as it was the only kitchen-related job that Charles had ever helped her with. He had always insisted that it was the man of the house's job to carve the meat. He did also open jars for her, but only because if he didn't, then he wouldn't have been able to enjoy his beloved marmalade or mustard, seeing as his frail wife was simply not strong enough to do it herself.

The two women chatted happily as they prepared the lunch, giggling when they heard a Christmas cracker being pulled and Tracey cackling out loudly as she boisterously read out a classic old joke from the paper slip that dropped out when she'd won the tug-of-war battle.

"It's ready – come and get it," Belinda called out to everyone, popping her head comically through the 1970s serving hatch. Janet had laid out a buffet in her kitchen so that they could all help themselves and the dining table wouldn't be too cluttered with the various dishes of potatoes, vegetables and all the trimmings. The women enthusiastically traipsed in, lining up to load their plates, no one worrying about calories on this special day.

Back at the table, they took Tracey's lead, jovially putting on the paper hats and getting in the spirit, reading out naff jokes from the crackers and then getting excited at the silly gifts of nail clippers, mini packs of playing cards and bottle openers.

After a gratifying lunch, they all needed a hiatus before they even contemplated Belinda's desserts, especially as she never allowed anyone to just try one, so they retired to Janet's formal lounge, all satisfied, with very full tummies. Ever the perfect host, she had prepared an open fire, whilst an enormous real fir tree stood majestically in the corner of the room, adorned with extravagant baubles that clearly cost a packet.

With Christmas songs playing subtlety in the background, they began to hand out the gifts to one another, all expressing their thanks, touched by the thought that had gone into them. Janet was last to distribute hers. They were amazed, embarrassed even, at the expense that she had gone to. Tracey was given a set of very expensive wooden paint brushes complete with a vintage wooden palate. Louise was presented with an oil painting that she had admired in Majorca, totally unaware that Janet had sneakily purchased it after she had left the shop, discreetly slipping the merchant her home address to post it on to.

Carrie was astounded when she unwrapped hers to discover a Mulberry handbag, just like the fake one that she had wanted to buy on holiday, but this was the real deal, the real McCoy. The young girl burst into tears, having never been given such an extravagant gift, but mainly feeling emotional that Janet obviously cared enough about her to do such a thing. Janet apologised that she did not yet have the gifts ready for Amanda and Belinda, explaining that they were something that she'd had to order. The two women were puzzled as to what it could possibly be, but Janet also informed them that her neighbours, the Smiths, would be delivering the gifts shortly as she had also invited them over to join them all for a drink.

The day continued as they all sat around relaxing in Janet's lounge, telling tales of Christmases past, ones that they had enjoyed, or not, from when they were children, to previous years, sharing recollections of good ones and bad ones, with most of them telling funny stories of disasters whilst attempting to cook turkeys.

Another hour passed before the doorbell rung, and when it did, Janet requested that Belinda and Amanda be kind enough to go and let the Smiths in and help them carry in their presents. The two ladies obediently got up, wondering what on earth she had bought them that would require help to lift into the house. The others were also extremely eager to find out what gift Janet could have possibly got for their friends that could either be that big or so heavy. Their curiosity was made even greater when they heard Belinda scream out loud from the hallway, followed by Amanda doing the same. Janet remained seated, smiling serenely. The others all shot up from their chairs and ran out to see what the commotion was all about.

Standing in the hallway was Belinda, clinging onto her son Max and Amanda hugging her daughter Sophie tightly. Both women had tears of joy streaming down their faces. Janet had arranged flights for them, swearing them both to secrecy. Both offspring had pretended to be too busy to come home, purely to be able to surprise their mothers, and it was all set up, and paid for, by Janet, determined to get them home, knowing how much it meant to her friends. It was the best gift they had ever received.

With the youngsters settled in, they all returned to the warm lounge where Max and Sophie were provided with belated Christmas lunches served casually on trays for their lap. After travelling all day, they gratefully and hungrily wolfed down their dinners, as the widows eagerly waited to listen to stories of their travels and adventures.

The sight of Max resembling Roger so much affected Carrie. Already feeling emotional after a lovely day and a touching present, the sight of him caused all her memories to come flooding back. She was already tipsy from drinking champagne all day, but now she started to knock back even more, keen to calm herself and to stop herself from crying. With everyone in high spirits and the attention on Max and Sophie, no one noticed that Carrie was getting absolutely sloshed.

After a while, she excused herself for a loo break and on her way back, nipped into the kitchen to top up her glass, where she discovered, to her disappointment, that the champagne had run out, so she came back and popped her head around the lounge door to tell Janet that they had run out of champagne and to enquire if she had any Prosecco. "No Prosecco, dear, but there are a few more crates of champagne down in the cellar."

Carrie looked alarmed at the thought of going down to a cellar, so Janet, seeing the panic on the girl's face, asked Max if he would do the honours and fetch a box up for them.

Max emerged from the cellar and carried the box straight to the kitchen where he unpacked it, placing one bottle in an ice bucket, then stacking the other five into the wine cooler fridge. He looked around to let Carrie know that they were now restocked, but she was nowhere to be seen, so he went into the lounge with the chilled bottle, expecting her to have sat back down, but she wasn't there. Regardless, he topped up all the ladies' glasses, before returning to the kitchen where he grabbed a fresh glass and poured himself one too. He turned round to put the now half-empty bottle back into the ice bucket when he suddenly spotted Carrie through the kitchen window. She was outside, sitting on the garden bench crying.

Alarmed at the prospect of facing a repeat of her hysteria from the funeral, he quickly grabbed the glass that he had just filled with the cool, bubbly liquid for himself. Then he gentlemanly took it out to her. As he approached her, she attempted to disguise the fact that she was crying, but he kindly told her, "It's OK, we've all been there," handing her the drink. Then, he sat down beside her and looked up at the full moon at which she gazed intently. "You still miss him, don't you?" Max asked, regarding his father.

Carrie shrugged, unsure whether she even did anymore. "I just feel so lonely sometimes."

"Yeah, I know what you mean…" Max nodded back in empathy. "But he wouldn't want you to be sad. He'd want you to get on with your life. To be happy."

Carrie began to cry again and rested her head on his shoulder.

"Shush. It's all gonna be OK," he reassured her, leaning in towards her and stroking her head affectionately, meant as an entirely platonic gesture, but as he did so, he smelt her hair, her perfume smelling so good, and it ignited something in him.

In return, Carrie felt the manly shoulder that her head lay on. She nuzzled her face into his soft cashmere jumper, enjoying the closeness and the comforting security of masculinity. Realising that they had gotten too close, Max went to move away, but Carrie had other ideas. Swept away by the moment, and the bravado of the drink, she grabbed him, then kissed him.

Max was alarmed, aware of where they were, and he leapt up. "I am so sorry, Carrie. Maybe we're both a bit too emotional tonight," he apologised, even though it was actually her kissing him.

She too jumped up, and went to speak, but Max pulled her to the side of the house and away from the kitchen window, mortified that they might have been seen. "Careful, they'll see," he warned. He expected her to calm down, to be embarrassed of her mistake, but she didn't. Instead, she pushed him up against the wall, and she kissed him again, this time more urgently and passionately. To his surprise, he kissed her right back. Feeling incredibly guilty, he suddenly stopped to remind her, "Carrie, stop. I'm *not* Roger," he told her firmly, not wanting to take advantage of the distressed girl, with him being a decent man and nothing like his father in character.

"And I'm *soooo* glad you aren't," she replied, brazenly staring him in the eyes, letting him know that it was him that she desired, not the memory of his dead dad. Then, she passionately kissed him again.

THIRTY-TWO

CHRISTMAS KISSES

After the most passionate embrace that either of them had ever experienced, Carrie dragged Max into the nearby summer house. The glass windows steamed up against the cold winter's night as, on Janet's wicker chaise longue, they had animalistic, electric sex. Desperate, quick and frantic. Before either of them could catch their breath, they suddenly realised the enormity of what they had just done, and more so, remembering where they were.

Carrie suddenly sobered up. "*Shit!*" she exclaimed, rapidly getting dressed. "How did this just happen? Your mum has forgiven me for Roger. I can't do it again to her. I'm so sorry." Then, without looking at him again, she dashed off in the direction of the house.

"Carrie. Wait," he tried to call her, but she was gone. A gobsmacked Max also quickly dressed whilst trying to gather his own thoughts. Suddenly concerned that his absence might be noticed, he too returned inside, but back in the house, he remained in the kitchen. Carrie was nowhere to be seen so he began tidying up plates and glasses in order to give himself an excuse to have been away for so long.

Unheard by him, Janet entered, and at seeing him doing his good deed, she fondly scolded him, making him jump out of this skin in the process. "You *naughty* boy!" she shouted out loud. He spun around in alarm. "You are meant to be my guest. Come and sit back down with your mother." She hooked arms with him and returned him to the lounge, where she informed Belinda, "Guess what I caught your naughty son doing?"

Carrie had slipped in beforehand and was sat huddled in the corner chatting to Sophie, deliberately attempting to blend into the background. Her head shot up in panic at what she was witnessing.

"This naughty boy was tidying and cleaning the kitchen, bless him," Janet continued, to Carrie's immense relief.

"He doesn't do that at home," joked back Belinda. Carrie observed her friend gazing at her son proudly and felt tremendous shame for the carnal act that she had just committed. First her husband, and now her son. How could she have betrayed this wonderful woman, and twice?

What sort of a slut are you? she secretly berated herself.

Carrie suddenly felt sick. She couldn't even look in Max's direction, so she discreetly slipped out, then rushed towards the bathroom. Safely inside, she splashed cold water onto her face. What on earth had she done? Whilst she knew that Max wouldn't tell a soul, and would no doubt be going off abroad again soon, she felt such shame at having her first one-night stand, if you could even call the brief sexual encounter that, but more so at betraying dear Belinda. Again.

After a while, a flush-faced Carrie came out of the bathroom, bumping smack bang straight into Belinda, who was patiently waiting to go in next. Upon seeing the state of Carrie, she was genuinely concerned. "Are you OK?" She reached out protectively to hold her arm. "You look a bit peaky. Aren't you feeling very well?"

Carrie could hardly look her in the face. "I, err, I feel a bit sick," stuttered a flummoxed Carrie.

"Oh, you poor thing, Let's get you a glass of water," said Belinda, leading her to the kitchen.

The room was spinning for Carrie. She must get away. "I think I'll call my cab now," she spluttered.

THIRTY-THREE

HAPPY NEW YEAR

Carrie had beaten herself up every day since Christmas. What should she do? Confess? The widows were back to being the best of friends again, stronger than ever, so she did not want to upset anyone, especially the kindest one of all, Belinda. Selfishly, nor did she want to lose what she had with them all, but how could she face them now, knowing what she had done? She felt so deceitful keeping her dirty little secret, but she must keep it inside. Surely if she admitted it, it would cause even more damage.

It had only been six days since she saw last them, but tonight she would have no choice but to face everyone again because it was New Year's Eve. The host for tonight was Belinda. *Of all the houses*, she thought to herself as she got dressed for the occasion. She couldn't even get out of it by pretending to have other plans because they had already discussed it over Christmas lunch, when she had admitted to everyone that she usually stayed in on New Year's Eve, immensely disliking that particular night of the year, finding it utterly depressing. Being the lovely people that they all were, they had made her promise that she would come along regardless, and they told her that they would cheer her up, so she had accepted the invitation. But that was before the Max incident, and besides, if she didn't go tonight, she would end up putting it off forever.

It was 7.15pm. Turning up late, she was the last to arrive. She nervously knocked on Belinda's door, preparing herself for what she would say to her when she opened it, having practised beforehand how to act so that she would appear normal and not the monster that she was. Getting no answer, she rung the bell this time, the twenty seconds it took to open seeming like an eternity to the anxious girl.

Finally, it opened, and nothing could have prepared her for what faced her. Max stood grinning at the door. The sight of him took her breath away. "Don't worry, I'm not staying," he whispered to her. He seemed amused by the situation, as he stood back and gentlemanly allowed the trembling girl to enter.

A flustered Carrie walked past him and headed straight into the kitchen where she handed a large purple hyacinth plant to Belinda, trying her best to appear casual. Her choice of flowers, signifying forgiveness and regret, did not go unnoticed by clever Janet.

The others were already there, excited for the night ahead, all in jolly moods exchanging gossip. "Are you better, dear?" Janet asked, examining the girl thoughtfully, seeing as she appeared to not be herself.

"Oh, I'm fine now, thank you," Carrie replied, trying to sound casual, then she deliberately changed the subject, turning to ask Tracey, "How's the painting coming along?"

The women were all still having drinks in the kitchen when Max entered the room to ask his mother, "Have you seen my denim shirt, Mum?"

Belinda, the dutiful mother that she was, took a freshly laundered and immaculately pressed shirt from out of the adjoining utility room and handed it to her handsome son. "Give me that one you've got on then, and I'll wash that as well." The others laughed fondly at her fussing over her precious son.

"No wonder he decided to stay home for another week," laughed Amanda.

Max obediently pulled off the shirt that he was wearing and replaced it with the freshly laundered denim one. Carrie took one look at his bare chest and immediately felt herself blushing, aware of the effect he was having on her. Janet noticed and watched her, deep in thought.

With Max leaving to go out and meet his friends, the women retired to relax in Belinda's lounge. They had already decided that an informal night was called for after the extravagance of Christmas. Belinda had made a huge pan of chilli con carne, so it was going to be bowls on laps when they got peckish later. She had also thought that Max might need a midnight snack when he got home later, and chilli was his absolute favourite.

Everyone relaxed as they sat around the large oak coffee table that was now cluttered with wine glasses, chocolates and various nibbles, with the women all discussing their plans for the forthcoming year. Louise had nipped to the bathroom and returned sniffing her hands as she rubbed in some hand lotion. "The toiletries in your loo smell divine," she told the host, who laughed, admitting, "They were a recommendation from Amanda, and now that all our money isn't being spent on golf, I thought I would treat myself." Belinda then regretted that she had said something so negative, so she immediately apologised, "Oh, I really shouldn't have brought that up again, should I? I am so sorry."

"It's certainly been an eventful year," Janet responded. "And talking of golf, I have some interesting news."

The others expected her to tell them how her golf lessons were getting on, but she astounded them by adding, "About Thailand." The room fell silent as they all looked up, intrigued. "As you know, we all had to sort out the men's business affairs… I have been waiting for months to hear about a mysterious property that one of Charles's businesses owns. It appears that it is the villa in Thailand that we stayed at twice a year. I've discovered that it actually belonged to us all along."

"*What?*" shrieked Tracey, echoing the thoughts of the others.

"Charles had told me that they were going to stay at a different villa to our usual one, but it turned out that they were going to the exact same one. He must have lied because he didn't want me to get suspicious or for me to find out that we owned it."

"But I don't understand? Why on earth would he keep that from you?" Belinda was confused.

Janet explained, gobsmacking the women, "I found his instructions in black and white, as well as several love letters from his lover."

"*Noooo!*" went the gasps around the room, Carrie feeling uncomfortable that mistresses were about to be the topic of conversation.

"Who the hell is she?" Amanda asked angrily.

Janet gave a simple one-word answer: "Johnny."

The whole room was in shock. The silence of the flabbergasted women was broken by Tracey. "Oh my God! That is *hyst-er-i-cal*," she cackled her head off. "The major, queer?"

Belinda glared at Tracey for being so insensitive, but thankfully, Janet was not at all upset. "That's right, Tracey," Janet stated matter-of-fact. "Johnny the pool boy from our villa. The one who Charles went off with every afternoon to play golf."

"No wonder you hardly ever had any rumpy-pumpy then," Louise commented, turning the subject to sex as usual.

"Clearly," said Janet. "Apparently, he was going to leave Johnny the villa, but he hadn't got round to changing his will. Or maybe he planned to run off one day and live there with him?" She shrugged.

Belinda reached out for Janet's hand. "I'm so sorry, Janet."

Carrie stayed quiet. She felt even worse, wondering how Belinda broke the news to everyone about her and Roger.

"Please don't be, dear," Janet assured Belinda. "I'm *so* over that now. I will not be grieving for Charles Cavendish a moment longer."

"Good on you, Janet," piped up Amanda cheerfully.

Janet retrieved a pack of photographs from her handbag, passing them around. They were of the Thai villa. It was absolutely stunning. "Furthermore, it now belongs entirely to me," Janet smiled excitedly. "And I am inviting you all to join me there in January." Then she sat back calmly and waited expectantly.

"Wow. That's fantastic. I've always wanted to go to Thailand. Thank you *so* much." Amanda was the first to accept, having been desperate to visit for quite a while.

"Yes!" chorused both Louise and Tracey in unison.

Belinda looked shell-shocked. "I don't know what to say, but congratulations on your new holiday home."

"Just say yes," laughed Janet.

Then they all turned to look at Carrie, who almost burst into tears. "I don't know if I can," she said, trying to get out of it, believing that she did not deserve to go with them.

"Why not?" Tracey, blunt as ever, demanded.

"I'm really busy at work, and I have so much on my mind at the moment."

"You have to," pleaded Amanda. "It'll do you good, and maybe you should be the one who misbehaves this time? Finally move on from Roger?"

Carrie looked awkward, mortified by the topic of conversation. Janet sensed that there was more to Carrie's upset than met the eye so she rescued her, telling everyone that they could all sleep on it and discuss it the following week over lunch.

"I have a question," Belinda queried. "What are you going to do about the pool boy? He can't stay, surely?"

"I've already sorted it," Janet explained. "I really don't want to have to face him, so he's been generously paid off, and a new job has been arranged elsewhere for him. I don't blame him, the poor lad. He's probably a victim himself."

"You're very kind, Janet. You always do the right thing," Belinda said approvingly. Carrie saw that they both were.

"It also explains something else," Janet chirped up, keen to divulge more… "Why I once caught him wearing my nightie!"

Belinda covered her face with her hands in shock as the others erupted into fits of laughter, Janet most of all.

"Fancy that of Major Charles. And to think I was always rather frightened of him," admitted Belinda. "I wish I'd known. I would have just imagined him in it." She laughed out loud, joining in with the others' fits of giggles.

"That's a sight I *don't* want in my head," added Louise in jest.

By the time midnight came round, Carrie had downed rather a few too many glasses, needing the alcohol to help her relax and appear back to normal.

Suddenly, Tracey jumped up. "Come on, it's that time." She grabbed the TV remote and turned up the volume, then she urged them all up onto their feet. "Ten, nine, eight, seven…"

They were all in high spirits as they saw in the new year together, the chimes ringing out from the TV, courtesy of good old Jools Holland, as they hooked arms and sung 'Auld Lang Syne' out loud.

They had just began to exchange post-midnight hugs and kisses, when they were unexpectedly joined by the arrival of Max.

"What are you doing here?" exclaimed a delighted Belinda.

"I wanted to see the new year in with you, of course," he told his mother, pulling her in close for an enormous hug. One by one, the widows all greeted him with a new year kiss and a hug. Last of all, he went over to Carrie. Their hug was far briefer than all the others, both keen to avoid anyone suspecting what they did, but he did manage to whisper, "Happy New Year, Carrie," to her as he kissed her cheek, causing her to melt upon hearing his voice.

She wished desperately that he would go back abroad as soon as possible, not sure how she could contain herself any longer when he was around. She had never felt anything like this before. Unable to cope in his presence, and worried sick that someone would notice, Carrie told a fib to her friends, "I promised my parents that I would pop in and wish them Happy New Year on my way home, so I really should be off so that I can catch them before they go to bed." She needed to get away from him.

"Party pooper," screamed out a drunken Tracey.

"Oh, that's a shame," Belinda said, but she totally understood that her parents would want to see her, even if she wasn't that close to them. "Shall I order you a taxi?"

Janet had a better idea. "Max, I don't suppose you would mind running Carrie to her parents' house, would you? Seeing that you've only just turned your engine off and you haven't been drinking? They only live five minutes away and the taxis are charging triple rates tonight."

Max managed to act casual. "Yeah sure. Come on, then," he beckoned to her.

Carrie was traumatised, but she couldn't get out of it without causing suspicion. She didn't know how, but she managed to walk across the room without her legs buckling. She kissed everyone goodbye and walked out to the car where Max waited for her, secretly chuffed at Janet's intervention. Truth be told, he had only come back to the house early to see Carrie again, having not being able to get her out of his head since Christmas Day. They drove off, with Carrie giving him directions, unable to even look at him.

As they drove down a quiet country lane, Max pulled over in all innocence. "Carrie, I've been wanting to speak to you. Don't you think that we should at least talk about what happened?"

Carrie looked up at him, with her big, sad, brown puppy-dog eyes and went to speak, but no words could come out. Before she knew it, she was kissing him again.

THIRTY-FOUR

DREAMS CAN COME TRUE

It was a brand-new year and six new lives had already begun.

Amanda had joined Janet and the others in Thailand, and it was everything that she had ever dreamed of and more. The delicious food, the fantastic massages and sense of freedom she felt inspired and elated her. It had certainly made her mind up about what she wanted, needed, to do in the next chapter of her life. Immediately after she had returned home, she had handed in her notice at work, taken her house off the market and had arranged for Louise to rent it out instead of selling it. Then she went off travelling.

Janet had offered that for any visits home, there would always be plenty of spare bedrooms available at her home, for both Amanda and her daughter. Sophie had just come to the end of her own travels, so Amanda had paid for her girl to fly over to Rio de Janeiro, and she had joined her there. Together, they planned to explore the whole of South America, in style, on a mother-and-daughter adventure. Amanda was going to use the time to finally write her book.

Louise had dumped Steve the window cleaner. He'd been getting a tad too clingy lately, expecting to see her every night, and even worse, he was constantly turning up early in the hope that he would get his dinner cooked each evening. It had really got on her nerves and was 'as bad as being married again', she complained to Samantha.

He still cleaned her shop windows though, and they had managed to remain friends. She and Samantha now wanted to snigger rather than lust after him when he turned up every Monday morning in his double denim to swish his silver wand across the huge panes of glass of their shopfront. She wasn't that mean though, so as soon as they heard the clanging sound of his metal bucket and ladders arriving, Louise would always use that time to nip into the back office and catch up with paperwork, hiding herself away until after he had finished.

She had begun to update the office and make changes to the business, improving it greatly. Samantha had been a great help, and with such inspirational ideas, Louise had sold her half of the business. They were now officially fifty-fifty partners. Louise knew that Samantha had planned to open her own estate agency one day, and she was wise enough to know that she would be far too dangerous as her competition. Working together, they were a force to be reckoned with, and their estate agency remained as the finest in town and would now, without doubt, continue to be so.

With the help of a partner who pulled her weight

instead of being off on a golf course all the time, their business was flourishing, and she was finding more time for herself, which was just as well, as she planned to be busy. Following an appointment with Janet's doctor, she'd managed to resolve her embarrassing problem, giving her a new-found confidence, so she'd downloaded a couple of dating apps, and her spare time was now spent excitedly swiping away, like a kid in a sweet shop, and she certainly had a sweet tooth! She was determined to thoroughly enjoy herself before she ever contemplated settling down again.

Janet was the happiest she had ever been. She didn't bother swapping her big house for a little cottage in the end, seeing as she had ample funds to pay for it now, and having her gardener and good friend Burt to assist her meant that she was easily able to manage it with his help. Her grand house was also the favourite meeting point for the girls. 'Widows HQ' Tracey had jokingly called it.

She also had a new companion. He was a little pug that Carrie had sent her a photo of from the local rescue centre. As soon as the photo had pinged up on her phone, of the little chap looking all abandoned in the centre, she'd got straight in her car and rushed over there to collect him. She hadn't needed to go car shopping either, because she'd purchased Amanda's smart convertible that she'd always admired, and which Amanda had sold to her before she left to go travelling.

It turned out that the little dog was four years old and named Dougie or 'Doug the pug' as he would be forever affectionately referred to by the others. His previous owner, an elderly lady, had sadly died. Janet took one look at him and, without any hesitation, had agreed to adopt him on the spot. She thought she had saved him, but they had actually rescued one another.

She was also now a fully paid-up member of the golf club and had joined the Senior Ladies' B Team. She wasn't the best player, still needing to catch up, but she thoroughly enjoyed it, and she went back to the old club now twice a week, once for a lesson, then to play with her team every Friday. They never did win any competitions though! To her surprise, she was getting lots of attention from admirers, one of whom was a distinguished-looking widower called George who was taking her to the theatre the following week. Life was finally fun.

Tracey had behaved herself in Thailand. She still drank more than anyone else, but she had cut back and calmed down, much to the relief of her friends. After Thailand, she had returned to Majorca a couple of times to check out different resorts and had viewed several apartments, finally deciding to buy one in the same resort that they had visited the year before. Louise had sold her house for her, and she had swapped her four-bedroom detached house in Seale for an easy-to-manage, one-bedroom lock-up-and-go apartment in Guildford; then she'd purchased a deluxe sea-view penthouse apartment on her favourite Spanish island. She planned to spend her time living between the two properties.

The foreign pad had three double bedrooms, so there would be plenty of room for all her friends to visit whenever they desired. Between her flash Majorcan pad and Janet's swanky Thai retreat, the women had plenty of excuses to get away together. Right now, she was thoroughly enjoying life in España. She was up on her spacious rooftop terrace, her sturdy wooden easel stood waiting for her daily creation. Her location, and the choices of stunning scenery around her, greatly inspired her. She painted every single day when she was out there, improving all the time. Unbeknown to everyone, she had a secret plan to host her own exhibition on the island once she had enough of her work completed, and she wanted to hold it when all of her friends were visiting. She was keen to surprise them, and she wanted her friends of be proud of her.

By her side sat the love of her life, Spanish, smooth and chilled. She reached out, ready for her daily treat. It was a bottle of *cava!* And she enjoyed a whole bottle daily, whether she needed it or not.

Later that day, she would be joined by another Spanish friend. Fernando. What the others didn't know wouldn't hurt them, she reckoned. She was enjoying a blissful love affair with her experienced and skilful Spanish hunk who, in return, was besotted by her, his 'crazy English lady'.

However, he had been told very firmly that whenever any of the widows set foot on Spanish soil, he must disappear completely, with her explaining to him, "They wouldn't approve. Boring bastards!"

Belinda had finally done it. She was the proud director of 'Artisan Catering', suppliers of fine food and desserts for private parties and special occasions. Three months in and her cakes were already renowned across her county, with a few local restaurants ordering all their puddings from her. Thanks to Janet recommending her, she also supplied all the birthday and celebration cakes to the golf club whenever they were required.

To her delight, her son Max had stayed in England, sensing that she needed him and finding that he no longer wanted to be away from home. With her business expanding rapidly, he now worked with her, making all the deliveries, doing her marketing and was currently setting up a website and online ordering service for her delicious wares. He had planned to go out and get himself a regular job, but they were so busy with Belinda's business, he simply didn't have the time, and anyway, there was no one she would rather have working beside her than her beloved boy.

Carrie was still trying to fix her up on a date with her widower neighbour, but she was far too busy and far too content on her own with her son, her dog and her baking. What more could she possibly want?

Carrie had been very quiet in Thailand. Everyone could sense that she wasn't herself. Belinda was concerned that she had PTSD from the men's deaths. Amanda thought she was depressed. Tracey just thought she needed to loosen up and have a fucking drink. Not only was she already too much of a flippin' goody two shoes, but now she was on a health kick as well and wouldn't even join in and have a proper drink.

She hadn't really wanted to go, now feeling even more guilty and ashamed of herself, seeing as she had enjoyed sex with Max for a second time. It had happened on New Year's Eve when he had given her a lift home. Once was a mistake, but twice? She couldn't even blame him. It had been her that had not been able to resist him, or help herself, so even though he had made no advances towards her, she had leapt on him once more. So, she only had herself to blame, not that he seemed to mind.

Janet had, in her usual generous and extravagant style, surprised and treated them all by booking first-class flights. After seeing the price of her non-refundable ticket, she had felt obliged to go. Once she was there though, she was glad that she had. The country was breathtakingly beautiful, but the stress of the last few months had finally caught up with her, and she felt overwhelmed and ill. She had no energy and had moped around by the pool all week, her head stuck firmly in a book. She had felt so two-faced whenever she looked at Belinda, and to make matters worse, she knew that everyone thought she was still depressed over Roger, whereas she knew that the only reason she was in a state of turmoil was because all that she could think about was Max.

Janet had wanted to go to and visit the local temple, so she asked Carrie if she would accompany her, having pre-warned the others she was going to take Carrie off by herself to try and cheer her up. The others had got the hint that they weren't invited, so they had all spent the day together shopping at the local market instead.

With them all alone in the quiet, serene temple, Janet had looked at Carrie, her young, pretty face staring up the giant Buddha statue, deep in thought, but looking so sad, and she'd spoken softly to the young girl, "What's wrong, Carrie? You can tell me."

Carrie had immediately burst into tears. "I've done something so awful," she blurted out. "To Belinda."

"You're in love with Max, aren't you?" Janet had come straight out with it.

Carrie had been gobsmacked. "How do you know?"

"What makes you think you can't tell Belinda? I think she would be OK with it," Janet had tried to reason with her.

"Oh *no!* I can't. Please don't tell her, Janet. Anyway, I don't even know if he likes me as much as I like him," Carrie had exclaimed in a panicky voice.

"Carrie, I might not be the most experienced person in matters of intimate relationships, but I can tell *love* when I see it."

"You think he loves me?" Carrie immediately perked up.

"Why do you think I got him to give you lift home on New Year's Eve?" laughed Janet.

"You knew?" Carrie was confused.

Janet then went on to explain the whole story, of how she had found a pair of men's boxer shorts in her summer house on Boxing Day, and knowing that Burt her gardener would never fit into a pair of medium pants, nor was trendy enough to be a wearer of Calvin Klein's, she had realised that they must belong to Max. What's more, when she went to remove the offending garment, she had also smelt a familiar smell in there. Chanel No. 5. She explained that she had observed the tension between them and how they were going out of their way to avoid each other. She then told Carrie of a conversation that she had with Belinda after church on Christmas Eve, when Belinda had joked that she was so fond of Carrie, she wished she could fix her up with her Max.

"She actually said that?" Carrie had said in glee. "She really likes me that much?"

"She does. The only reason she didn't push it was because he was due to go off abroad again. But he is staying at home now, so who knows?" Janet winked to Carrie.

Carrie felt much better, but she still hadn't wanted to ruin the holiday by telling anyone yet. She had been avoiding Max's calls since New Year's Eve, despite his many efforts to call her. He had been pining for her and thought she wasn't interested. She had been desperate to answer, but her loyalty to Belinda was greater than her desire for him. Even though it was killing her.

Janet and Carrie retuned to the villa, and to everyone's surprise, Carrie was upbeat and cheerful for the rest of the trip. She had decided to go and see Max as soon as she got home. She desperately needed to talk to him.

Six months later

It was Belinda's turn to host Sunday lunch, and she didn't think she could be happier if she tried. Her business was booming thanks to Max's marketing skills, and they had even had to take on staff to help. With the desserts for today having already been prepared, and before her guests arrived, she used her last free hour to add the finishing touches to a wedding cake that she had been diligently working on. To complete her creation, she placed the tiny groom statue on the top tier to join his little miniature bride, then she shouted out into her lounge, "OK, you can come and look now."

In came Max and Carrie, who both rushed in excitedly to see the cake that she had made for their forthcoming wedding. "Cheers, Mum," said Max, giving her a grateful kiss on the cheek.

"Thank you so much," squealed an excitable Carrie. "I love it. It's so beautiful." As Carrie went to hug her, they laughed together at the obstacle in their way. Carrie's large, pregnant tummy. It turned out that on the evening of Christmas Day, in Janet's summer house, both Carrie and Belinda were given an extra gift that year, one that they both so desperately desired. They hadn't found out yet whether she was having a boy or a girl, but they had all agreed on one thing. If it was a boy, they would *not* be calling him Roger!

Amanda now relaxed on the tranquil wooden terrace of her holiday rental cabin, deep in the rainforest of Costa Rica. Clad in her white spa robe, she took a sip of the pina colada cocktail by her side, then she reclined her chair in readiness of the masseur she had booked for her foot massage, her new weekly treat. As the handsome Luca worked his magic on her toes, she closed her eyes in bliss and she smiled to herself with a facetious thought in her head, *it's better to be a golfer's widow than a golf widow.*

This book is printed on paper from sustainable sources managed under the Forest Stewardship Council (FSC) scheme.

It has been printed in the UK to reduce transportation miles and their impact upon the environment.

For every new title that Matador publishes, we plant a tree to offset CO_2, partnering with the More Trees scheme.

For more about how Matador offsets its environmental impact, see www.troubador.co.uk/about/